ISBN: 0-9552957-0-X

False
Treason

Brian Sanders

Brian Sanders

"False Treason" is dedicated to

Bonny and Ken

with thanks for their encouragement

Contents

CHAPTER ONE

Treason!

Sir Richard Kempe looked through the small, barred window of his cell in the Tower and watched three men testing the scaffold. In a few hours two prisoners were to be hung for treason. Afterwards they would be drawn and quartered and their heads would be rammed on to the spikes of the southern gateway to London Bridge half a mile away.

Staring at the men Richard reflected that since his first fencing lesson at the age of twelve he had longed to serve his Queen, Elizabeth. Like his father he would be happy to die for her. Now, seven years later, he was to die – not as he had imagined, on the battlefield – but on the scaffold.

It was just two months since he had accidentally stumbled on part of a plan to kill the Queen. But his attempts to discover more had been cleverly turned by the plotters to get him accused of treason. It would be only weeks, perhaps days, he thought, before his own head was impaled on one of the spikes to provide food for the ravening birds of prey that scavenged the filthy streets of London.

He knew of no one who could help him. The only other members of his family, his younger brother Mark, and his sister, Catherine, were in the far north of England and knew nothing of his plight.

The clash of foils rang loudly as it echoed and re-echoed from the walls of the house close by.

Mark Kempe felt pleased as he parried the attack of the man fencing with him. The 'right of way' was now his. He lunged forward into the attack but after the third stroke was himself parried.

The right of attack passed again to his sallow-faced, black haired opponent and Mark felt himself being driven back into the shadowy corner where the extension built by his great-grandfather joined the older pele tower.

Peering over the battlements at the top of the tower Catherine watched her brother moving slowly backwards as he defended himself.

'It would be nice if Mark could beat Cain Webster just once,' she thought. Her fifteen-year-old brother and his tutor practised nearly every day but the man always won. She had watched the two previous bouts and Webster had won the first by five hits to one and the second five to none. Now he was leading four to two.

Mark felt the blunted end of his opponent's foil touch him on the chest. The man pushed until the blade bent.

"Another hit!" said Cain Webster, stepping back and relaxing. "That's enough for to-day; I have matters that require my attention. Shall I take your foil?" Webster strode into the newer part of the house.

Mark crossed to a garden seat to collect his jerkin and heard his sister's voice calling from above.

"Come up, Mark. I can see something!"

"Coming, Kay!" He opened the stout wooden door near one corner of the pele tower and stepping into the shadow waited for his eyes to become accustomed to the dim light. How cool it was inside the thick walls!

He frequently marvelled at the strength of the tower with its battlements and arrow slit windows. It had been built two hundred years before by an ancestor on his Mother's side of the family as a protection from the marauding mosstroopers: bands of men who roamed Northumberland, the wild country of the Cheviot Hills and the border with Scotland, plundering and killing. At such times of danger cattle were driven into the bottom room of the tower for protection. Mark thought it ironic that at present this room contained two barrels of salted meat.

By now he could just make out the rough vaulted ceiling of the room and he began climbing the stone staircase built into the thickness of the tower wall.

He reached the first floor. Once the living room it was now seldom used, for the arrow slit windows gave little light. The extension built by his great-grandfather was lighter and more comfortable.

He continued up to the second floor and passing through the room used by Francis Hemmings, the servant, ran up the stone stairs and on to the battlemented roof.

Bright, warm air greeted him and he joined his sister at the south corner of the tower. The stone parapet was warm in the August sunshine.

"Look," said Catherine. "Someone's riding this way!"

Mark looked over the roof of the more recent building, which was a few feet below the battlements, and across the fields to where the Alwin stream wound its way towards the river Coquet. About a mile distant was the village of Alwinton and to its left the track from Harbottle. Mark saw a small cloud of dust approaching the point where the track forked, one branch going to Alwinton and the other coming towards the house.

Catherine and her brother watched in silence until the cloud of dust moved on to the track leading to the house.

"Do you think it's Richard?" Catherine asked with excitement in her voice.

"I doubt it. He would have sent a messenger ahead of him."

"Perhaps it's the messenger then."

"We'll have to wait and see."

They watched in silence again. Catherine was inwardly praying that at last they would hear something from their elder brother. Mark was recalling an incident between Richard and Cain Webster over two months before when Webster had been summoned to his brother's room. Mark had heard voices raised in anger. Later Webster strode from the house, his face white and taut.

Richard made no reference to the disagreement but the next day he told Mark and Catherine that he had something of great importance to do and that he would be away for about three weeks. Since then they had heard nothing.

When questioned Webster always denied knowledge of Richard's whereabouts and said they must remain in the north and await news. Occasionally dusty or mud-spattered messengers arrived at the house but they were always shown straight to Webster. Later he would say that they had only come on routine matters concerning the family house in Warwickshire. Several times Mark had asked if his brother was at their Warwickshire home but Webster always said he was not and that he had no idea of his whereabouts. He twice suggested that Sir Richard might well be at court in London enjoying himself but neither Mark nor Catherine believed this. They were sure that Richard would have sent messages to them if this were so.

Mark wandered to the west corner of the tower and looked at the hills that flanked the house and its adjoining farm to the west, north and east. He could see the sheep grazing around a circular pen of stones in the field that sloped up to the shepherd's hut. Then Webster came into his mind again. It irked Mark that this man had so much power over them. As a young man of twenty-two Webster had joined his father's staff just before his own birth. Three years later Lady Kempe had died giving birth to Catherine. The next year his father had been killed serving with the Earl of Leicester in the Netherlands and Webster had assumed the responsibilities of steward. He had been tutor to Richard and himself.

Mark knew that Webster had worked well for his father but like Richard and Catherine he had never warmed to him. He was efficient and polite but cold and humourless.

Mark rejoined his sister and together they watched the horse and its rider turn sharply away from the Alwin stream and approach the house. Hens from the farm scattered fearfully in all directions, clucking loudly.

The rider dismounted about a hundred yards from the house and called to a farm lad. "You! Rub this horse down and feed him! I have a long journey again to-morrow!" It was a command, not a request.

"It's Gervase Ford," said Catherine disgustedly. They disliked this arrogant young man whom Webster had employed as an assistant for the past three years.

"Let's go and see what we can find out," said Mark. "And anyway, I'm hungry!"

They went down into Hemmings' room and through the doorway that their grandfather had opened in the south-west wall of the pele tower. This gave immediate access to a passage on the second floor of the new building that lay alongside.

"I'll leave this jerkin in my study," said Mark. He entered a room across the passage and walked over to a low chest near one corner. Lying on the chest was a small knife and the model of a fish that he had been carving out of a rough piece of wood. Glancing out of the window nearby he looked down to the left where he had been fencing with Webster only a short time before.

'I'll beat him one day,' he thought. He dropped the jerkin on top of the knife and returned to the passage.

"Where are you, Kay?"

"In my room. Just coming!" His sister's room next door was coloured a brilliant gold in the late afternoon sunshine.

Together they went down the stairs. On the first floor they passed Webster's closed door and then Richard's room – which was beneath Mark's. At the foot of the stairs they turned and hurried to the kitchen at the back of the new house.

"Where's Ford gone?"

"Has he said anything about Richard?"

"Master Ford is cleansing himself," said Francis Hemmings, a grey-haired man. "As to his news – well, we shall have to wait and see what Master Webster thinks fit to tell us."

"But we're never told anything," said Mark, angrily. "Twice during the last month Webster went away for several days but he never told us where he was going, or why. Messengers arrive but they go straight to him. We never have a chance to talk to them. If we ask Webster he always gives the same reply: 'Matters of no importance! Nothing for you to worry about.'"

"Richard's been gone since early June and we've heard nothing" added Catherine. "Francis, you've been with the family longer than anyone – longer than us even. Why doesn't Master Webster tell you what's going on?"

Hemmings smiled. "I've served the family since I was a boy, but I'm only a servant."

"That's nonsense!" Mark's eyes flashed with temper. "My father trusted you more than anyone: Richard always said that. You fought with him in the Low Countries and received a special commendation from the Earl of Leicester when you retrieved his body from the battlefield in face of the enemy and prevented a ransom."

Francis Hemmings set some apple pasty and cheese on the table but said nothing.

"And why can't we return to Warwickshire?" said Catherine. "We've been here since the spring. It's beautiful by the Cheviots but we're so cut off."

"I've asked Webster enough times as you know, Kay, but he says that the house is being completely re-roofed. It would be inconvenient to return." Mark imitated Webster's clipped consonants and added, "Inconvenient for him perhaps. I believe he's up to something."

"Now don't let your imagination colour your good sense," said Francis Hemmings. "We'll all hear something soon, you'll see."

At that moment Gervase Ford entered the kitchen and the conversation ceased abruptly.

"I hope you had a pleasant journey, Master Ford," said Mark in his loftiest tone. "Have you come from Warwickshire? What's the news?"

"Nothing of particular interest, Master Kempe."

"It is a long way to come with nothing of particular interest," goaded Mark.

Ford glowered. "If you'll excuse me I'll eat the food Master Hemmings has prepared."

"Let's get some fresh air, Kay," said Mark pointedly. "We'll eat outside in the sunshine."

They took some pasties and cheese and went outside through the kitchen door. Tall trees nearby threw long shadows over the side of the house and the two walked over the rough grass until they could sit in the sun and eat their food.

"You were rather bold with Gervase Ford just now," observed Catherine.

"He's too arrogant for a servant," replied her brother. "He would never dare to put on such airs before Richard. Why should he before us?" Mark was aware that if anything happened to his brother he would be head of the family and through the feudal system of land-owning he would become Sir Mark Kempe. He felt that servants should show respect even if one was friendly with them.

"He looked very angry," Catherine cautioned her brother. "Do be careful, Mark. Don't let your feelings get the better of you. It isn't worth it."

"Well it grieves me. After all I am ...." he began. Then, seeing the expression on his sister's face he stopped and grinned. "Cautious Catherine! You've got a bit of a temper too, you know. Your hair isn't that auburn colour for nothing!" He chuckled and lay back on the grass.

Catherine stroked her shoulder-length hair. "The Queen's is the same colour!" she said in a mock hauteur.

They had just finished eating when they saw Francis Hemmings approaching from the house.

"Master Webster is asking for you both."

"Perhaps it's news of Richard!" cried Catherine excitedly.

They hurried back into the house and found Webster waiting in the kitchen.

"I am sorry to disturb your afternoon. I wondered if you would both be kind enough to go on a small errand to the village."

'He's at his most charming,' thought Mark. 'What's he up to?'

"The smith's wife is most unwell. As they are our tenants I thought you might like to take a chicken and some eggs and honey from the farm. I would come with you but Gervase Ford is waiting upstairs for me and I must check the accounts before he leaves in the morning."

"Of course we'll go," said Catherine. "Poor woman. I wonder what's the matter with her?"

"Tell me when you return. I haven't questioned Ford yet and there might be news of Sir Richard."

Hemmings had packed the food in a small basket.

"Is she very ill?" asked Mark as they heard Webster going up the stairs.

Hemmings shrugged slightly. "I saw Armstrong in the village yesterday and he said his wife had been sick after eating mutton though he hadn't been upset. Perhaps it wasn't the mutton and it's more serious."

Mark looked thoughtful. "Come on, Kay. While we're there we'll see how Susan and Will are getting on with their reading. If it's dark before we leave the village we can borrow a lantern from Armstrong."

They left the house and soon reached the Alwin stream.

"Kay, there's something odd going on. Let's sit down on the bank for a minute."

They sat by the edge of the stream and Mark looked round before continuing.

"Ford comes all the way from Warwickshire just to get the

accounts checked. That's unusual to begin with. And suddenly Cain Webster shows great interest in the health of the smith's wife. He's never bothered before. In any case Hemmings says that she's only bilious."

"We don't know for certain. She might be very ill"

"Well I've got a feeling that we've been got out of the way so that Webster can talk to Ford without fear of being overheard. Remember that he asked us to see him as soon as we returned from the village? That way he'd know when we got back to the house. You go to the village and see the Armstrongs while I go back to the house and listen to their conversation."

"I'm coming with you," said Catherine immediately.

"No, Kay," said her brother firmly. "One of us must go and see Mrs. Armstrong. After all she might really be ill and we must deliver the food. If there's nothing secret about Ford's news then I can leave the house and meet you on the way back from the village."

"All right. I suppose that's sensible. Boys do seem to have the most fun though. Please be careful, Mark. Even if it is only about the household accounts there'll be a dreadful scene if Webster finds you spying on him. And if it is something secret and he catches you..."

"Don't worry – I'll take care of myself. If you don't see me on your way back from the village wait here until I appear or until you can get hold of Hemmings."

Before Catherine could say anything further Mark hurried back towards the house. Reluctantly she turned and walked along the stream's bank towards the village. Gradually the calm and beauty of the early evening overcame her fears and she began to wonder if her brother was not being over-dramatic. Webster was a curious man but he had always treated them quite well. Ford had come north before with the household and estate accounts. At least that was what they had always understood. Why should it be any different this time? As she walked her fears fell away and she began to enjoy the freedom of the countryside.

In the meantime Mark was approaching the house with a thumping heart. To avoid passing beneath Webster's windows on the first floor he would go by the north corner of the house and the two outside walls of the pele tower. If he were seen he would say that he had slipped back for something. His fish carving – that was it! He wanted to show the smith his woodcarving.

He opened the door near the south corner of the new building, slipped inside, pulled it shut and stood still for a moment with his breath held, then he walked quietly up to first floor. Webster's door was shut and although he could hear voices he could not distinguish the words spoken. He put his ear close to the door but the words were still indistinct.

He tip-toed upstairs, entered Catherine's room which was immediately above Webster's and moved to the window which was partly open. A window in Webster's room must also have been open because now he could hear quite clearly. He opened Catherine's window wide and stuck out his head. An unpleasant drawl reached him. Ford was speaking.

" ... can be sure that Armitage will not fail us. His loyalty to the Queen is not suspect and he is good at playing this double game."

Mark held his breath and waited for Webster's reply.

"He may be too good, that's what worries me. If anything should go wrong with our plan – then he might blab the whole plot to Cecil."

Mark knew that Sir Robert Cecil was the Queen's Secretary of State.

"However, he cannot deny his part in the false accusation against Richard Kempe."

Mark leaned further out of the window.

"I congratulate myself," Webster continued, "on getting Kempe falsely accused of treason and shut in the Tower. But without the help of Armitage it might have been difficult to convince Sir Robert Cecil and the other lords of his 'guilt'. As it is they are demanding further proof before taking final action against him. I confess that I shan't feel happy and secure until Richard Kempe's head is rolling down Tower Hill!"

"When will Cecil get the further proof he requires of Kempe's 'guilt'?"

"Armitage is working on that now, but it's a tricky business what with forged documents and bringing one of our confederacy from Spain to testify. It'll be another four or five weeks before Kempe is executed and then the plot against the Queen herself will be sprung.

Believe me, Gervase, there are going to be some big changes in England and I shall be assured of a high office. You, too, will get your just reward."

"What are you going to do with that wretched boy and his sister?"

"They are a problem. However, this is a wild, lonely part of the country and the mosstroopers are a law unto themselves. When the time comes they can be disposed of without much fuss. I shall have to shut Hemmings' mouth as well. The loyal family servant will go with the children he's so devoted to."

This last sentence was uttered with a snarl and Mark realised that Webster would do anything to forward his own plans. It all seemed like a nightmare. He'd known Webster all his life. The man had served the family since his own birth fifteen years ago. What could cause a person to change like this? How was it possible to trust anyone in the future?

Mark drew his head back into the room. He must go immediately to Alwinton, find his sister and tell her what he had heard. Or should he tell Hemmings first? He stood undecided. He was supposed to be with his sister, therefore he would go straight to the village. He would try to tell Hemmings later. Preoccupied, he turned awkwardly towards the door and struck his shin against a wooden stool. The stool crashed over and Mark, twisting and doubling with the sudden pain, lost his balance, fell and struck his head against Catherine's bed. Half-stunned he desperately tried to get to his feet but he could already hear voices and footsteps on the stairs.

Seconds later Gervase Ford was holding him with his arms twisted behind his back. Webster was standing in the doorway.

"I thought I sent you to the village. Where's Catherine?"

Mark said nothing and Ford twisted one arm still further. Mark cried out in sudden pain.

"Where's your sister?" repeated Webster.

"Find her!"

"I shall," Webster hissed, "And take good care of you in the meantime."

He moved towards Mark and stood close in front of him. "How much did you hear?"

"Enough to know the kind of person you are," Mark answered defiantly. Immediately he regretted having spoken.

"Bring him to his room," muttered Webster, leading the way.

Struggling uselessly against the older man, Mark was dragged unceremoniously out of the room and along the passage. Webster stood by the door and Ford propelled Mark into the room and thrust him sprawling on to the floor. Before he could recover the door had slammed and the lock was turned.

How much did you hear?

CHAPTER TWO

Escape

M ark scrambled to his feet and hammered on the door. No one heard him but it relieved his feelings.

He felt angry and frustrated. His pride was wounded by Gervase Ford's treatment of him. He had a score to settle with that arrogant servant!

He paced about the room, his thoughts confused. He was always the same when thwarted or crossed. His brother, Richard, had often told him to keep calm and to concentrate. "Think and then act" was Richard's advice.

Mark sat on the edge of his bed and tried to relax and concentrate.

What would Kay do when he failed to meet her? How long would she wait by the stream? She must return to the house eventually and then she would be caught.

They could expect no help. Hemmings could be effectively silenced. Their nearest friends were over two hundred miles away in Warwickshire. There were two armed and ruthless men against Kay, an old servant and himself. They would be taken to a band of mosstroopers who would be paid to cut their throats and leave them to rot in the Cheviot Hills.

Mark found himself pacing the room again. 'Think! Think!' There must be a glimmer of hope somewhere. He sat down.

He must try to escape as soon as possible. He could not get through the stout, locked door. There was only one other way – through a window.

Of the three small latticed windows only one opened and that was on the south-west side of the house and just above Webster's room. There was no escape there! The other windows were on the south east side. They looked just large enough for him to squeeze through but how could he remove the lattice? One small square of glass had been left out of each window to allow a flow of air but the empty square was only large enough to put a hand through.

He crossed to the window above the chest and in moving his

jerkin to sit down he knocked his knife and wood carving on to the floor. The knife struck the boards with a loud clatter.

Mark picked up the knife, hurried to the door and stood listening. There was no sound. He crossed back to the window, knelt on the chest and tried to prise the leaden lattice away from the window frame. This was not successful but the point of the knife went into the lead fairly easily. Worried that his pressure on the knife might send part of the window crashing to the ground about thirty feet below he put his left hand through the empty square and pushed gently inwards from the outside. Then he drew the knife slowly but firmly down a section of lead strip. He found that he had made a cut in the lead but it required more pressure if the knife was to go through. He tried once more and this time the point sank clean through that section of lead.

So far so good! Mark felt elated. He put down the knife and drew in his left hard. Supposing he was able to get out of the window – what then? He couldn't jump down thirty feet or more,

Then he remembered that one of the main stems of the ivy that clung to the walls of the pele had grown away from the tower and up the corner of the house about five or six feet from his window. If he could reach this he might climb down. But even if he hung from the sill by his arms the ivy stem would be too far away to reach with his feet. He wanted something tied to the window from which he could hang and then manoeuvre himself along the wall until he could reach the ivy.

He looked round his room: table, stool, bed, cupboard – the bed! The stuffed woollen mattress on his stump-bed was resting on interwoven strips of leather!

Mark pulled the mattress to one side.

There was one strip of six feet and three of about two and a half feet. Tied together they would make a length of eleven to twelve feet. That should be enough!

The light in the room was becoming dim. He would wait until it was nearly dark and then he would cut away the lattice from the window. No! Now was the time to cut through most of the lead leaving only one side to remove when he was ready for his escape in the dark. If anyone came into the room they would see nothing unusual about the window unless they examined it closely.

He replaced the mattress, crossed to the door and listened.

The house was silent. He went swiftly to the window, knelt on the chest, put his left hand through the empty square and pushing the lattice gently inwards resumed his work.

He placed the point of the knife into the slit he had made and with a gentle sawing action began cutting through the lead. After three minutes he had cut through three inches. He shifted his position on the chest and continued. After another two minutes he had increased the slit to five inches.

He touched his forehead with the back of his hand and found that he was perspiring with the effort of concentration. He inserted the knife again and repeated his sawing action. Five minutes later he had cut right down one strip of the lattice.

He crossed to the door and listened. There was no sound.

He returned to the window and began cutting the lead strip on the other side of the lattice. This time he worked with more confidence and after four minutes he had completed cutting that side.

Next he would cut across the lowest strip leaving the whole window hanging by the topmost lead. He prayed that it would remain hanging and would not fall out to smash on the ground below and give his plan away.

Putting his hand once more through the empty square he inserted the knife at the side of the strip and began cutting horizontally.

At that moment there was a dull thud from somewhere in the house. He withdrew quickly from the window and stood in the middle of the room. He must hide his knife in case Webster should enter and search the room. He made a small slit in the woollen mattress and slipped the knife inside.

He heard Webster's voice on the stairs. Then the lock was turned the door opened and Webster marched a struggling Catherine into the room and threw her on to the floor. Mark rushed towards the doorway but Ford appeared, thrust him roughly back and shut the door. Ford had a cut above his left eye and the area around it was swelling.

"I hit him with a leather drinking bottle!" said Catherine.

Ford stepped towards her but Mark stood between them and faced up to the young servant.

"That's enough!" snapped Webster. "You two will remain here for the night. I'll deal with you both tomorrow."

Mark faced his tutor. "For a servant you take a great deal on yourself, Master Webster."

Webster hit Mark across the face with the back of his hand, then he turned and stalked from the room followed by Ford. The door was shut and locked.

Mark did not move. His right cheek stung and his eyes were filled with tears. He could have cried out in pain but he did not. He would not give Webster that satisfaction.

He turned, his cheek still smarting, and sat beside Catherine. "What happened after I left you?"

"I found Mrs Armstrong almost completely recovered so I made an excuse to get away as quickly as possible. I was waiting by the stream when Ford suddenly came up behind me. Did you discover anything."

Mark told his sister all that had happened.

"We must get to London, find someone of importance and tell them the truth about Richard and the plot against the Queen's life," Catherine said, making it all sound very simple.

"We've got to get out of here first." Mark told Catherine of his plan. "Removing the window is the least of our difficulties. We've somehow to reach the ivy and then climb down and get away without being seen. And then we've got to get to London. It takes us three days by coach from here to Warwickshire. London is further than Warwickshire and we haven't got a coach!"

"When do you think we should start?" asked Catherine, who still did not realise the difficulties and dangers of the task ahead of them.

"We must start now," said Mark, taking his knife from the mattress. "If we wait until it's pitch dark it may be impossible to find a hold on the ivy."

"If it isn't cloudy we should have some moonlight. It was quite bright last night when I went to the farmhouse with Francis." Catherine crossed to the door. "I'll listen while you work on the window."

Mark was able to concentrate fully on his task now that Catherine was keeping guard and he soon cut through the bottom lead. Now came the trickiest part of the operation: the cutting of the top lead from which the whole window now hung. If he kept his wrist through the empty square it would prevent the whole lattice from crashing on to the ground outside or on to the floor inside.

As he began cutting the top lead the whole panel of window moved backwards, forwards and sideways and made the job increasingly difficult.

Eventually the knife cut through the last half-inch of lead and spreading the fingers of his left hand wide open Mark carefully drew the whole lattice into the room and laid it on the mattress.

His next task was to remove the small panes around the outside edges of the window. This was comparatively easy as each one could be removed separately. In two minutes the job was completed.

"I've done it!" Mark whispered. "If anyone comes in now we're in real trouble!"

Mark leaned out of the window and looked down to his left. Drawing his head in again he said, "It's too dark to see the ivy. I hope you're right about the moon."

"What do we do now?"

"Cut the leather strips from the bed and tie them together."

After cutting the lead lattice this was a simple task.

"We need to tie one end to something in the room. We'd better shift the bed and tie it to that. You take the foot. Lift it carefully and don't drop it. I'll take the head and swing it round to the window. Oh! We'll have to move the chest out of the way first. I hope no-one comes!"

They lifted the chest to one side and swung the bed round so that the head was immediately under the window. Then Mark tied one end of the leather riband to a leg of the stump-bed, tested the knots and dropped the other end out of the window.

"We might wait ages for the moon. I'm going to chance it, Kay. I think it will work. Stay by the window and when I've reached the ivy I'll tell you and you can follow."

"What shall I do if Webster comes?"

"Get out of the window and climb down immediately." It was a great deal to ask of his young sister. "Can you?"

"Of course!"

Mark took the leather riband with both hands, squeezed

through the window and climbed on to the sill. Slowly he lowered his legs and body from the ledge and then gripping leather with hands and ankles began to climb down. Several times his knuckles scraped against the wall.

Then the moon appeared from behind a cloud and illuminated the side of the house. He was level with a window on the first floor and about six feet to his right was the thick ivy stem. There were crevices in the stone wall. He must use these to edge his way along to the ivy. His left foot found a crack and he explored the wall with the other foot until he found a crevice about two feet to his right. He wedged the toe of his leather shoe in the crevice and searching the wall with his right hand, dug his fingertips into a slit between two stones. Then he transferred his left foot next to his right one. Clinging to the leather with his left hand he edged further to his right in the same way: right foot, right hand, left foot to right. If he lost his grip on the wall his weight would turn the leather riband into a long pendant and he would swing helplessly along the side of the house.

The moon went in and he remained still, clinging to the riband and the wall. How large was the cloud? The strain on his left arm was intolerable.

The moon appeared again and he looked to his right. The ivy was about two feet away and almost beyond the limit of his reach. He tried to edge further along the wall but the angle of the riband would not allow this. He must reach out for the stem with his right hand. If he missed he might well overbalance and fall to the ground. He must take the risk.

The moon went in again. As soon as it reappeared he would go for the ivy.

He waited. It grew light again. He looked to his right, took a deep breath, steadied himself, stretched to his right and clutched the ivy. He felt spread-eagled on the wall like a gigantic insect.

He must keep hold of the riband with his left hand so that he could tie it to the ivy to help Kay to climb down.

Then the door below him opened and he heard Webster's familiar clipped tones. "You're certain of the place, Ford? I don't want any bungling."

The two men stood on the gravel path outside the door. Ten

feet above them, in bright moonlight, Mark clung desperately to the leather and the ivy.

"Quite clear, Master Webster. I'm to ride to Windyhaugh and find a man named Thirl."

"There's only one dwelling. Thirl lives there with his wife. Tell him Master Webster has work for the mosstroopers."

"Very well!"

"Make sure you take a fresh horse from the stables. And mind your way; the track's very rough."

"I'll be all right." Ford's voice died away as he turned the corner of the house.

Mark heard Webster moving just beneath him and held his breath. His arms ached; his toes were losing their grip on the wall. He felt as though he was falling backwards.

Then he heard the crunch of gravel, a moment's silence and the slam of the door below.

Mark waited in case Webster should re-appear. Seconds passed. There was no sound.

Feeling with his toes, he edged along the wall until he was able to grip the ivy stem with both ankles. Then he slid his left hand carefully along the riband until it reached his right. He found that he had just enough leather to tie to the stem. Now Catherine could climb diagonally from the window to the ivy.

"Kay," he whispered towards the window above.

"Yes?"

"You can come down now."

He watched Catherine climb out. She had removed her skirt and was wearing her velvet bodice and petticoat. She climbed slowly down towards him with her legs twined round the leather riband. When she reached the ivy Mark climbed down to make room for her.

As soon as she was clinging to the ivy immediately above him Mark whispered, "Well done! Follow me down."

A minute later they reached the ground and hurried away from the house into the shadow of some pine trees on the north-east side of the tower. Glancing fearfully towards the house, whose grey stone walls reflected the brilliant moonlight, they half ran towards an outhouse on the edge of the farm buildings and stumbled inside almost breathless.

"Oh Mark! When they came out of the house I was sure they'd see you!"

"So was I. I felt that I would fall at any moment."

"I took my skirt off to make climbing down easier."

"If we're lucky our escape won't be discovered till morning. That'll give us a good start. But we'll have to watch out for Gervase Ford. Once we're clear of Alwinton Webster won't know which way we've gone."

"I'll need something else to wear. I didn't think of that when I took off my skirt."

"We ought to disguise ourselves in rough clothes. I think you should be dressed as a boy: it'll be safer."

"How splendid to be a boy!" said Catherine. "And you can still call me 'Kay'. There's a knight called Kay in the King Arthur stories. But where shall we get the clothes? Can Francis help?"

"It would be far too dangerous to go anywhere near the house. We need clothes of fustian or rough woollen cloth and old shoes. And we must dirty our faces and hands."

"Could the Armstrongs help?"

"I doubt it. And Webster's sure to question them. He'd make them talk. It's got to be someone he wouldn't think of questioning."

"What about Gabriel?"

Mark considered. His father had given Gabriel a job on the farm ten years before. He had heard of a boy wandering about the village starved and ragged and had taken pity on him. Mark knew there were many children, boys and girls, who had no homes and who begged by the wayside. Many died in the ditches where they begged. Gabriel had been fortunate: he was now the shepherd. He rarely spoke to anyone and kept away from the village, preferring the company of his dog and the sheep to that of people. All creatures seemed to trust him and he mended their broken legs and wings.

The previous year he had been ill and they had taken food to his hut. In this way Gabriel had come to trust them and was always pleased to see them. They had begun to teach the young shepherd to read and write. Webster had been away at the time and knew nothing of all this.

"Of course," said Mark, "He'll help. The villagers have given him bits and pieces of clothing that were almost worn out. He had some on his bed when he was ill if you remember?" Catherine nodded. "And Webster would never think of questioning him. Even if he did Gabriel would act dumb. Let's go and see him."

They left the outhouse and keeping in the shadows of buildings and trees hurried towards the Alwin.

They glanced back to the house and could see the flickering of the pale rush lights in Webster's room and in the kitchen beneath. Crossing the stream by stepping-stones they climbed a path under more pine trees and reached the long upward slope of lush grass that led to Gabriel's hut.

As they climbed up out of the shelter of the Alwin valley and on to open ground they felt exposed to all kinds of danger. Each step took them away from the house and from Cain Webster and yet on the hillside hundreds of pairs of unseen and unknown eyes seemed to be watching. The grass at their feet was alive in the breeze. The shadows of clouds scudding across the moon were creatures moving in the long grass. A sheep rose up suddenly in front of them with a loud bleat and ambled to a circular pen of stones. Other sheep rose out of the ground and followed. An owl screeched from the trees: a wild dog howled.

They walked much faster, tripping and stumbling on tufts of grass in their anxiety to reach the safety of the small grey stone hut. They imagined things unseen pursuing them up the long moonlit slope.

As they approached the hut the door opened and the young shepherd stepped out. In the moonlight his blond hair looked almost silver. His sheepdog followed and stood close at his heels.

"I heard the sheep tussling about and wondered what was the matter." He saw Catherine in her petticoat. "What's happened? Come inside."

The stone interior was lit only by moonlight through the door until Gabriel removed a piece of sacking from the square gap in the wall that served for a window.

"Will ye not sit doon," he said, indicating the wood bench that was his bed. He shut the door and sat himself on a plank supported by two tree stumps that served as a table.

The sheep dog sat beside Catherine and pushed his head on to her thigh.

"Hello, Johnnie! Good boy!" She scratched his ears.

"What's happened?" repeated Gabriel.

Mark told him briefly of the day's events. "We must go to London and save Richard but we need some rough clothes to help our disguise. And Kay must travel as a boy."

"You're welcome to anything I have though I haven't much." Gabriel reached up to a small hayloft above an open fire in one corner of the room and took down a large bundle of cloth. He opened the bundle on the floor to reveal a ragged cloak torn around the edges and several other rough garments with patches and holes.

"Let's see how these'll do. C'mon, take off yo'r bodice and petticoat?"

Catherine stood up, took off her bodice, slipped out of her petticoat and shivered.

Gabriel measured the old cloak against her and said, "Now Master Mark, let's hev the shears, if ye please?"

Mark took down a pair of sheep shears hanging from a nail and handed them to the young shepherd.

"Now will ye thread us some twine? Ye'll find it and the bone needle on the shelf ower there."

Gabriel made a slit in the cloak and pulled it over Catherine's head. After some skilful cutting with the shears he took the needle and thread from Mark who watched in admiration as the shepherd gradually converted the old cloak into a rough jerkin.

Next Catherine pulled on a pair of patched breeches that were far too large for her. Gabriel worked steadily, kneeling first on one side of Catherine and then the other, cutting, snipping and sewing. Mark sat on the plank table and Johnnie, the dog, his tail never still, watched every move of his master.

At length Gabriel stood up. "There, what d'ya think of that?"

"That's splendid, Gabriel! Stand in the moonlight, Kay." Mark looked carefully at his sister. "There's just one thing, Kay."

"What's that?"

"Your hair; it's much too long."

"Oh." Catherine touched her long auburn hair. "Must it be cut?"

"I'm afraid so."

"Oh." It was the end of something precious. The end of a life. But it was for Richard. "When must it be done?"

"Not now. Not here. Webster might come. When we're on the hills. Don't worry, Kay. It'll grow again."

"I know. It's just that ... Oh, never mind. We'll do it to-morrow."

Gabriel found an old leather jerkin that he had long since grown out of. "It's a funny thing, it was yo'r father that gave me this a long time since."

Mark removed his velvet jerkin and tried on the old leather one. "It's very tight under my arms."

"I'll see to that," Gabriel said. "Take it off." He made some careful cuts with his knife.   Now try it."

"That's better."

They could find nothing else to suit Mark and agreed that he would soon dirty his velvet breeches on the journey.

"I shall have to carry the leather jerkin until I can get rid of my velvet one on the hills. And we must take Kay's bodice and petticoat: they mustn't be found here! What about our shoes?"

"The Cheviots'll roughen them up soon enough," answered Gabriel. "Y'u'll want some food for the start of your journey. I've some apples – they're windfalls, and cheese." He wrapped the food in some cloth and gave the bundle to Catherine. "Are you all ready then?"

They nodded and Gabriel opened the door and led them outside. The dog followed.

"Thank you for all your help," said Mark. "We shall never forget your kindness." To his surprise he found himself putting out his hand to Gabriel. It was not usual to shake hands with servants. After some hesitation Gabriel took it and they shook hands warmly.

"Which way will you go?"

"Across the hills to find the road running south from Scotland," said Mark. "We'll take the track through Harbottle to Holystone and then follow the course of the old Roman road to Otterburn. My brother and I used to spend hours walking the hills. That will help us to find our way."

"My but I'll miss ye both," said Gabriel. "Be sure to come back safely now."

"Goodbye!"

"God bless ye then."

They left the hut and walked up to Clennel Street, the name of the rough sheep track that went from Alwinton over the Cheviots to Scotland.

Looking back down the slope and beyond the pine trees they saw the pele tower and the house bathed in bright moonlight. Everything looked serene. They wondered how long it would be before they saw the house again.

Gabriel waved. They waved back and set off down the sheep track towards Alwinton and London.

They waved back and set off down the sheep track towards Alwinton and London.

chapter three

The Cheviot Hills

Catherine gasped suddenly and stumbled forward. "What is it?" Mark turned quickly to see his sister, crouching and clutching her left ankle.

"Oh! – It's all right. I twisted my ankle on a stone. For a moment I thought I'd wrenched it badly."

"We must walk carefully. The sheep track is full of holes and stones. They're difficult enough to see when the moon's out but in the darkness it's impossible. If one of us should break an ankle....."

Catherine straightened up. "It's better. Let's go on down to the village."

They lost sight of the distant pele tower as Clennell Street dipped steeply towards Alwinton and entered a narrow gully. Mark struck a stone with his right foot and the clatter reverberated between the high banks. For the next quarter of an hour they negotiated the steep, rough descent with great care.

Then the track levelled out and they entered a grove of ash trees just as the moon went behind a cloud. They could see nothing.

Catherine touched her brother's hand and felt relieved as he grasped it firmly. Hand in hand they moved through the darkness trying to make no sound in case things unseen should hear them.

Moonlight brought relief. The track ended and they walked on to rough grass. "'We must watch out for Gervase Ford returning from Windyhaugh" muttered Mark. Skirting the village they crossed the Alwin for the second time that night and passed near the church, ghostly and silent among the trees.

Ahead they could hear the shallow water of the Coquet splashing continuously over small rocks. They reached the left bank and saw the water reflecting the moonlight.

They looked back towards the village and listened. All was still and silent save the splash of the river behind them. "I wonder if they've discovered our escape," whispered Mark. They glanced fearfully at each other. "Come on," he said and led Catherine along the left bank of the Coquet.

The moon was high when they reached Harbottle twenty-five

minutes later.

"We'll cross the river here," said Mark, sitting on the bank to remove his shoes and hose.

Catherine did the same and they waded into the river.

"Its cool and refreshing" said Catherine, kicking the shallow water. "My feet were beginning to feel tired."

"We'll dry ourselves on the velvet jerkin and I'll put on the old leather one Gabriel gave me. It's strange that it should have belonged to father."

Forty minutes later they reached Holystone farm and refreshed themselves from spring water.

"This may be the last chance to drink for some hours, Kay. I hope we can find the course of the old Roman road across the hills towards Otterburn."

Leaving the farmhouse they followed the cattle track leading to the wild, desolate moorland. An owl hooted from the trees above and then came a sound that petrified them. It was a long thin scream. Catherine clutched Mark's arm in fear.

"It's a stoat killing a rabbit," he said, nervously.

Mark's mind began to race with fears. Were they mad to attempt the hills at night? Wild dogs, the descendants of wolves, roamed the Cheviots. Hunger often drove them into villages where they killed and ate cattle and sometimes children. Could their night walk end with them being torn to pieces?

Then he thought of Webster who might yet catch them; and he thought too of his brother in the tower. Richard faced certain death; they must take their chance.

As they emerged from the trees another owl hooted and passed over their heads and down towards a burn on their left. In the moonlight they saw rough grassland rising steadily in front of them. In the distance was the dark outline of hills.

"The moon's already sinking! We must get as far as we can before it goes behind the hills. This cattle track won't last much longer."

"Can you hear burn splashing? That will guide us for a while."

"At least it will prevent us from walking in a circle," said Mark. He feared they might lose their sense of direction and end up back at Holystone, or, worse still at Alwinton.

After another mile the cattle track was lost in the rough grassland.

"If we look carefully we might make out the course of the old Roman road." They studied the ground ahead. "Yes! Look, Kay! Can you see – in the moonlight – there's a strip of land ahead that looks different from the ground on each side." He knelt down and explored with his hands. "It's all grass on the strip, there isn't any heather. In daylight it would show up green against the purple heather on each side. And look! Here's a large flat stone. It might have been the surface of the old road. Just think – someone laid it here over a thousand years ago for chariots to drive along!"

"Here's another stone!" cried Catherine, walking forward and bending down. "And there's another over there!"

The discovery helped them to forget their fears.

Mark stood up. "The course of the road leads down the hillside and into that wood. It must cross the burn further on."

On their way down to the wood they passed several more stones showing white against the dark ground.

A mile further on they crossed the burn by a fallen tree and began a steady ascent. The moon was just above the hills slightly to their left. Mark was anxious to reach higher ground so that they might make use of the moonlight while it lasted.

Heather and bracken made their climb even more tiring. They had either to drag their feet through a tangle of sprigs and stems or lift them well clear of the ground. Their legs ached. Each new step became more of an effort than the last. They struggled on until Catherine said, "Can we rest for a little, Mark?"

Mark looked at his young sister. "I'd hoped we might got further but it's tiring, and we'll lose track of the road completely. Yes, let's have some food and go on when we've rested."

They sat in the dry heather, opened Gabriel's bundle of food and ate some cheese and an apple. Then lying back on the springy heather to rest for a short while they both fell asleep.

They awoke chilly and sat up.

The sky was misty-grey and the air moved coldly about them. Somewhere a wild dog bayed like a lost soul. Mark shivered and rubbed his legs.

"I'm frozen." said Catherine. Her cheeks felt cold and her

clothes were damp.

"Come on, Kay. We'll get warm walking."

They rose stiffly and stamped their feet on the wet heather. Then Mark led the way as they climbed vigorously upwards through the tangled undergrowth. He hoped they were going in the right direction but it was impossible to see far because of the mist everywhere.

Upward they climbed, Catherine struggling to keep pace with her brother who stopped occasionally to let her catch up. The physical effort warmed them. Imperceptibly the light grew stronger and the mist dispersed.

"Look, Kay! There are more of those whitish stones. We're back on the track of the Roman road! Race you to the top of the hill!"

After two hundred yards they were breathless and they walked together until they stood on the crest.

"We must be very high up," said Mark. "Over a thousand feet I should think."

All around them, behind and beyond, the Cheviots were a vast grey rolling sea. Looking back they saw, low in the sky, a faint russet colour.

"That's the dawn."

They watched in silence.

Suddenly, nearby, a skylark sang as it rose and hovered high above them.

"Mark, have you the knife?"

The strands of Catherine's auburn hair fell gently on to the heather or drifted down from the hilltop on the slight breeze.

"I think that's short enough. Don't worry, Kay, it'll grow again."

Catherine smiled. "I don't mind now."

They left the summit and walked together down the hillside. "I recognise that place," said Mark, pointing to a large pile of stones some distance ahead. "It's the ruin of an old pele tower. I've explored it with Richard. We'll stop there and have some breakfast. Come on!"

The fresh morning air gave them buoyancy and they raced over the heather towards the ruined tower.

Arriving with their faces glowing they sat on some fallen stones beneath a wrecked wall and undid the bundle of food.

"We should reach Otterburn by midday but we'd better save an apple each and some cheese in case we don't get any more to eat for a while."

Mark was not sure how they might obtain food. They had no money but he thought they could help farmers and other people and earn themselves a meal.

After breakfast they bundled up the remaining food. "I'll hide our velvets and your petticoat under these stones."

Leaving the ruin they began the steep descent to a burn. The sun had risen and they felt the air growing warm. "It's going to be a lovely day, Mark."

A movement to his right made Mark look up the valley and he saw two horsemen about half a mile away riding swiftly towards them. "Mosstroopers! Run, Kay!"

Catherine ran down the hillside, while Mark stood to face the horsemen. He thought he could try to detain them and give Catherine a chance to escape. The reaction of the men was immediate: one continued galloping towards him while the other plunged his horse into the valley after Catherine.

'This is the end of our journey,' thought Mark. 'They'll find out who we are and tell Webster.'

As the mosstrooper approached Mark saw he was a powerful man dressed in thick brown clothes with a leather jerkin and riding boots. On one side he wore a sword and on the other a dagger. Mark stood resolutely and looked up at him.

"Ye're a long way from home," said the man in a broad Northumbrian dialect, which Mark could only just understand. "Which way are ye going?"

Mark hesitated. What was happening to Catherine? If she had been hurt … He glanced down the hillside. The other man was riding towards them with Catherine seated in front struggling fiercely.

"This one's a fierce little besom!" he called, in mock agony. "I'll be black and blue!"

"Let me down!" shouted Catherine.

"If ye go on like that ye'll fall doon," said her captor, adding grimly, "Except that I won't let ye!"

When Catherine saw that Mark was standing by the other

trooper unharmed she stopped struggling.

Mark's horseman spoke again. "I don't like the idea of leaving two little lads in this wild place," he said mockingly. "'There are some rum people about. I think ye'd better climb up behind me. And don't try any tricks, if ye please."

Catherine's captor, who had a short livid scar down his left cheek, stationed himself so that Mark was between the horses.

The feelings of elation and confidence that Mark had felt minutes before had changed to one of hopelessness. He was trapped. The towering horses snorted and stamped and shook their heads vigorously on each side of him. It was useless to argue; impossible to run. Mark looked from one man to the other.

"Don't let's waste any more time," said the first horseman, disengaging his left foot from the stirrup and extending his left arm. "Put yo're foot in the stirrup and hoist yersel up."

Mark did as he was told, taking hold of the man's hand and pulling himself up to sit behind. The horse, worried by the extra rider, backed up and moved in a circle. "Steady boy." The trooper's voice was suddenly gentle and he patted the horse's neck. When the animal was still he looked round and said to Mark, "That's a soft pair of hands ye've got." He glanced over at his companion. "There's something queer about this!"

Catherine felt sick and Mark sat silent. Both expected to hear the name Webster.

"Ye've come from Harbottle way, I fancy, so ye must be travelling west or south. Now that's a bit of good fortune for ye because we're going south and then west!" He moved his legs against the horse's flanks and the animal leapt forward. The other horse followed and both galloped down the hillside. The going was hard and rough and Mark clung grimly to his trooper. Catherine, who was in front of her captor, was firmly pinned by the man's elbows. She bent her head slightly forward to avoid contact with his chin and felt glad she could not see his scar.

Reaching the burn at the bottom of the hill the men reined in to allow the horses a drink.

"Shall we go by Gallashiels or through Otterburn?" Mark's trooper asked his friend.

"I don't think we're over popular in Otterburn at the moment," replied scar face and both men roared with laughter.

Catherine and Mark guessed that the men had been involved in a raid on the village and had probably looted farmhouses and cottages and set fire to them; or worse.

They crossed to higher ground on the opposite bank and, following the course of the burn, cantered away to the south. The morning was fine and warm. In other circumstances Catherine and Mark felt they would have enjoyed the ride but neither knew what lay at the end of their journey.

Descending from rough moorland to rough grassland they came to a broad stream. The horses pranced across splashing the riders' legs, scrambled up the low bank on the other side and were urged into a gallop.

The riders leaned forward into the wind as the horses sped surely over the steadily rising ground. Bracing themselves at first against the fury of the ride Mark and Catherine gradually relaxed and allowed themselves to be carried by the strong rhythm of the gallop. The valley to their left broadened and deepened until they lost sight of it. The sun rose high in front of them.

After four miles fierce riding the horses slowed to a canter and just before midday the riders looked down a steep hillside into a broad river valley. Near the bottom of the slope cattle and sheep were grazing and further along the valley were farm buildings. The horses slowed to a leisurely trot.

"Now, me bonnie lads, which way are ye headed?" Mark and Catherine looked across at each other in bewilderment. "What do you mean?" asked Mark.

"Don't you understand the language? I know I don't speak yo'r southern. Where are ye headed? I mean which way are ye going?"

"I understood you," said Mark, "but I didn't think we were free to choose."

"What, not free to choose? Ye've been listening to too many minstrels' tales!" Both men laughed. Mark's horseman became serious. "Ye can reckon yourselves lucky being found by us. Some of our friends might not have been so helpful! Now, which way are ye headed?"

"Corbridge."

"Ye see that track?" The man pointed to a greyish streak running up the other side of the valley. "That's all that remains of Dere street, the old Roman road. It leads to Corbridge and the south."

Catherine and Mark could not believe they were free to go.

"Well – off ye go then! We're going westwards."

Mark slipped easily from his horse while Catherine's trooper lifted her into the air and bending from his saddle set her on the ground. "Oh – thank you!" said Catherine with surprise.

"Don't get yersel's into mischief!" called Mark's trooper and with another shout of laughter they both galloped away.

Brother and sister watched until the brown clothes and the horses merged with the colour of the hills. "I thought mosstroopers were wicked men," said Catherine.

"Some are worse than others apparently," replied Mark. Then he added bitterly, "Until yesterday we thought all tutors were honest."

They climbed down the hillside towards the farm buildings. "Shall we find out if anyone's going in the direction of Corbridge or shall we begin walking?" Catherine's legs felt weary after crossing the Cheviots.

"We might as well ask," said Mark.

They approached a flock of grazing sheep who trotted away bleating and baa-ing. "Silly things!" observed Catherine. "One runs and they all run."

Reaching the level of the valley, Mark led the way to a barn from which came sounds of snuffling, clanking and clucking. Various animal and earthy smells drifted from inside.

They peered into the semi-darkness as a young man came out of the gloom carrying a wooden pail containing eggs. He was sturdily built and had a mass of dark brown hair which fell about his forehead and ears. His bare arms looked very powerful.

"Hello! Where did ye two come from?"

Mark and Catherine stepped back to allow the young man into the open.

"We're trying to get to Corbridge and we were wondering if a farm cart was going that way," said Mark. "We haven't anything to offer in way of payment I'm afraid," he added quickly and rather shyly. He was not used to begging for anything.

"Corbridge?" grinned the young man. "I'm going there mesel this afternoon. Me grandfather's been poorly and I'm going to work for a few days on the farm. There's nothing to stop ye comin' with us if ye like." Catherine and Mark could hardly believe their luck. The young man looked keenly at them. "Could ye do with somethin' to eat?" They nodded. "Come with us then."

He led the way to a grey stone cottage with small windows. They saw that the windows had wooden shutters but no glass and Mark thought grimly and with an empty feeling in his stomach that there was a window without glass at the house near Alwinton. Their escape must have been discovered hours ago. His thoughts were interrupted by the young man's voice. "Mam, we've got company."

They entered a room full of warmth and life. There was a strong smell of leeks. In the middle of the room was a large rough wooden table. The floor was covered with rushes that looked as though they needed replacing. Along one wall was a large open fireplace where two black pots hung on chains over the blazing logs. A woman was preparing a meal.

"Who is it, John?" she asked, turning round. She was a dark little woman, her face red and perspiring from the heat of cooking.

"Two lads on their way to Corbridge," replied her son. "I've promised to take them on the cart this afternoon."

"Where ye from?" The question was natural enough, not really inquisitive.

Mark looked at Catherine, then at John and then at the woman again. "We're on our way south," he said awkwardly.

"Ye don't belong hereabouts – by the sound of ye. Well, there's no call for me to ask questions. We don't have much company and ye both look harmless enough to me – though it's never wise to go by looks. Ye're brothers – I can see by yo'r faces."

Catherine smiled and felt pleased.

"This is Kay and I'm Mark."

"Well, Kay and Mark, as soon as me man returns from the hillside we'll have some food. There's plenty for all of us. Then John can take ye to Corbridge."

"Thank you," said Catherine. "Can we do anything to help?"

"Why sartainly Master Kay, ye can give us a hand with the dinner. Ye'll find some wooden trenchers on the dresser; get them doon. Then ye can fill this flagon at the well."

"And Mark can help me to load the cart. C'mon, Mark."

Mark followed John into the farmyard. He was glad to escape from the hot, smelly kitchen where they were to have their food. He was used to eating with his sister in a cool room that was apart from the kitchen. 'I hope Kay remembers she's a 'boy',' he thought.

"We'll pull the cart into the barn and then pitch the hay doon from the loft."

Mark stood and admired John's skilful use of the pitchfork: plunge, swing, flick, with the hay dropping neatly on to the cart below.

"See how ye get on," said John handing the pitchfork to Mark.

At his first attempt Mark swung the hay back into the loft. At the second try the hay missed the cart and fell near several hens that scattered in all directions clucking loudly. "It's not as easy as it looks," he said to John, who grinned.

The third attempt was more successful but after a few more swings Mark was pleased to hand the pitchfork back to John.

"That's all the hay," said John when the cart was nearly full. "I'm taking a rabbit and some eggs and cheese but we'll put them up just before we leave. Let's see if me dad's back yet. I'm hungry!"

The smell of cooked mutton wafted from the kitchen and Mark realised how hungry he was too.

John's father had just returned and they sat very close together on a bench along one side of the table. The two men discussed the coming harvest while they ate a thick broth.

They wiped their platters afterwards with hunks of dark bread.

"There's plenty more if ye like," said the farmer's wife.

"Ta!" said John. His father nodded and they continued talking.

"Master Kay?"

"No thank you. It was delicious!"

"Mark?"

"Yes please!"

"Ye can help us serve out, Kay," said the farmer's wife as the platters were being wiped again with bread.

In the relaxed family atmosphere Mark and Catherine soon forgot the heat and smells of the kitchen.

Conversation ceased as they devoured mutton, leeks, tares and turnips and was resumed over mugs of ale when the meal was finished. As they listened, Mark and Catherine realised how much they missed the family life that had once been theirs.

The provisions together with some bundles of fleece were placed in the cart and then Mark and Catherine thanked their hosts and climbed on top of the hay. They waved goodbye as John shook the reins and the horse and cart moved forward.

Slowly they were drawn up, out of the river valley and along Dere Street towards Ridsdale and Corbridge. The cart bumped and swayed over the rough track and this motion combined with the large meal of mutton, the mug of ale and the warm afternoon had a soporific effect on them. Before the cart had travelled two miles they were asleep.

Catherine awoke first to see leafy branches apparently passing over the top of the cart. She blinked, sat up and saw that they were going down into a lush green valley. Mark was still asleep and Catherine moved forward over the hay and spoke to John who was humming quietly to himself.

"How much further to Corbridge?"

"A couple of miles."

Catherine flopped back and shook her brother awake. "We're only two miles from Corbridge."

After some time the track forked and John halted the cart. "I go left here; the road to Corbridge goes straight on. Ye'd be welcome to stay with me grandma for the night. They haven't much room but ye could sleep in the kitchen."

Without hesitation Mark replied, "Thank you but we must get on as quickly as we can." He was thinking not only of his brother under sentence of death but also of Cain Webster who must surely be searching for them.

John nodded. "Ye know what's best. But mind how ye go. The ways are dangerous. Ye can trust the farmers but hardly anybody else. Good luck to ye!"

"Goodbye!" they called as he drove away.

The early evening sun sent long shadows across the ground as they walked into Corbridge.

"Where shall we spend the night? I thought we could have stopped with John's grandparents."

Mark told her his fears. "We might manage a few more miles

tonight. In any case it's better to stay the night outside a village. People take note of strangers and if Webster arrived someone would be sure to tell him about us. We might even be treated as vagrants and chased out of the village or put in the stocks!"

They reached the market square and stood wondering which way to go.

"We don't want to start walking in the wrong direction. Look, there's a pele tower standing by the churchyard wall. Perhaps the vicar lives there. He could show us the way south. Let's go and see."

They walked towards the tower and did not notice three men watching them from the shadow of an Inn.

"They look a bit young for the work," said a heavily built man in ragged clothes and with a grimy face, "They've no muscles on them."

"They've two pair o' hands, " growled the short pale youth next to him.

The third man, who was cleaner and better dressed said quietly, "They can be made to work. Get them."

The small wooden door at the bottom of the pele tower was open. Mark walked into the barrel-roofed ground floor room and called up the stone stairs. There was no reply.

"It's just like our tower at Alwinton," observed Catherine.

"We'll see if anyone's upstairs," said Mark.

The first floor room contained a truckle bed, a table and two stools. It looked very untidy. They climbed up to the second floor. Here was a larger bed, a wooden chest and a small table with one stool. A black gown was lying on the floor near the bed and there was the same air of untidiness. In the far corner of the room a shaft of evening sunlight was streaming through an opening in one wall. They went over to investigate. The opening was so shaped to direct the light from outside across the corner of the room and on to the next wall where a sloping desk had been hollowed out of the stone. Upon the desk lay an open book. They could read the print quite easily in the bright shaft of sunlight.

"It's the vicar's reading and writing desk," said Mark. He stiffened suddenly. "Listen!"

"What?"

"I thought I heard something downstairs."

They crossed the room and went down to the first floor. "I'm sure I heard something."

They descended to the ground floor and turning to walk into the open Mark felt himself gripped from behind. A rough hand was slapped across his mouth. He heard a gasp and a moan from his sister.

"Keep still or have your throat cut!" hissed a voice in his ear.

"This one's swooned," said another voice. "He won't be much use getting pit-coal."

"Give me a hand then."

Mark was swung round and forced to kneel. Then he was held by one man while the other gagged him and tied his wrists and ankles. Lying on the floor he watched the two men gag Catherine and tie her wrists. Then they were lifted up and carried into the open.

The third man was waiting outside. "There's no one about. Put them in the wagon." They were taken to a covered cart nearby and flung on the floor inside. Mark landed heavily beside another body, which was also bound and gagged.

"Let's go. They may live here and be recognised and then we'd be in trouble."

From the floor Mark watched his captor climb into the back of the cart and heard the others getting on the driving seat. Then the cart moved slowly off.

"They'll crawl along the low tunnels easy enough," said one of the men in front. "And if they can't do the work they can be got rid of!"

"Keep still or have your throat cut!"

ChAPTER FOUR

Pit-Coal

The wagon lurched into potholes, heaved and slid over large stones lying on the rough road. Each shudder jolted the three bound bodies lying on the dirty, splintered floor of the covered cart. Mark made a short anguished noise in his throat, shook his head and tried to bite through the gag that numbed the corners of his mouth, but it was securely tied. He glanced at his sister who appeared to have fallen into an exhausted sleep. Attempting to ease the pain in his right shoulder which struck the floor whenever the cart lurched, he rolled on to his back but this proved more uncomfortable for he was forced to lie on his tied hands. With some difficulty, for his ankles were also bound, he manoeuvred himself on to his left side and looked into the face of the young stranger who was also gagged. He saw a mass of black hair, dark eyes and a grubby face that looked pale and thin under the dirt.

The two boys stared at one another and each took some comfort from the sympathy that seemed to flow between them. Then suddenly Mark felt very tired and everything including the pain began to drift away from him. The face watching him became misty, the sound made by the cartwheels blurred and faded. Like his sister he slept exhausted while the face under the black, curly hair continued to stare at him.

For half an hour the curly haired boy lay watching, until the last rays of the setting sun shone into the back of the cart. Then he heard the driver cry, "Whoa!" and the cart crunched to a halt.

Mark and Catherine became aware of voices shouting and calling. Scarcely awake they were dragged from the cart with the other boy and carried to a dingy storeroom at the end of a barn. They were dumped on the earth floor, their gags and bonds were untied and the wooden door was slammed and barred. Fading light filtered in from a hole in the door.

Mark's wrists and ankles felt sore. The insides of his lips were dry and the corners of his mouth were raw where the cloth gag had chafed his skin. He turned to his sister who looked very pale in the poor light. "Are you all right, Kay?"

"Yes, except that I ache all over. What do you think they're going to do with us?"

"Make us dig for pit-coal."

"Where?"

"There's a place called New Castle not far from Corbridge. A lot of coal comes from there I believe."

"Why should they make us do the work?"

Mark shrugged "I don't know. Cain Webster once told me that the pit-coal owners can make a lot of money. Perhaps they can't get enough people to dig for it."

"What happens to all the pit-coal?"

"It's taken by sea to London and other big towns."

"London!" they exclaimed together, their faces suddenly bright with joy. Then both glanced guiltily towards the door. Was anyone listening?

Mark lowered his voice. "If we could escape and get aboard one of the ships," he whispered.

"A ship to London! I wonder how long the journey takes?"

A slight movement made them look round. In the excitement they had forgotten their new companion. He was sitting cross-legged near a corner of the small storeroom and looking at them with large dark eyes from under his tangle of hair. Mark went to him and saw how dirty and scratched were his arms and legs.

"Where do you come from?" he enquired as though addressing a young vagrant. The boy looked at him but said nothing. "Where do you come from?" The question was repeated severely for Mark felt irritated at receiving no answer. Still the boy said nothing and turned his face away.

Catherine's reaction was gentle and compassionate. "My brother doesn't mean you any harm," she said, going over to the boy. "It's just his way of talking. We're all in this trouble together and we must try to help each other."

The boy looked at her.

Mark, inwardly regretting his sharp tone and learning humility from his sister, overcame his aversion to talking to such a grubby mass of tatters and said, "My sister's right. We must help each other and try to get away."

"Only I'm not your sister," interrupted Catherine. "I'm your brother, Kay!"

"Oh Lord!" muttered Mark. He regretted his slip for it put him under an obligation to the boy. Could a young vagrant be trusted? "Look – we can't explain now – we're pretending Kay is my brother. Will you keep our secret?"

The boy's eyes opened wider and he looked from one to the other but still he said nothing.

There was a crash as the wooden bar was removed and the door flung open. The burly man who had driven the cart looked in and said, "Here's mite food." He placed a large bowl and half a loaf of dark bread on the earth floor. "When you've finished that get some sleep; there's some straw in the corner to lie on. You'll be up early tomorrow with a hard day's work ahead of you!" Then the door slammed shut and they heard the bar replaced.

Catherine picked up the bowl of broth and the bread. There was one spoon between them. "We must share this equally. Here, Mark, you eat first. I'll divide the bread."

"No Kay," said Mark firmly. "You have what you want." He divided the bread into three, gave his sister one piece and offered another to the boy who took it in silence.

Catherine ate some broth and then forced herself to eat the dry rye bread. Mark ate his share from the bowl and passed it to the boy who ate quickly, glancing at them occasionally.

Meanwhile Mark dragged the stubbly straw from the corner and spread it on the floor for Catherine and himself. Then he placed the rest in a pile near the boy.

It was now almost dark and Catherine and her brother stretched out near one wall. They half watched the boy wipe the inside of the bowl with a piece of bread and then place the bowl on the floor. Next he arranged his bed of hay and settled down upon it.

All was still. The moon rose and its light filtered through cracks in the wooden door and the hole in the roof. Then Catherine heard what sounded like a stifled gasp from across the room. She sat up. Mark had heard it too. Propped up by their elbows they heard other short gasps. Motioning Catherine to remain still, Mark moved across the small room and crouched down.

The boy had heard him coming and had turned to face the wall but it was clear to Mark that he was in tears and trying not to sob loudly.

"What's the matter? Can we help?"

The thin form shook with another sob and the boy turned on to his stomach, his face covered by the crook of his left arm.

Mark returned to Kay and said softly, "What can we do?"

"Nothing, we must wait until he trusts us enough."

They lay back on the hay. Soon Mark heard his sister breathing deeply and rhythmically. It was not long before he too fell asleep. But the dark-haired boy lay tense and troubled far into the night, his head still shielded by the crook of his arm.

Early next morning they were taken to the covered cart that had brought them from Corbridge. "You're going to the new pit-coal workings near New Castle."

Clinging to the back of the cart as it swayed and bumped over the uneven ground they passed fields and meadows glistening with dew. The treetops of a wood shivered orange, green and gold in the early sunlight. The air was light and filled with birdsong.

They emerged from the wood into a sunlit valley. But the beauty of the valley had been scarred. The once green floor was furrowed brown with cart tracks and the sides were disfigured by several black and brown pyramids: huge mounds of coal and earth.

Two men were shovelling at the base of one black heap and were throwing coal on to a horse-drawn wagon.

Near each mound of coal were three wooden sheds. The driver stopped the cart near one group of sheds, dismounted, walked over to some men and touched his forehead to one of them. The man pointed to sheds a short distance away. The driver nodded and returned to the wagon.

"You've to go down number four pit to-day." He flicked the reins and the horse jolted the wagon forward.

They reached the pit-sheds and the driver jumped down. "Out ye get!" He walked towards the largest of the three sheds. "Hey! I've brought some extra help!"

Mark, Catherine and the boy climbed from the cart and stood wondering what sort of person would be in charge of them.

In answer to the cart-driver's call a pleasant looking man emerged wiping his hands on a piece of cloth. He stopped short when he saw the three children and frowned. "Ye're not expecting these youngsters to work doon the pit, are ye? What does Master Tresswell think he's doing?"

"I don't know about him – he owns all this doesn't he?" replied the driver. "The children are Mister Fenwick's business. He found one in Chester and the others in Corbridge."

"Well, Master Tresswell should be told about it. Children for this sort of work! It's all wrong!"

"I know exactly what I'm doing!" They all looked round and the children saw the tall thin man from Corbridge. "You look after your job and I'll attend to mine. Get them below and working immediately. Your job, Martin Hartley, is to get coal to the surface in large quantities and not to question the methods used." He turned to the driver. "Follow me with the cart and let's waste no more time gossiping!"

The driver climbed on the wagon, urged the horse around and followed Fenwick up the valley.

Hartley looked from one to another of his new recruits. "What do they call ye?"

"I'm Kay," said Catherine, before her brother could accidentally give away their secret. "And this is my brother, Mark."

Hartley turned to the other boy.

The curly-haired lad looked at him in silence as though trying to make up his mind about something. Then he said, "Tom."

Hartley nodded. "It'll be a minute or two before ye can go doon. Come and have a look at me pump." He led the way into the biggest shed where Mark, Kay and Tom saw a large wooden cogwheel. The shaft had a handle at each end and was hold in position by two wood blocks.

"Men turn the handles and this big wheel revolves. Its wooden teeth fit right into the grooves in the little wheel underneath. Aren't they beautifully carved? See how neatly the teeth fit into the grooves." He was obviously very proud of his machinery. "It needs a lot of grease to keep it running smoothly. That's what I was doing when ye came. Because the wheel underneath is smaller it spins round much faster. These shaped bits at the ends of the small wheel shaft make the rods move up and down and they draw water up the pipes from the pit below by suction. Turn the handle, Tom, and listen what happens."

Tom's face lit up for the first time and he took hold of the handle at one end of the shaft. He turned slowly and they heard gurgling and sucking noises coming from below. But no water appeared.

"There are five sets of pipes and troughs for this pit," Hartley continued. "The water is drawn up the bottom pipe and into the first trough. Then the next pipe draws it from that trough up into the second trough. When the water reaches the top trough it's carried away to a small stream that runs doon one side of the valley. It's quite simple really and keeps the pit tunnels from being flooded when there's heavy rain."

"When was it last used?" enquired Mark.

"Two days ago. We've had very little rain recently. Come and see the other workings."

He led the way out of the pumping station to the next shed. "That's where ye'll go doon but let's see this one first."

He crossed to the third and smallest shed that was open at both ends. Outside the shed on the far side was a pyramid of coal. "This is where the coal comes up. It's like a well – a coal well. Ye turn the handle, the rope winds round the spindle and a large bucket filled with coal comes to the surface. A few days ago one of the tunnels was dug as far as the side of the valley about a quarter of a mile away. They've just started to use that new opening to get the coal out in small wooden wagons; it's easier and quicker. They'll do anything for speed. The more speed the more coal; the more coal the more money. But we still winch up the coal to help out."

They walked back to the second shed where two men had arrived. One peered down the hole, cupped his hands to his mouth and yelled down, "Are ye coming up?" After a slight pause, during which the watchers heard nothing, the man, who had his head in the hole, turned and said, "They're ready." There were two jerks on the rope causing the shaft handle to move. "There's the signal!"

The men grasped the handle and began turning. After much effort and what seemed a very long time, two heads appeared from the hole in the ground. Seconds later the men stepped off the wooden platform drawn up by the rope. They were dirty and covered in sweat. Their faces, chests and arms were filthy with coal dust and the lines on their faces were encrusted with black. They staggered slightly, blinked their eyes in the bright daylight and stumbled away up the valley.

Hartley and the children watched them go. Then Hartley said, "Ye'd better go doon. But I'll see to it that yo're not there long. When the owner hears about youngsters working in his pits I bet there'll be some skin and hair flying."

He moved away and spoke quietly to the man at the winch. "Mind ye go canny with the three lads now. Two men were killed last week and another had his legs broken because the winders were careless. Lower them slowly."

The men at the winch nodded and spat on their hands. Mark, Catherine and Tom stood close together on the platform holding on to each other as well as the rope, and the contraption was lowered slowly into the hole.

Over one hundred feet below ground the children waited for the platform to return with Martin Hartley. The atmosphere was hot and sticky. They felt they were breathing dust and not air. In the pale light of the rush dips they could see to reach up and touch the roof of the tunnel that was supported every few feet by stout timber props. Mark stretched out his arms and found he could reach the wall on either side. They peered along the tunnel into the black distance and heard scraping and knocking sounds.

"There's someone working along there," said Catherine.

"This is where they pull up the coal," said a voice.

Catherine and Mark turned to see Tom staring up towards the roof a few feet behind them. It was the first time he had spoken to them. Mark glanced at his sister and they joined Tom under a hole in the gallery roof. They looked up and could just make out the tiniest speck of light far above them.

There was a bumping sound from the descent shaft and small stones fell down into the tunnel. They heard Hartley's voice calling, "Mind oot the way below!" Moments later, bumping and scraping the sides of the shaft and with more falls of stones and small rocks, the wooden platform, secured from above by rope, grated on to the tunnel floor. Hartley stepped from it and stooped into the tunnel with the children. Then from nowhere two more stooping figures appeared, stepped on to the platform and pulled twice on the rope. A moment later they were hauled up out of sight as more stones fell down the shaft.

"Ha'way," said Hartley, and he bent forward into the darkness ahead. Tom, Catherine and Mark, who was last, followed the pit-coal worker along the tunnel and it was not long before Mark too was stooping to avoid the low roof. In the close atmosphere sweat broke out over their faces and they felt hot and clammy.

Hartley stopped and in the light of two rush dips they saw that the tunnel forked.

"That tunnel joins with another from pit number two. This one leads to the side of the valley and the open air. The coal from this tunnel is taken by truck to the tunnel mouth. Coal from this other tunnel goes either to pit number two or is taken back the way we'ave just come and gets hauled up by bucket. We'll go along by here first."

Martin Hartley led the way stooping along the tunnel towards pit two. The sounds of picking grew louder and soon they reached a low wider area where two rush dips showed a man lying on his side and chipping into the wall.

"Yon's Jack Hetherington," said Hartley.

A wooden truck half filled with coal stood nearby.

"Here's a pick and a shovel. Sort them out between yoursel's."

Mark took the tools and handed the shovel to Kay.

"There's only room for three to work here. Tom, ye come back along the other tunnel with me. I'll be back shortly to see how yo're getting on. Jack," said Hartley, addressing the man working on the floor, "Go canny with yo'r new mates; they're only youngsters. They'll not be doon here long if I can help it. Ha'way wi' me, Tom."

The man grunted by way of reply and continued chipping. Mark knelt down on the floor and began picking at the coal in the wall opposite Hetherington. Kay, who was also forced to stoop slightly now, started shovelling coal into the truck.

After some minutes Mark found the kneeling position very uncomfortable. His knees felt sore. He lay on his side, supported himself on his left elbow and continued working. A little later he shifted his position and supported himself with his right elbow.

It grew hotter and dustier. Both Catherine and Mark felt their noses becoming blocked with coal dust and their throats growing parched. Their arms and backs ached and Mark, whose pick seemed to have become four times heavier since he first used it, put the tool on the floor and leaned against the wall. Kay continued shovelling.

Hetherington stopped work and looked at the children.

"Hot work isn't it? I'm hungry. Fancy a bit of cheese? I might even find an apple for ye each."

Mark found he could only croak, "Please."

"The food's along here, I'll be back in a minute." Stooping low he crawled into the darkness towards pit number two and disappeared, although Mark and Catherine could still hear a faint scuffling noise as the man scraped his way along the gritty floor of the underground passage.

They listened intently for the man's return.

Suddenly there was a loud explosion and the tunnel erupted all around them. Earth, rocks and coal flared off the walls, timber props collapsed and large sections of the roof caved in. Both children felt themselves flung several feet before they were buried under the debris of coal, stones and pit props.

The noise subsided and was followed by an awful silence. Then there was a rush of earth and rocks as more of the gallery roof collapsed. Then there was silence again.

In the darkness Catherine had the strange impression of being upside down. She was lying across something hard. Trying to sit up she realised that her feet were above her head. Searching carefully with her hands she touched thick, rough wood and realised she must be lying across a pit prop. She stretched her arms above and around her but could contact neither roof nor walls. She felt very frightened. "Mark?" There was no answer. She called again but still there was no response. She attempted to move and the pit prop tilted suddenly putting her head even lower.

Feeling downwards beyond her head Catherine's hands encountered a hard, rough surface. Could it be the tunnel floor? She called again, softly, as though fearful that a loud sound might bring more roof crashing down. "Mark?" But still there was no reply.

'I can't lie here,' she thought to herself. 'I must get on my feet.' She eased herself slowly downwards towards the hard rough surface and the pit prop tilted again and some rubble slithered and fell down with her. If only she could see! Easing herself along by bending and stretching her legs she found herself sitting on the hard surface. She felt around and her hands touched something solid behind her. She presumed it must be the tunnel wall. She reached slowly upwards and moved into a crouching position. Her hands touched the tunnel roof. This section must have remained intact – roof and walls alike. But where was Mark? And which way should she go? She had lost all sense of direction.

For a short while fear took hold of her. She was trapped, entombed.

She called again, "Mark!"

The atmosphere was thick with dust stirred up by the explosion and Catherine coughed and choked. She sat on the floor again and by making herself think clearly shook the fear from her. She thought of her elder brother, Richard, who was also entombed in the Tower of London. His position was worse than hers. Chained to the wall by his legs, no doubt tortured upon the rack and with thumbscrews, or worse, he had no hope of escape. But her legs were not chained. She could help herself.

Catherine crouched on all fours and keeping the wall on her left began to move slowly along, feeling her way all the time. She had moved about five feet by her own reckoning when she encountered a pile of rock in front of her. She felt upwards and found that it sloped away from her. She started clambering up the slope of rock and rubble but her head came into contact with the tunnel roof. She felt her way to the right and what she thought must be the middle of the tunnel. Then quite suddenly as she put her weight on something solid there was a movement and Catherine found herself propelled forward as all beneath her gave way. Putting her arms out in front she could feel solid ground again. Her weight must have dislodged a pit prop that was supporting a pile of rubble and it had all collapsed beneath her.

She began to crawl forward and to her horror put her hand on a human leg. She withdrew her hand, trembling violently. Someone groaned just in front of her. Still trembling she put her hand out again and gripped what felt like an ankle.

"Mark? Oh, Mark! Oh, are you hurt?"

"I feel all right but I can't move. Something's on top of me, holding me to the floor. Are you all right?"

"Yes. I wish I could see you. I called you several times."

"I think I was knocked out for a few minutes. I can't remember anything but a bang."

Catherine crawled forward. Feeling around in the dark she concluded that a pit prop had fallen across her brother. She tried to move the prop but it would not budge.

"I can't help you," said Mark. "My arms are trapped."

Catherine traced the length of the prop and found that one end was buried in a pile of rubble. She pushed it again but there was no movement.

"I'll see if I can free this end," she said and began to claw at the rubble. But it was a hopeless task in the dark. As fast as she dragged away lumps of coal and rock more slithered from above and took its place. After a few minutes she felt that she had made no impression and the pit prop was as firm and tight as ever. She crawled back to Mark.

"Can't you move at all?"

"Only my legs, slightly. And I can roll my head about. But the prop is holding me by the waist. I can't move up or down. It's lucky that the prop is jammed in rubble; if it had crashed down to the floor...."

Mark left his thoughts unspoken. He was lucky to be alive.

"I must loosen it somehow," said Catherine, with great determination. She crawled back to the pile of rubble and began clawing at it once more.

Then she stiffened with fear as she heard another slithering sound followed by a low rumbling crash somewhere in the darkness just ahead. More of the tunnel roof must have fallen in. Even if she did free Mark their way out of the mine was hopelessly blocked. There were further sounds of rumbling and slithering and then quiet.

In the silence and the blackness Mark tried to push himself from under the wooden prop with his legs but he was held tight.

Catherine knelt on all fours, despairing. And then from the blackness a gentle voice called softly, "Mark: Kay: Are you there?"

"Oh, Tom! We're here. But Mark's trapped."

There were more sounds of falling rubble. Catherine, who was staring into blackness in the direction of Tom's voice, suddenly seemed to see something. It was a very faint light like a pale smudge in the air. As her eyes grew accustomed Catherine could see a small gap near the roof through which the light was coming. The hole seemed to grow larger. Then Catherine made out the outline of a head in the gap: an outline surrounded by a mass of black curls.

The gap in the rubble grew larger and minutes later Tom had pulled himself through. The hole was just wide enough to allow him passage. He leant back through the hole and collected the rush dip that was the source of light.

Mark was lying on the floor with his head towards the gap in the rubble. The pit prop was wedged against the wall less than a foot from the floor on one side, and on the other side it was buried in the heap of rubble that Catherine had torn her hands trying to clear.

Tom took one look at Mark and then began to work on the mound of rubble with the speed of a terrier. Catherine joined him. After a few moments Tom pulled upwards at the prop but there was no movement. He jumped back to the rubble and cleared some more coal and rocks. Another heave at the pit prop and this time there was a slight movement.

"Can you get out?" Tom said to Mark.

Mark tried but shook his head.

Tom bent down, placed both his hands under the wooden beam, gritted his teeth and pulled upwards. This time there was further movement. Mark pushed with his feet but was still stuck.

"Next time I lift you try to slide out," said Tom.

Another desperate heave from Tom, the prop lifted a fraction and Mark was free.

Tom returned to the gap and placed the rush dip on the other side. Then he turned and looked at Catherine. She scrambled up the rubble and pulled herself slowly through the hole. Mark tried to squeeze through but Tom was slimmer and the hole was not big enough. The boys removed some more rubble and Mark pulled himself through followed by Tom.

Mark and Catherine found themselves in another small chamber and Tom indicated a narrow tunnel in the wall of rubble that faced them. Mark and Catherine looked at each other. Tom must have worked frantically to reach them and at considerable risk.

They could see a light at the other end of the short tunnel and after the hole had been made larger for Mark to get through the three found themselves standing beside a relieved Hartley in an undamaged gallery.

"Are ye all all right?" he asked.

"Yes thank you," replied Catherine and Mark together.

"What happened to Jack Hetherington?" said Hartley.

"We forgot about him," gasped Catherine. "He went the other way just before the explosion."

"I'll look," said Tom.

'No, ye won't," said Hartley. "I'll get a man through to search for him. Ye've already done more than yo'r fair share me lad. Let's get into the air."

Where the tunnel forked they met two pit-coal men carrying a rush dip on their way to help.

"Jack Hetherington may be trapped somewhere towards pit number two," Hartley told them. "Ye'll find two gaps in the rubble. Ye'll have to make them bigger. Go through and see if ye can find him."

Then stooping he led the way along the tunnel where Tom had been working before the explosion. Gradually the air became less dusty and the children could feel a draught on their sweaty faces. Once or twice they pressed, stooping, against the tunnel wall to allow pit-coal men to pass on their way to work. Then, at last, they were aware of daylight and moments later, blinking in the glaring light, they emerged on to the side of the valley.

Mark and Catherine dropped exhausted on to a rough patch of grass and lay on their backs with their eyes shut. Tom sat blinking a few feet away and chewed a piece of grass. Hartley sat beside him.

"What caused the bang?"

"I don't know, Tom. It happened once before – about three months ago in one of the other pits. It might be something to do with the lights. That's why I didn't want ye to go back along that gallery. Yo're a very brave lad. There might have been another explosion. But if it hadn't been for ye yo'r two friends wouldn't have come out alive."

'My two friends,' thought Tom. He looked at the ground and continued chewing.

"The three of ye aren't going down any more pits," said Hartley, firmly. "I'm going to see the owner, Master Tresswell. He's not going to allow it!"

Mark and Catherine found themselves in another small chamber.

CHAPTER FIVE

New Castle

Mark lay in the rough grass and felt the sun warm his eyelids and cheeks. As he rested he recalled the events of the last hour. Kay and he had come close to death. They might have been killed immediately by the explosion or, trapped for many hours between the massive roof falls, they could have suffocated slowly. Tom had risked his life to save them. 'But why?' thought Mark. 'He's known us less than two days. Why risk your life for two strangers?'

Mark wondered if he would risk his life for someone he scarcely knew. He would risk everything for Richard but that was different: Richard was his brother! But was it right to think that the life of one person was more precious than that of another? He lay back and closed his eyes again. Tom's unselfish action had made him think deeply.

Lying beside Mark, Catherine tried to forget the worst moments in the pit when, in the darkness, she had called in vain to her brother. Instead she thought of the men who had to work daily under the ground in such appalling conditions and danger. And she thought of Tom. At home in Warwickshire her few young friends were the sons and daughters of other rich families. The only servant that she and Mark had come to know well was Gabriel, the young shepherd, and he seemed different from others of his class. There was a sense of mystery about him that set him apart from everyone else. Now they had a friend who seemed little more than a vagabond and there was a sense of mystery about him too. But vagabond or no Catherine felt sure he could be trusted.

"Ha'way!" said Hartley. I'll take you for a wash in the river."

They walked along the rutted track that led out of the scarred valley with its mounds of pit-coal and earth. "The carts carry the pit-coal along here to the river," said Hartley. Turning from the track they followed a footpath across a cornfield and a meadow to a hamlet of five cottages with a farm nearby.

"Wait here while I get some soap." Hartley entered a grey stone cottage with a tiled roof.

Mark wanted to thank Tom for saving them but could not find

the right words. He would have found it easy to thank his equal but what should one say to this ragged boy? He wanted to give him something but he had no money. Should he give him his pocket knife?

Hartley reappeared with a small woman who wore a woollen bodice with a rough woollen skirt reaching almost to her ankles.

"This is Mistress Hartley."

"Ye poor bairns," she said. "Ye look as though ye could do with some food. I'll heat some barley broth while yo're away at the river and see what else I can find for ye to eat."

Martin Hartley handed the soap to Kay. "That'll help to clean ye up, young man! Ha'way!"

Catherine was worried. If Hartley remained while they washed he might learn the truth about her. Although he could probably be trusted, the fewer people who knew their secret the safer they would be.

As they walked through a grove Catherine pulled Mark's sleeve and they allowed the others to walk ahead.

"It's going to be difficult for me washing in the river if Mr. Hartley stays."

"Oh goodness!" Mark frowned and thought for a moment.

"Could you keep some of your clothes on?"

"Mr. Hartley will think it very odd. Besides they'll take ages to dry even in this warm weather."

"Let's see what happens. If necessary we'll have to confide in him."

They caught up with Hartley and Tom who were chatting amiably. Tom seemed positively animated.

"Here we are," said Hartley as they came to the edge of a steep bank. "I'll leave ye here. Ye'll find yo'r way back to the cottage all right?"

"Easily!" replied Catherine and Mark together.

"Champion! Mistress Hartley will have the dinner ready by the time ye get back." And with a smile and a nod Martin Hartley turned and walked back towards the trees and his cottage.

"I've got the soap!" shouted Catherine. She felt suddenly jubilant. "I'll see you both in the water." She skipped a few feet along the bank and slid down to the river on the other side of a large bush. The boys jumped down to a flat piece of ground by the water's edge. Tom froze as a flash of sapphire flew swiftly downstream.

"Look! A Kingfisher!"

They watched until the bird was out of sight and then Tom began dragging off his dirty, ragged shirt.

Mark removed his jerkin now smeared with pit-coal dust and began taking off his shirt. He noticed how small and how thin Tom was. His ribs seemed to be pushing through from beneath his skin and his arms and legs were wiry and had little muscle on them.

Tom glanced with envy at his more mature friend.

They stood for a moment, naked. Then a splash from the other side of the bush told them Kay was in the water and together the boys plunged into the river.

The water felt cold and exhilarating. They passed the soap between them and washed thoroughly to remove all trace of the black filth of the pit-coal. It was like washing away a disease as their skins returned to the natural colour. Wet hair clung to their ears and necks.

Tom trod water and occasionally felt the gravel bed of the river with one foot. Mark, who could not swim, stood with the water just reaching his waist.

"Thank you, Tom, for saving us. It was a very brave thing to do. I hope that in time we shall be able to repay you."

Although sincere Mark felt his words hopelessly inadequate and was still conscious that he had a debt he must repay.

Tom blushed with pleasure. No one had ever treated him with such courtesy. He felt pleased to have saved his friends and wanted nothing in return.

They washed their shirts and hose and wrung them as dry as possible. Then they shook the dirt from their breeches. Some of this transferred itself to their bodies and so they plunged once more into the river. Eventually, stripped to the waist, they carried their other garments back to Hartley's cottage.

Although the bathe in the river had refreshed them the midday heat sapped all their remaining energy and by the time they reached the cottage they felt exhausted. Hunger gave them the energy to eat the broth, eggs and green vegetables provided by Mrs. Hartley but on completion of the meal they could scarcely keep awake. Martin

Hartley took them up the straight narrow staircase and then by an almost vertical ladder into the small loft where they fell asleep on the dry straw.

They slept for six hours and it was late evening when Mrs. Hartley called them. "Come doon for yo'r supper. There's more barley broth and some bread and cheese."

When they had eaten she handed them their dry clothes. "Now I think ye should go straight back to the loft. Ye look tired and washed out. With a bit more sleep you'll be fit for anything in the morning! And ye can rest easy. Mr. Hartley saw Mr. Tresswell, the pit owner, this afternoon and ye'll not be going down the pit any more. That Fenwick's in trouble and serve him right!"

They climbed happily back into the loft. Now that the threat of the pit was banished from their minds the idea of sleeping on straw in a loft was an enjoyable adventure for Catherine and Mark. For Tom it was a luxury to have somewhere dry and warm to sleep. He lay on the straw in the darkness and felt the presence of his two friends.

"Good-night Tom," called Catherine, softly. "Thank you for rescuing us this morning."

"Yes. Good-night Tom."

"Good-night."

How beautiful life could be! Tom turned on to his side and, looking towards his friends in the darkness, fell asleep.

After breakfast the next morning Martin Hartley sat on the edge of the wooden kitchen table and surveyed his three young visitors now refreshed and bright-eyed.

"Ye can go now. Mr. Tresswell says that ye must be helped back to yo'r homes. Can we do anything for ye? Where do ye want to go? Back to Corbridge?"

Mark glanced at his sister and stood up from his stool to face their host. He chose his words carefully.

"Mr. Hartley, I believe we can trust you."

Hartley frowned slightly and nodded.

"I would rather not say where we've come from. Kay and I are on our way to London. We must get there as quickly as possible"

"To London? On yo'r way to London?" Hartley sounded incredulous. He looked from Mark to Catherine. "How on earth do ye propose getting there?"

"We wondered if we could sail on one of the ships carrying pit-coal?"

"Well – I suppose it could be arranged. The ships dock at Billingsgate just beyond the Tower."

Mark and his sister felt an inward excitement when Hartley mentioned the fortress where Richard was imprisoned.

"How long will the journey take?"

"About fourteen days given the weather keeps up. The ships aren't built for speed but to carry as much coal as possible."

Mark thought swiftly. Fourteen days – two weeks: Webster had reckoned that Richard had about four or five weeks before sentence would be carried out.

"The North Sea can be very rough. Are ye good sailors?"

"We'll have to find out! How long would it take by road?"

"It's hard to say. It might take only a week; it could take a month or more. The roads are very bad. Besides ye might be taken for vagabonds and put in the stocks or the pillory. And there are cut-purses and worse. Ye might never get there at all. But by sea at least ye have a fair chance, and ye should be at Billingsgate in fourteen days."

'That's our way then if you would be kind enough to arrange it."

"And what about ye, Tom?" Hartley enquired. "We can take ye home."

Tom felt confused. "I – would you – could you ... " He faltered. "Corbridge would do, thank you."

Hartley frowned. "Are ye sure that's what ye want? Mr. Tresswell knows what a grand lad ye've been and he'll do anything for ye."

Tom felt empty. "Corbridge will do. Really."

Catherine, who had been watching Tom closely, said, "Would you rather come to London with us?" And then she wondered if she had spoken too hastily. What would Mark think?

Mark was wishing that he had thought of the invitation first. Perhaps this was a way of repaying Tom. "Would you, Tom?" he said.

"Oh yes! I would!"

Hartley grinned and looked at each of them in turn. "Well,

I canna make head nor tail of it. But I suppose ye all know what yo're doing. Three young adventurers! But if yo're serious ye must know someone in London. It's an unfriendly, dangerous place I hear tell."

Mark nodded. "Believe me, Mr. Hartley, we have a very good reason for going."

Catherine looked with pride at her brother who appeared so confident. Tom felt great happiness: he was travelling to London with his new friends! What an adventure it would be!

Hartley left immediately to see Tresswell and the three friends spent the day helping Mrs. Hartley in her vegetable plot.

Late in the afternoon their host returned. "There's a ship leaving for London in three days. We'll travel to Newcastle the day after tomorrow and ye can spend the night on board. The next day ye'll sail with the tide."

The three travellers were delighted although Mark was worried about the delay. One day could make all the difference in saving Richard. He slept badly that night. Try as he would he could not get comfortable on the straw bed. Eventually he dozed off but slept only fitfully and awoke at first cock-crow.

The next day passed slowly for him. Catherine and Tom seemed cheerful enough but Mark kept glancing towards the sun. Would the shadows of the trees never lengthen? He threw himself frenziedly into repairing a stone wall for the neighbouring farmer.

Eventually night came and exhausted by their labours the three friends slept long and deeply.

After breakfast they climbed on to an open cart. Mrs. Hartley handed up some apples, pears and cheese. "That'll keep you going until you're on board. The Lord bless you and bring you safely and blithely to the end of your journey."

"I'll see you sometime tomorrow," said Hartley to his wife as he mounted the horse. "Giddup, Bess!"

"Goodbye! And thank you!" they called as the cart moved off.

They rejoined the rutted track used by the pit-coal wagons but turned away from the scarred valley. The wheel-gauge of the cart was not as wide as that of the coal wagons and they proceeded at an angle with one wheel in a rut and the other bumping over the rough ground between the ruts. They were shaken vigorously and clung to the sides of the cart for support.

"Sorry it's a rough ride. It'll get better when we reach the Tyne. The track there is much wider and we can choose our way."

They jolted on beside a broad stream for several miles and just before midday reached a wide river. "That's the Tyne. It flows through New Castle and into the North Sea."

Now the cart ran quite smoothly and they stood up and looked ahead. About half a mile away hung a low black cloud of dust. As they drew nearer they saw a jetty with four flat wooden barges moored alongside. A small army of men was shovelling coal into the barges from large black mounds piled nearby. Further off three more barges filled with pit-coal were very low in the water.

"Our pit-coal is brought here, loaded on to those keels and then taken by the lightermen down river to New Castle where it's transferred to the three masted merchantmen tied up at the staithes."

Inside the dust cloud everything lost its natural colour and looked grey. And it was colder. The black specks got up their nostrils and down their throats and they coughed. The horror of the pit came vividly back to them.

They held their breath as long as they could to avoid taking the pernicious dust into their lungs.

Finally they emerged from the filth and the colour of the day returned.

A mile further Bess pulled the cart on to a stretch of high ground and looking downstream they saw in the distance a bridge leading to a town on the opposite bank.

"That's New Castle. Only a few miles more to go. Let's have something to eat."

Bess was taken from the shafts to graze and they sat on the grass and ate some of Mrs. Hartley's fruit and cheese.

Two hours later they emerged from the arch of a building, on the southern end of the bridge and saw on the opposite bank part of the magnificent fortified wall that surrounded the town. Standing on a hill in the town's centre and dominating everything was the Castle.

Hartley drew their attention to several coal-laden keels that were negotiating the narrow arches of the bridge. Then he pointed downstream to the harbour where they could see the masts of several sea-going merchantmen.

"That's where we're making for!"

They turned right at the north end of the bridge and clattering and jolting over the hard cobbled street in the shadow of the high wall they made their way towards the harbour.

"The finest town wall in England," said Hartley.

"Why is it called New Castle?" enquired Mark.

"I heard tell that the Normans built a new castle on the site of an old Roman fort."

"Did they build the wall as well?

"No. That was begun about 1280 or 1290 to keep the Scots oot."

"Like our pele tower," said Catherine, who immediately bit her lip and blushed.

Hartley glanced quickly at Catherine and smiled but said nothing.

The harbour was a frenzy of activity. Two men, obviously wealthy and looking splendid in their slashed doublets and coloured hose, appeared to be arguing with several other men also well dressed but in less colourful material. Their doublets were not slashed to allow any bright-coloured shirt to show through.

"They're trying to agree on the selling price of the pit-coal," explained Hartley. "The two bobby dazzlers are Mr. Tresswell's sons. The others are some of the chief citizens of New Castle. They belong to the company of hostmen who manage all the ships sailing on the Tyne."

They dismounted from the cart and walked towards the water's edge. The tide was in and the river was at its height with water lapping near the top of the wooden jetties. The coal-laden keels, although low in the water, were level with the jetty tops and a dozen men were busily transferring pit-coal from keel to shore. Four huge mounds of coal were already stacked near the edge of the river. Everything looked black, brown or grey and the Tresswell sons stood out gaily in their fine clothes.

Moored close by several heaps of pit-coal were two three-masted merchant ships standing high out of the water on the flood tide. Their high sterns dwarfed all the buildings close by.

"One of those will take ye to London," said Hartley as he led the way to the two ships. "Do ye see those wooden shoots lying on the heaps of pit-coal? When the tide has ebbed and the river is low the ships will be below the level of the jetty. Then the men will slope those shoots so that they let the pit-coal roll straight down into the hold of each ship. It must be carefully loaded so that the weight is evenly spread otherwise it might shift in heavy seas, or a storm, and the ship would capsize. It's the job of the ship is Master to see this is done."

A sturdy man with a splendid beard strode up and greeted Hartley with a booming voice.

"Welcome to New Castle. What brings you here?"

"These young friends of mine are travelling to London with the authority of Mr. Tresswell. Can you take them?"

"I'd be delighted but the 'Ann' is taking her cargo to Hull this trip."

"Sailing home, eh?"

"Aye. She's due farra fair overhaul. The 'Susanna' there is bound for Billingsgate. Good sailing!"

The 'Ann's Master boomed his farewell and joined the group surrounding the Tresswell sons.

Hartley and the travellers walked in the shadow of the towering 'Ann' to the stern of the next ship where they saw the names 'Susanna' and 'London'. As they reached the steeply sloping gang-plank the huge figure of a man swung over the ship's side and descended swiftly.

"That's Simon Lee," said Hartley.

Lee greeted Hartley at the bottom of the gangplank. "What' s this – a deputation?"

"I've three extra hands for ye. They want to travel to London and Master Tresswell hopes that a ship's Master will agree to take them. Will ye do it, Simon?"

The Master of the 'Susanna' studied the three young faces gazing hopefully up at him.

"If it's a request from Mister Tresswell then I reckon I can squeeze them in somewhere. Are you good sailors? The North sea can be rough even at this season. What do you want in London?"

"They've very important business there," interposed Hartley.

"Master Tresswell wants them to get there as soon as possible."

'What a friend Martin Hartley is proving,' thought Mark. From their first moment of meeting he had shown great kindness and had never asked awkward or searching questions.

"So be it," said Simon Lee. "Follow me!"

They climbed on to the main deck.

"You'd better be quartered in the locker room. It's below my cabin in the stern."

Simon Lee led them up the steep wooden steps to the half deck and moving towards the stern they walked through a doorway. Just inside Mark stopped to inspect a thick wooden staff that passed through a hole in the deck above and down through a hole in the deck on which they stood.

"Please – what's this?"

Simon Lee stopped and turned back towards Mark.

"That's the whipstaff: shaped from the trunk of an oak – toughest wood there is!" He clouted the staff affectionately with a huge hand. "It enables the helmsman who stands on the quarter-deck above to assist the steering of the ship. Below this deck the whipstaff is attached to the tiller – that's the lever which turns the rudder."

"Thank you."

"Now here's the locker room." The ship's Master threw open a varnished door and they crowded into a small cabin whose walls were lined with lockers and chests. "All the spare tackle's kept in here. Those long chests are filled with sails."

A large black cat was curled on the chest under the casement window in the stern. "Come along, Tommy, wake up, you've got visitors," said Simon Lee, scratching the animal's back. Catherine and Mark looked at Tom and laughed and he grinned with delight.

The cat stood up, stretched to an incredible length, yawned, jumped off the chest, flicked his tail and walked out of the room. "The terror of the rats on board! Best ship's cat I ever had."

Simon Lee heaved open the lid of one chest and pulled out three filled sacks. "There's a palliasse for each of you. Lay them along the chest lids to sleep on. The rocking of the ship'll do the rest."

"I must be going," said Hartley, quietly.

All the excitement, which had built up in the children since boarding the 'Susanna', evaporated.

They gathered miserably at the top of the gangplank to say goodbye but even Mark, who had been taught matters of respect and grace which were part of a young Gentleman's learning, could not find words to express their gratitude. He was too upset to speak. They had known Martin Hartley for only three days and yet he seemed their dearest friend.

"Take care of yersel's", said Hartley, as cheerfully as he could. Although he managed to hide it he felt as miserable as the children for he had none of his own and these had filled a gap in his life, if only for a short time. He shook hands all round and hurried down the gangplank.

Mark called, "goodbye – thank you!" Catherine stared mistily down at the quayside and Tom wished that life were not filled with so many 'goodbyes'. They watched until Hartley had reached the horse and cart and then Simon Lee, sensing how they felt, said, "Let's visit the cook room and find some food." They gave a final wave and went below.

They awoke the next morning to sounds of rumbling and shouting. Looking out of the small casement window in the stern of the locker room Catherine announced that the jetty was now high above them. The tide had ebbed and the Tyne was at low water.

"They'll be loading the ship with pit-coal down those wooden shoots," observed Tom.

The door of the cabin swung open to reveal a young man about Mark's age. "Two bells! Food's ready in the cook room!"

On their way down the half-deck steps they could see the sun had not yet risen and judged the time to be between five and six o'clock.

Breakfast consisted of fish, bread and butter and milk. "Make the most of the milk," the ship's lad told them. "You won't get any more once we're at sea."

After breakfast they watched the men working at the staith. This was a rough wooden staging astride the huge mounds of pit-coal. One end of a wooden shoot was tied to the staging and the other end placed over the ship's hold. Pit-coal was then shovelled on to the shoot where it rumbled down into the hold. Simon Lee was directing the positioning of the lower end of the shoot so that the cargo was evenly distributed in the hold.

Once more they observed the cloud of black dust that hung over the work. The men on the staith with grimy faces, arms and hands, were coughing and spitting to rid their throats and lungs of black grit.

"I hope they pay them well," said Mark and Tom nodded vigorously.

By midday the 'Susanna' was level with the jetty and the work was finished.

"We sail just before high tide – that's in four hours," announced Simon Lee.

"We sail just before high tide."

CĐAPČER SIX

Shipwrecked

That afternoon, just before eight bells, Mark Catherine and Tom joined Simon Lee on the quarterdeck.

"We're about to cast off. Stand abaft the helmsman. There you'll see everything without being in my way!"

They moved to the stern and watched eagerly as Simon Lee stood forward on the quarterdeck and directed operations.

The helmsman stood quietly awaiting orders while the other nine men swarmed up the shrouds of the main and fore masts where, high above the deck, they bent the sails on to the spars and yards. Then the ship was cast off and while two men hove in the cables the remainder unfurled the sails.

"Hard to larboard!" said Simon Lee.

"Hard to larboard it is, Master Lee!" replied the helmsman.

The 'Susanna' rocked gently and drifted slowly towards midstream. Gradually the sails filled, the ship turned and running before a gentle west-south-west wind she slipped towards the mouth of the Tyne.

The rate of knots increased as the turbulent river narrowed between high cliffs.

The three passengers remained on deck long enough to inhale their first whiff of salt-sea breeze as the wind freshened slightly.

Later that night, clear of the treacherous sand bar in the estuary, the ship anchored off the Tyne mouth and her gentle rocking motion helped the children into a deep and relaxed sleep.

They awoke to the sound of distant shouts.

"What's that?" said Catherine.

"It's still dark," reported Tom, scrambling up on his locker and peering out of the casement window.

There was another shout and they felt the ship swinging round.

"They're weighing anchor," said Mark. "Let's go on deck."

They hurried out of the locker room, past the whipstaff, on to the open half-deck and tasted the morning air salt-sharp. Above they saw the pattern of sails, masts and shrouds against a sky showing the first pale light.

"Good day!" called Simon Lee from the quarterdeck. "Come up abaft!"

Mark led the way up the steps to the quarterdeck and they stood well to the stern of the helmsman.

With the anchor weighed and the cable hove in and neatly coiled the crew mustered for the next order.

"Make all plain sail!"

Topsails were unfurled above the fore and main sails, the mizzen was raised above the quarterdeck, and a spritsail bent to the yard slung under the bowsprit.

"In this fresh sou'wester with 'Susanna' balanced we'll be running down the coast," said Simon Lee.

"How do you 'balance' the ship?" asked Tom.

"By angling the sails to catch the best of the wind," replied the Master.

For two days the weather and wind held good and a large flock of gulls were in constant attendance around the stern, wheeling swooping and ascending; always changing formation. The coast was just visible on the starboard horizon.

Early on the third day the Master pointed to a castle standing high and magnificent on a headland. "That's Scarborough Castle. I always look out for it when the weather's good."

That evening they shielded their eyes and looking into the sun they saw the chalky cliffs of Flamborough Head. "It's a dangerous place for ships in bad weather," said Simon Lee. "My brother was drowned there. The ship went down with all hands."

The fourth day began sunny with a fresh wind still from the southwest and the gulls remaining in attendance. Mark, Kay and Tom were on the stern castle. Kay was playing with the ship's cat and Mark was talking to the helmsman. The ship's cabin boy, an apprentice sailor, was showing Tom how to tie various knots.

A sailor on the mainmast shrouds called down, "Wind's freshening!" At the same moment the bows dipped and a spume of white spray rose over the forecastle from the starboard beam.

For the next hour the wind increased, and from the land away to starboard the children saw a build up of black clouds.

"Haul the topsails!" cried Simon Lee to the boatswain who was on the half deck.

"Aye! Aye!" replied the boatswain, hurrying down to the main deck.

"I don't like the look of it," said Lee quietly to the helmsman.

"Shall we go down – shall we go below?" asked Mark.

"No lad. You can stay on deck for a bit. It may come to nought though my bones don't think so."

There was a zeal of activity as the topsails were taken in. Although the ship's company numbered only ten, twice as many seemed to be at work: swarming over the decks, up the shrouds and along the yards.

The 'Susanna' continued south-east, plunging and heaving through the growing seas. Half an hour passed and all the time the black mass over the land seemed to lower and thicken and come closer.

"Wind's backing to south-east!" observed the helmsman.

"Aye, it is," muttered Simon Lee. We'll make for the Humber and shelter there." He leaned over the quarterdeck rail, cupped his hands round his mouth and bellowed, "Reef fore and main!"

The children watched as the crew rolled up a section of each sail in order to reduce the surface area and give less resistance to the wind.

"Look!" cried Tom. "All the gulls have left!"

"Aye. So they do before a storm. They seek shelter inland and that's what we're going to do!"

The wind grew fiercer, howling through the ratlines and shrouds and the 'Susanna' rolled, plunged and heaved with the sea breaking across the bows. Spray blew across the ship and drenched the figures on the quarterdeck.

"Lower main and fore sails!" yelled Simon Lee through the rising gale. "You lads go below and remain in your cabin!"

They went immediately, clinging to anything for support as they clambered down the steps to the lurching half deck. Everything below was groaning and creaking. They staggered into their cabin and found the ship's cat asleep on Mark's palliasse. "I expect he's used to rough weather," said Tom, scratching behind the cat's ear with a finger.

The cat awoke, uncurled, stretched on his back and awaited

further attention. The children laughed and Tom tickled its stomach. The cat purred loudly with pleasure. Kay watched Tom with a gentle expression in her eyes while Mark peered out of the stern casement.

'"The sea's rising and falling a tremendous distance," he called. "Come and look!"

Catherine and Tom crossed to the casement and peered over his shoulders. One moment all they could see was surging water and spray; the next moment the sea had fallen far below them and only the sky was visible. Then the sea rose again splashing the casement glass only to fall back almost immediately.

The children staggered forwards and backwards with the pitching of the ship, Catherine losing her balance and falling against a locker.

"I shall lie on my bed; it's easier!"

The boys continued staring out of the stern casement and Mark put his arm round Tom's shoulders to steady them both. On deck Simon Lee pointed to a low section of coastline away to the southwest that seemed to end abruptly in the middle of the Sea. "That'll be Spurn Head. There's a deep-water channel that runs close to the Head and leads to the Humber. We'll keep the wind abeam with spritsail and mizzen." The sky above the ship was still blue although the mass of black cloud was drawing ever closer.

For the next hour the 'Susanna' fought her way towards Spurn Head. In their cabin Tom showed Catherine and Mark how to tie knots he had learned from the cabin boy.

Presently the boy himself appeared with hot drinks. "Cook says to down this. It'll help you through the rough weather."

They drank and pulled wry faces. The drink had a peculiar taste but it made them warm inside.

The boy withdrew and Tom continued with his lesson of knots while the cabin rose and fell and tilted from side to side. They were sitting on Kay's locker but kept toppling on to one another as the ship heaved and slid and rolled. The groaning and creaking of the ship's timbers sounded like a huge creature in distress. The 'Susanna' seemed to be tearing herself apart as she buffeted through the ever-growing seas.

On deck the noise was far worse. The sky overhead had turned black and a mixture of sea-spray and rain was lashing about Spurn Head, now close on the starboard beam, but no longer visible.

Suddenly, as the bows rose into the air and the stern fell, there was a roar of water. A mountain of wave swept over the stern castle smashing the helmsman against the ship's rail and then thrusting him overboard. He was immediately lost to sight in the turbulent sea as the stern rose up high out of the water.

Simon Lee and the boatswain, both of whom had been knocked down, climbed to their feet again, the boatswain struggling to the deserted whipstaff.

As the stern rose again Simon Lee caught a glimpse of land through the driving rain. The next moment it was gone as the stern fell into another chasm of roaring water.

There was an explosion like a cannon roar and the spritsail burst and shredded in a sudden gust of hurricane force wind.

"All hands astern!" yelled Lee above the roaring sea and shrieking wind. "I'll take the helm!" Only the mizzen sail remained, stretched this way and that by a frenzy of wind.

The boatswain partly clambered and partly fell down to the half deck, yelled the order amidships and lurched to the locker room.

One by one the ship's company struggled up to the stern castle whilst the boat, now under only one sail, careered helplessly. The children held on to each other and under his arm Tom clutched a bundle of canvas. It was a large kit bag inside which was the ship's cat.

The 'Susanna', now out of control, was being driven to leeward by both the wind and the flood tide. Suddenly the coast loomed up directly ahead. A loud grinding noise rose above the wind and sea as the ship struck Spurn Head. There was a shudder and everyone was thrown to the deck. At the same moment the foretopmast carried away on the impact and crashed to the deck in a tangle of shrouds.

The ship was dragged sideways and away from the coast. Then suddenly she was flung once again towards the land. There was a dreadful tearing, cracking sound and with an angry roar the sea broke over the side and flooded into the hold.

"Her back's broken!" cried the boatswain.

"Jump for it!" yelled Simon Lee. "Abandon ship!"

"Abandon Ship.'" cried several voices.

"Follow me, lads!" shouted the boatswain who scrambled for the side nearest the shore. Kay and Mark followed with Tom clutching his wriggling canvas bundle. The sea burst over the ship, knocked them down, and dragged them rolling over each other away from the side.

There was another grinding roar as the 'Susanna' shuddered and slewed her stern seawards.

"Keep with me!" yelled the boatswain.

They crawled along the sloping deck but the sea burst again over the breaking ship and they were knocked down once more, dazed and soaked. Then the deck tilted violently hurling them to the side. Shocked and frightened they clambered over the rail and jumped after the boatswain into the foaming mass of water.

Kay instinctively took a deep breath before hitting the water. She went under and everything about her roared. She threshed about with her hands and suddenly her head broke the surface. She had no control over her movements for the sea took her, pushing and dragging her at its will. In a moment she felt herself grasped by firm hands and was aware of a body moving just under her own. Something that felt like an arm was under her chin and a voice bawled in her ear, "Keep still!"

Seconds later she was aware of a large piece of wood floating nearby. It was the foretopmast. "Hold that!" Kay put both arms round the mast and then saw the boatswain swimming beside her. He tied one of the shrouds that were still attached to the mast around her and yelled, "Don't worry – you can't sink now. Keep holding on!"

The mast and it's passenger rose and fell in the huge waves and the man disappeared.

Together Mark and Tom met the water, which leaped to greet them. Down they sank, side by side, and up again to break surface together. Tom was still clutching the canvas bag and Mark attempted to hold Tom's free arm to help support him but the power of the sea wrenched them apart. Mark fell with the momentary ebb of water and then rose as the sea surged, foaming furiously. He caught a brief glimpse of Tom before he sank into another valley of water. When he rose again on the next surge he could see nothing of his friend.

Unable to swim Mark sank with the sea roaring in his ears.

He broke surface gasping and choking, was aware of the 'Susanna' close by, a squalling mass of wood, and then he sank again. The water roared in his ears, and his chest felt as though it was being crushed. He came up too winded even to choke and then through his stinging eyes he saw a ship's cask floating by. The sight gave him new strength. With a tremendous effort and helped by the sea he reached the cask and clung to it. Coughing and choking and with his head only just out of the swelling sea Mark wondered how long he could hold on. Already his fingers felt tired and numb and were losing their grip. Then something in the water close by attracted his attention. It was the cabin boy. At first Mark thought he was swimming but then he realised that it was only the movement of the water. There was a gash on the boy's forehead.

Beating the sea with his legs Mark propelled himself along until he reached the boy. Then grabbing him by the shirt scruff with his right hand Mark somehow manoeuvred him on to the opposite side of the cask and hung on.

They rose and fell with the sea. Mark saw the boy's eyes flicker open.

"Hold on to me!" yelled Mark above the storm.

Up went the cask on a fuming crest of wave and down into a valley of water.

"Hold on to me!" yelled Mark again. With a look of agonised determination the boy pushed his right arm across the cask and grasped Mark's jerkin. This drew them closer together over the cask and Mark got his hands under the boy's armpits. Then by hugging the boy towards him Mark clasped his hands together in the middle of the boy's back. The boy reacted instinctively and put his arms round Mark's neck and with the current bearing them along faster and faster the two young men clung on to each other across the cask.

Tom, who in the past had so often to look after himself, clung to the canvas bundle and pushed at the sea with his legs.

He was surprised to discover that although part of the bundle was under the surface most of it had swollen like an air-filled bladder and would not sink.

Tom held on and stretched his head out of the water as the sea rose and fell. He felt himself being pulled or dragged along and through the foam and rain-mist saw a dark shape not far away. The pull increased and Tom found himself powerless in its grip. He clung to the bag containing the cat and tried not to be frightened. He thought of his dead father, the only person he had ever loved until now.

Then something bumped his shoulder and twisting round in the water he saw a long piece of wood. Clinging to the other end was Catherine. Tom made to call out and got a mouthful of water. He released one arm from the bundle and curled it round the topmast.

The tow of the current grew stronger but the mountainous waves had ceased. The topmast with its passengers had swept round Spurn Head and was being carried up the mouth of the river Humber on a strong tidal flow. The shrieking gale still lashed the children's faces with rain and slashed up water all around them but it was now much easier to cling to the topmast.

Several hundred yards seawards Mark was still holding grimly to the cabin boy who kept fainting and reviving. Mark felt both his arms stretched beyond endurance and he thought that he must let go before long. Then his brother, Richard, came suddenly into his mind. Mark recalled their farewell when Richard had left Alwinton for London. Looking down from his horse his elder brother had said, "Keep Faith!" It was the family motto. He would keep faith now. He felt a new lease of energy and renewed his strong grip on the boy. Then with relief he saw that they were no longer rising and falling on huge seas. The same tow that was speeding the topmast up the Humber estuary had taken hold of the cask.

Shooting up the estuary Tom and Catherine found themselves joined by the boatswain and another of the ship's company. The men, who were strong swimmers, had been level with the mast about two hundred yards away. As they were all carried into a channel between submerged sandbanks they were brought closer together and when the two men saw the mast and the children it took them little time to steer themselves alongside.

Catherine was helped up so that she was astride the wood but Tom refused to let go of the canvas bag.

The channel grew wider and the current less strong. As the rain began to ease the visibility grew and boatswain cried, "Boat ho!"

He pointed ahead to larboard. They saw a large rowing boat some distance ahead. "When I say 'now' all yell!" And so they did. "Again!" and the second time Catherine waved as well and fell back in the water.

Someone in the boat waved back and shortly four sailors and a cat were hauled aboard the large, sturdy rowing boat.

"How many altogether?" asked a rescuer.

"Eight men and a boy – No! Seven and a boy. We lost the helmsman overboard. And three lads – passengers," said the boatswain. "We're from the 'Susanna', London bound with pit-coal."

"My brother's out there," said Catherine, her anxiety crushing her joy and relief at the rescue.

"They'll be swept this way on the flood tide," said the man cheerfully. "You'll see."

"There's something!" said Tom, who had been scanning, the rough water carefully.

The four men strained at the oars and the rowing boat was manoeuvred directly into the path of the object. A few moments later they could make out three men clinging to a large piece of wood.

"It isn't Mark," said Catherine despairingly and she began shivering with cold and anxiety.

With the cook and two others hauled on board the rowing boat was overfilled and dangerously low in the water.

"We'll have to pull back to Grimsby," said the man in charge surveying his passengers all of whom were ashen and shivering.

A feeling of horror swept through Catherine and Tom.

"Couldn't we wait a little longer?" pleaded Tom.

Before there was time for reply a loud shout signalled the arrival of another rowing boat. Explanations were given and the second boat assumed responsibility for further rescue while the first returned to Grimsby fishing village.

An hour later Catherine and Tom were drinking hot broth in front of a blazing fire in the kitchen of a fisherman's cottage. Normally Catherine would have thought a fire and hot broth in August quite extraordinary. So too would the fisherfolk of Grimsby but on occasions like this their only concern was the safety and comfort of others whose living depended, like their own, on the sea. Preparations were made for extra sleeping space and warm clothes and covering were collected for use whilst clothes dried.

Four more boats had rowed out into the estuary but only one drowned sailor had been hauled out of the water. Mark and four members of the crew including the Captain, helmsman and cabin boy were still missing.

That night Catherine and Tom could think only of Mark. Neither of them spoke but it gave especial comfort to Catherine feeling that Tom was sharing her fears. Exhaustion eventually overcame them both and they slept until dawn. The ship's cat, which had refused to be parted from Tom, was sleeping soundly by his side.

The morning was bright and warm and but for the strangers and the clothes drying before the fires there was nothing in the village to show that there had been a fierce storm and shipwreck the previous day.

Catherine and Tom had to force themselves to eat some breakfast.

They wandered about in an agony of suspense followed by the cat. The fisherman's wife who had looked after them thought they would worry less if occupied. She took them down to the jetty and encouraged them to help mend the nets but their interest was half-hearted.

At midday a fishing boat put in from Kingston upon Hull with the news that two boys had been picked up on Sunk Island sands the previous afternoon by a fishing boat sheltering in the lee of Spurn Head. Both boys were completely exhausted and one of them was very ill indeed.

"It must be your brother and the ship's boy," said the boatswain to Catherine. "Where are they now?"

"At Hull. They're being well taken care of," replied the fisherman.

"Has anyone else been picked up?"

The fisherman shook his head. "Sorry, I'm afraid not."

The boatswain looked grim. "I think these two lads should come to Hull with me and see how things are," he said.

"I'm returning straight," said the fisherman. "I only came over wi' t'news about t' wreck. Boys were found clinging to a cask with 'Susanna' on it."

"My ship. Leastways it was. Three crew including the master, Simon Lee, are still missing."

Twenty minutes later the boat left Grimsby for Hull sixteen miles further up the Humber. "How slowly we're sailing," said Catherine to Tom who gave her the cat to look after. Both of them were wondering which boy was 'very ill indeed'.

They saw a large rowing boat some distance ahead.

CHAPTER SEVEN

Witchcraft

Catherine and Tom watched from the stern as the boat nosed its way through a maze of sails and masts. On every quay fish were being landed from boats of various sizes. The smell was overpowering.

Catherine passed the cat to Tom and clambered up the slippery steps of the quay.

"Where are the boys staying?" enquired the boatswain as the fisherman led them away from the quayside.

"They're being looked after by Mistress Coleman. She's t'wife of Cuthbert, brother of one o' town's Aldermen. They're a respected family and right well-off. I believe they've called their physician to attend to t'lads."

They walked along a lane called the 'Land of Green Ginger' and arrived outside a timbered house whose upper storey projected over the lower by two feet. The fisherman's knock was answered by a young servant girl in a simple dark blue dress, an apron and a small white cap.

"Good day! We've come to see the boys."

"Who is it, Susan?" called a voice from inside.

"Some gentlemen to see the boys, Mistress."

"Ask them to step inside."

"Mistress Coleman says to come in," said Susan standing to one side.

Catherine followed the two men into the house and saw a grey-haired lady rise to greet them. She wore an embroidered bodice topped by a ruff and a stiffened skirt with a farthingale. "Good morning, John Sproatley."

"Morning ma-am," said the fisherman.

Tom hovered outside the front door, clutching the cat and wondering if the invitation to enter included him. The servant girl stood holding the door open.

"What's the matter, Susan? Oh." Mrs. Coleman laughed gently. "You can bring the cat inside. We've one of our own but he's out at the moment so there won't be any fuss!" She smiled at Tom who entered and stood beside Catherine. "Take the cat, Susan, and give it some milk." Turning to John Sproatley she said, "You've come to see William and Mark?"

"Yes, ma-am. This is 'Susanna's' boatswain."

"John Bryan at your service, ma-am."

"These two lads are friends of William and Mark?"

"Mark is my brother. Is he badly hurt?"

"I don't think so. Both boys are exhausted and poor William had a nasty wound in his head. The physician is with them and we'll have to wait until he's finished examining them. Please sit down all of you."

Mrs. Coleman sat in a carved wooden armchair and the four visitors on a wooden settle.

"How old is your brother?"

"Mark is fifteen."

"And William?"

"'I'm not sure, ma-am," replied the boatswain. "He's fourteen I think."

A white-haired man in a long black gown appeared on the stairs and they all rose.

"One boy is very poorly. It's difficult to say at the moment how he'll get on. The other boy is improving. He's exhausted but nothing more. He keeps asking about Kay and Tom."

"That's us. He's my brother. Please, may we see him?"

"You may, but only for a minute."

They climbed the narrow stairs and entered a small oak-beamed room with white plaster walls. Catherine saw Mark lying on a low wooden bed. He looked pale and drawn. As she stood by the bed his eyes opened and he turned his head slightly and smiled.

"Hello," said Catherine softly. "The doctor says you'll soon be better. Mrs. Coleman's very kind. Is there anything you want?"

Tom stood awkwardly at the foot of the bed and felt he was intruding. He turned to the other bed where the boatswain was looking down at the still shape of William. A few wisps of fair hair were showing through his bandages. Tom turned back to Mark who was looking at him.

"Hello."

"Hello, Tom." Mark's eyes closed.

Catherine felt very distressed. Then a hand touched her shoulder and she heard Mrs Coleman say, "The doctor assures me he'll be quite well again in a few days. Let's leave him to rest now."

Downstairs Mrs. Coleman said to the boatswain, "Both boys may remain here until they are quite recovered."

"It's very kind of you ma-am. I shall wait for news of the 'Susanna's' missing crew and then board the next ship for New Castle. It's a bad business, ma-am. William can follow when he's fit. Mark with Kay and Tom here were travelling as passengers to London."

Mrs. Coleman showed surprise and turned to the children.

"Then you must stay nearby until Mark is quite well. I've no more room but I'll send a message to my widowed sister, Mrs. Darlby. I know she'll be pleased to look after you."

Two hours later Catherine watched Tom's expression of wonder as a delighted Mrs. Darlby showed them round her house. It was obvious that Tom had never set foot in such a grand place.

The walls of the main rooms were hung with tapestries. "They're pleasant to see and they keep out the draught. My late husband bought this open court cupboard just after we were married. Aren't the carved figures beautiful? All playing musical instruments, you see? Pipe, recorder, lute and viol."

They went upstairs. "Here is your bedroom," said Mrs. Darlby, leading them into a room half-filled by a huge four-poster bed. "My four grandchildren sleep together in that when they visit me so there will be plenty of room for you two boys!" She opened a carved wooden chest. "And here are your night-gowns."

Back at the Colemans' next morning Catherine and Tom waited anxiously for the doctor to complete his examination.

"William shows improvement but he'll be in bed for at least a week, perhaps longer. Your brother is much better. He should be up in two days and out of the house in four or five. You may see him but stay only a few minutes, he still needs rest. And William's asleep – try not to wake him."

Propped up by two pillows Mark listened while Catherine and Tom described Mrs. Darlby's house. Suddenly he interrupted. "We must make speed to London! I must get up! We can't afford to lose any more time!"

"You can't get up until you're completely recovered!" said Catherine firmly. "You'd probably be taken ill on the journey. And if you lie there fretting," she added, knowing her brother's disposition to impatience, "you'll delay your recovery further. Won't he, Tom?" Tom nodded. "Please be sensible Mark. The doctor says it will be only three or four days."

Mark looked grim. "Three or four days could make all the difference.'"

"Yes! They could make all the difference to your health!" She glanced towards William who still slept. Then in a quiet but firm voice she continued, "What could Tom and I do in London without you? And these people, Mrs. Coleman and the others, have been very kind. It would be selfish to undo all the good they have done."

She glanced at Tom who nodded emphatically. Then she looked back at Mark.

"You're right Kay. I'll do whatever the doctor says."

In the living room they found Mr. Coleman seated at an oak trestle table busily writing. The light from a window shone on his pate. On hearing them he turned and peered over his spectacles.

"Hello, you two! How's your brother? Eh?"

"He's much better, thank you."

"Good! Good! He looks a fine lad; a fine lad. I've just finished accounting numerous items for my brother. He's an Alderman you know. A most important man in the town. I must take this paper round to him."

They watched as he replaced his quill pen in the ink-horn and scattered sand from a silver dispenser on to the finished document. Then shaking the sand on the floor he folded the paper once and hoisted himself to his feet. "Don't get into mischief!" He twinkled at them over his spectacles and went out.

"I wish I could write and count," said Tom.

"Have you ever been tutored, Tom?"

"My father showed me what he could but no one taught him anything so it was difficult."

"Would you like me to help you?"

"Yes please!"

"We'll ask Mrs. Coleman if we can have a quill, ink and paper. We'll begin with writing words."

Lessons and visits to the boys helped the next two days pass quickly. Mark's frustration was eased when on the second day the doctor allowed him out of his bed and on the third day out of his room. William sat up in bed for twenty minutes and chatted with the others.

The next day John Bryan arrived.

"I'm afraid there are no more survivors from the 'Susanna'."

The children were shocked to think that Simon Lee and the missing crew were drowned. They thought of the wives and children of the men who might not hear the news for several weeks.

Later that day the doctor pronounced Mark fit enough to leave the house. As it was a sunny August afternoon they wandered down to the harbour to give Mark some exercise. During the short walk they decided to ask Cuthbert Coleman's advice about the next stage of their journey to London.

Sitting on his stool Cuthbert Coleman leaned back against the wall and puffed at his churchwarden pipe. "London? Mm! Roads can be very dangerous even for three young men." He grinned at them and puffed again at his pipe. "London. Can't think why anyone wants to go there! I was there once. It's a dirty, smelly place!"

Mrs. Coleman looked up from her embroidery and said quietly to Tom, who was sitting beside her, "I've never been there, Tom. It must be very interesting to see."

"Barge," said Mr. Coleman, suddenly. "By barge. A Humber Keel. That'll take you part of the way. It'll be safe and fairly quick. You won't be shipwrecked at any rate. But you'll have to go to York. That's north and west of here." He puffed at his pipe for a few moments, "Aye, that's it! We'll get a fisherman to take you up the Ouse to York. He'll introduce you to one of the men who sail their keels to Nottingham and Lincoln. You'll have to go to York because keel owners are very particular about taking passengers. There isn't much room on board either. You'll need an introduction from someone they know. It'll only take two days there and back."

Tom saw Mark and Catherine exchange glances. He knew what they were thinking: 'Two more days' delay!'

"Thank you, sir," said Mark. "That's what we'll do."

The next day Mr. Coleman made enquiries and found that John Sproatley was sailing for York the following morning.

That afternoon Mark went with Catherine and Tom to thank Mrs. Darlby for her hospitality. When they arrived Mrs. Darlby had a surprise for them. "These clothes belonged to my own boys when they were your ages. I think they'll fit you quite well. You can't go to London wearing shipwrecked clothes!"

Tom was thrilled; he had never worn garments as fine as these. Mark insisted on keeping his father's old jerkin.

Next day Tom cradled the ship's cat for the last time and handed him over to William who was sitting up in bed with his head still bandaged. "I know you'll look after him, Will. Perhaps I'll have another one day."

"Good old Tom,' said William. "He's yours really: you saved him. But I'll look after him."

The two boys shook hands. 'What a lot of friends I have' thought Tom.

"You're returning to New Castle in a few days aren't you?" asked Mark. William nodded. "Would you try to get a message to Martin Hartley – he works for Master Tresswell, the pit owner. Tell him that his three young friends are well and send greetings."

The Colemans saw them off from the harbour on John Sproatley's fish-laden boat. A lively breeze helped the boat up stream and also helped to disperse the strong smell of fish.

They passed Selby just before midday and tied up at Stillingfleet early in the afternoon. Sproatley was delivering fish to a relative and the children, feeling buoyant in the bright sunshine, accompanied him across the flat meadows to the village.

"While I'm with me cousin go and visit t'church. And look at t'model Viking ship nailed on t'big south door."

They walked to the Norman church of St. Helen and stood before the south doorway with its five series of mouldings, which arched over the entry.

"There's the Viking ship," said Catherine. "And look at those serpents growing out of the hinges."

"What's that near the top of the door?" asked Tom.

"The figures of two people who seem to be falling. I know! It's Adam and Eve."

"What do you think this is?" said Kay, pointing to a small design halfway up.

"It's rather like a knot. I can't think what it means."

Mark lifted the latch, pulled a small iron ring that went through the door and, pushing hard with his shoulder, slowly entered the church. Inside was quiet and cool. They stood in the half light and felt a sense of wonder that comes from antiquity.

The sun was still high when they first saw the magnificence of York with a battlemented wall around its perimeter. Dominating the river entrance to the city was a huge round tower set high on an enormous mound of earth.

"That's King's Tower," said Sproatley. "Some call it Clifford's Tower. It were built to guard York from a river attack. And there on t'far side o' t'city you can see three towers o' t'Minster. It's said to be one o' t' finest churches in Europe."

They tied up at King's Staith near a bridge and Sproatley tied up the boat and walked briskly to a cottage nearby. Two men came out to greet him and then a boy appeared from the back with an empty cart that was pulled to the quayside.

"You three help steady t' cart while we load it, You'll stink for days if you handle t' fish and there's no sense i' that. It won't tek four of us many minutes."

When the cart was loaded it was hauled to an open space near the cottages and one of the men ran one way and the boy another crying, "'ull fish! 'ull fish! Mack-rell! Tur-bot! Flounder 'n Cod! Come on then! Fresh fish! 'ull fish!"

Sproatley and the other man haggled fiercely over the price and by the time they were agreed men, women and children were appearing from all directions and were clamouring round the cart.

The man and the boy came racing back and Mark, Catherine and Tom watched spellbound as fish appeared to leap from hand to hand and from hand to basket. Customers pointed at fish; sellers named a price; customers named a lower price; sellers consented or refused according to their fancy. How anyone understood anything in the general babble was beyond the three watchers.

"Thar's dun well, lad," said a York man to Sproatley as the final customer departed. "Over 'alf sold. We'll put rest into t'cool cellar 'til mornin'. Then we'll tek it to t' Pavement."

"What's 'Pavement'?" enquired Mark.

"A street. It's got a gallows. We 'ang fish up to dry!"

When the laughter subsided Sproatley said, "Any Humber Keels sailing for t'Trent? Me young friends are travelling South."

"There's raw wool for Lincoln. Sailing tomorrer."

The York man pointed across the river. "One of them Keels. We'll row over and find out."

He led them to the quay and jumped down into a rowing boat. The children followed, stepping gingerly into the boat, which rocked uncertainly under them. Sproatley stepped in last, untied and the York man pulled smartly across the Ouse to the bow of a Humber Keel named 'Pyewipe'.

"Hoy! Are you there, Hugh Scothern? Hoy! Hugh! Are y' aboard?"

A ruddy face appeared through a hatch in the keel's stern.

"Oh 'tis you, Peter Scarcroft, making all that din. And John Sproatley. Ahoy, John!" They watched stocky Hugh Scothern climb on deck and walk easily along the narrow gangway to stand above them. "What can I do for yer?"

"Are you sailing for Lincoln in t'morning?" asked Scarcroft.

"On the morning tide. But I've a spot of trouble."

"What's that?"

"Me lad's ill and can't travel. I shall have to crew myself."

"Then I've good news. I've got a crew for yer; three of 'em," called Scarcroft. "You tell him, John."

Hugh Scothern was delighted and readily agreed to take the three to Lincoln. "Two will have to sleep in the Fo'c's'le store but we'll manage." He looked towards the three children. "Do you know anything about sailing keels?" They shook their heads. "Ah, it'll be good experience for you then!"

It was arranged that they should join the boat at daybreak when she would sail down the Ouse on the ebbing tide. That night they were to eat and sleep with Scarcroft and his neighbours who lived in the cottages near the river.

After the meal it was still light and Mark suggested that they should explore the large tower-standing at the river entrance to the city.

"Clifford's Tower," said Peter Scarcroft. "It's only been called that recently. Roger de Clifford, a rebel against Edward the second was 'ung in chains from t'top almost three hundred years ago. Leastways that's what I've bin told. It's not used now. In fact battlements at t' top seem to be falling down. Mind how you go. If you can find Robert Redhead, t'gaoler, ask him to show you round. Otherwise I wouldn't go to t'very top; it mightn't be safe."

The Tower seemed to grow more and more menacing as they approached. They stood at the bottom of the long flight of steps that were built into the mound of earth and led up to the entrance. As they looked upwards a raven detached itself from the battlements high above them with a loud croak and flew towards the river.

"Let's go up and see if we can find the gaoler who looks after it. What was his name? I've forgotten," said Mark.

"So have I," said Catherine.

"Robert Redhead," said Tom.

"Well done, Tom," cried Mark. "Come on. Let's count the steps to the top."

They counted sixty-six before they stood by the masonry of the fore-building, the entrance to the tower itself.

"Anyone about?" called Mark. "Master Redhead! Are you there?"

No one answered.

The interior looked dark and forbidding. They waited in silence. Mark took three paces inside the tower, paused and called again, "Master Redhead!"

From somewhere above them there was a faint slithering noise and then silence.

"Let's go, Mark," whispered Catherine. "I don't like the place." She moved towards the stone steps outside.

"Someone's had sand here," observed Tom, who was examining the floor near an inside wall.

Catherine re-appeared under the archway. "There are some men coming towards the tower. Perhaps Robert Redhead is one of them."

From the shadow of the entrance the three looked down the great flight of steps. The men were nearing the base of the mound and although daylight was beginning to fade it was still light enough for Mark and Catherine to recognise one of them. It was

Cain Webster.

They backed quickly into the tower pulling Tom with them. They were trapped.

To the left of the arch was a spiral staircase of stone built into the thick wall and leading upwards into gloom. "This way – quickly!" hissed Mark. "We'll have to hide up here."

They reached the first floor where some light was coming through an arrow slit window. Near them a doorway opened into a first floor room over the entrance. They entered the small room which contained the portcullis, its chains going upwards through the ceiling into the room above. In one corner a spiral staircase led down to the entrance.

"One way of escape," observed Mark grimly.

The sound of voices and footsteps immediately below drove them out of the portcullis room and up the stone staircase to the second floor where they paused again.

The murmur of voices continued but did not draw nearer; the sound of footsteps had ceased.

"Wait here for a moment," whispered Mark and he went swiftly up the next flight of stairs. Moments later he re-appeared. "It's a short flight to the roof, to the battlements."

A low, narrow archway on the second floor led into a small room where they saw the machinery of the portcullis; the chains for raising and lowering the contraption passing upward through the floor below. Beyond an arch on the opposite side of the room they found another stone staircase identical to the one they had ascended. "Another way of escape," said Mark.

They returned through the room to a corridor.

Their eyes had grown accustomed to the semi-darkness and Catherine noticed a small opening, like a spy hole, in the interior wall of the corridor. "Look here!" Peering down into a first floor room she saw a torch flickering in a wall hanger. The muffle of voices below grew suddenly louder.

Catherine withdrew her head and the three crowded round the hole and saw two men enter the room below. Mark put his ear to the hole in an attempt to hear what was said. He heard 'convince him' and 'should be satisfied' from a man wearing a sword, and 'a good performance' from the other, but nothing else that made sense.

Mark drew back slightly and the three crowded together once more and peered down. They saw that the triangular shaped room below occupied a quarter of the whole round tower: one curved exterior wall followed the outline of the tower itself and two straight interior walls met at the centre of the building. Screening this corner in the middle of the tower was a section of tapestry hanging by ropes from a wooden beam. A table and four stools stood in the centre of the room.

A door in the left hand wall opened and two hooded figures wearing long black gowns carried in a large iron cauldron. The table was moved to one side and the cauldron put in its place. The hooded figures left and returned with more implements: two smaller iron vessels shaped liked bowls which were placed on each side of the cauldron, and a wooden staff carved like a serpent which was laid in front of them. Two more bowls were taken behind the tapestry screen. Finally a rush light was set on the floor in front of the staff.

The man with the sword said, "Is everything ready?" The hooded figures nodded. "Good! Light t'rush candle and extinguish t'torch. Less light t'better. Mek it convincing. I'll bring Webster up."

The swordsman departed while his companion, a bearded man, moved the stools to the side of the room below the children and sat down. One cowled figure lit the candle and concealed himself behind the tapestry while the other took the torch from the wall bracket and disappeared through the door. The candle burned with a small flame and the children could only just make out the room and its contents.

The flame flickered in a draught of air as two men entered the room. One was the man with the sword and Catherine and Mark presumed the other to be Cain Webster. They sat down with the bearded man below the spy hole. The swordsman clapped his hands twice and the rush candle flickered again and almost went out.

From the darkness glided a black hooded figure. Around its neck on a silver chain hung the curled horn of a ram. The figure stopped between the watchers and the candle. The rush light flickered again and the figure's huge shadow rose and fell over the whole room.

"Your wishes are known to us", intoned the figure. "Your commands shall be executed with all the power we can summon. You have something belonging to the victim? A ring, brooch or neck chain?"

The children watched intently as a small ornament was passed from Cain Webster to the hooded figure.

"Remain still and silent", commanded the figure. The ornament, which glinted faintly, was placed on the floor near the serpent staff. Then the figure took one of the smaller vessels and, holding it up in front of him, chanted some strange words. He filled it from the cauldron with what appeared to be sand and held it up again. After chanting more words he moved around all the objects making a large circle of sand on the floor. He had to refill the small bowl several times from the cauldron and on each occasion he went through the same ritual with the bowl held high and strange words chanted. The children watched fascinated.

When the circle was completed he spread a heap of sand on the floor inside it, set down the bowl and took up the serpent staff. Standing in the middle, he held the staff with the serpent head pointing towards the sand circle. Then slowly he turned a complete circle himself, muttering and keeping the serpent's head just above the sand.

Next he reversed the staff and using the serpent's tail he drew a triangle, two crescents and some curious zigzag shapes in the heap of sand.

Tom's eyes opened wide and he drew back slightly. "It's witchcraft! They're hoping to bring bad fortune on the owner of that ornament!"

The hooded figure stepped outside the circle with both hands gripping the staff horizontally across his body. He walked slowly round the circle, stopping four times to mutter strange words in a low, harsh voice. Each time he raised the staff above his head.

This done he placed the staff on the floor, and, facing the silent and spellbound watchers, knelt down between the rush light and the second small bowl. Then he picked up the ornament – a chain with a pendant hanging from it – and held it with both hands over the fire in the bowl. The fire flared up suddenly and in its light Mark and Catherine recognised the ornament from the unusual design of the chain and the locket hanging from it. The locket contained a miniature painting of their mother done by the artist Nicholas Hilliard. It had belonged to their father and was now the property of their brother, Richard.

Mark felt his fury rising. How dare these villains handle a precious family possession! Webster must have stolen it from Richard's desk at Alwinton. He stiffened with rage. He wanted to dash downstairs and snatch it from them. He gripped Tom's arm in anger. Tom, who might have cried out at the sudden pain, gritted his teeth and remained still.

The brilliant light from the flaring bowl died down and the room became full of shadows and mystery again.

The figure rose, turned round and knelt facing the candle with his back to the watchers. He held the chain with its miniature high in the air and muttered some Latin words. From the darkness beyond the tapestry came a faint, greenish light. The kneeling figure spoke again but this time in a loud, high-pitched voice. Then from behind the tapestry there rose an awful figure with animal horns upon its head.

The kneeling figure shrieked more words. In answer the horned figure intoned some Latin and then uttered the name "Richard Kempe". The green light grew more brilliant and then two things happened suddenly and simultaneously that changed the whole atmosphere.

The children became aware of a man standing behind them in the darkness of the corridor and in the same moment there was a vivid flash and a loud explosion from the room below. The man lunged towards the children at the moment of the explosion but was taken off guard by the sudden noise and the flash. In that same moment the children reacted to their danger.

Catherine dodged to one side, Mark aimed a blow at the man's chin with his fist and Tom lowered his head and butted the man in the stomach. The large figure staggered backwards, struck his head against the stone wall of the corridor and fell heavily to the ground.

"Quickly!" hissed Mark and grabbing his sister's he hurried down the stone stairs.

Halfway to the first floor they smelt burning and arriving at the bottom of the flight outside the room of witchcraft they could see a small fire and were aware of figures coughing and staggering about inside.

A hooded figure ran out and, without seeing the children standing in the shadows, hurried down the stairs. Then they heard Webster's voice from inside the room shouting, "Where's the miniature? Fools! Where's the miniature?"

As Mark and Catherine moved forward to continue down the next flight of the spiral stairs Cain Webster appeared in the doorway gasping for breath. "Mark! You Brat!" He lurched towards them. At that moment another figure burst out of the room. Webster was knocked sideways, stood swaying for a moment at the head of the stone stairs, lost his balance and pitched downwards into the darkness with a yell.

Mark pulled Catherine into the portcullis room and down the staircase set into the corner. Moments later they reached the ground floor of the tower, hurried out into the dusk and ran down the steps of the mound.

Breathless they paused at the bottom to look back at the tower now a shadow in the fading light. Then together they cried, "Where's Tom!"

The figure then took one of the smaller vessels and,
holding it up in front of him, chanted some strange words.

CHAPTER EIGHT

Tom's Story

For a second they wavered. Then Mark began running back up the stone steps. Almost immediately voices sounded from the tower archway and he paused and crouched. The voices became more distinct and bending low Mark ran back down the steps.

"Under here!" hissed Catherine as she slid down the moat bank and crouched under the wooden bridge that crossed from the mound. Mark followed and they waited, their hearts thudding with excitement and fear.

As the voices grew closer Mark and Catherine put their arms tightly round one another making themselves as small as possible and hiding their faces.

"I expected better than this for the money I've paid, Master Sutton. Not only has the spell been bungled but you've lost the miniature."

"We shall find it." Sutton's reply sounded conciliatory rather than certain.

"You had better! And then I come face to face with that brat brother of Kempe's and that idiot of yours knocks me over before I can grab him. I want that boy found. Are you certain that he's not still in the tower?"

"Bilton saw 'im go out through arch with t'other boy."

"Why didn't he stop him?" demanded Webster.

"He was getting water to put out t'fire."

"Two boys wandering alone shouldn't be difficult to find. I wonder who the other was? And how they got here?"

"We'll do all we can but York is a large city and we can't do much in t' dark," muttered Sutton.

"I want the miniature portrait of Kempe's and I want that boy. Bring him straight to me when you find him. I'll take pleasure in dealing with him personally. And I want no more bungling!"

Mark and Catherine heard Webster thump across the wooden bridge and caught a glimpse of him as he strode angrily into the night. Sutton muttered something unintelligible and remounted the tower steps.

"Keep still, Kay," said Mark softly.

"Where's Tom?"

"He must be in the tower," said Mark. "We were ahead of him coming down the stairs. And the men only saw the two of us. Stay here. I'm going to find him." He eased himself on to his knees, stood up slowly and peered between the wood planks of the little moat bridge. It was now too dark to see the forebuilding and archway at the top of the steps.

Mark raised himself on to the bridge and was about to climb the steps when there was a commotion from above. Several voices were arguing fiercely. Mark slid back and rejoined Catherine under the bridge. The voices drew nearer. The men were quarrelling over responsibility for the mismanaged witchcraft and there were accusations concerning the whereabouts of the miniature. It was worth a considerable amount of money and Sutton was accusing the others of concealing it. They tramped over the bridge and stood on the ground just beyond still arguing.

Then Catherine and Mark heard more movement on the mound steps. Moments later the large figure of the man they had knocked down on the second floor of the tower crossed the bridge and joined the group.

"When do I get paid for t' use o' t' tower?" he demanded.

"You must see Maister Webster," said Sutton. "I've only received payment for t' witchcraft."

"I want my share. The city Aldermen would be interested to learn of toneet's little caper!"

"Hold your peace, Robert Redhead," retorted Sutton. "City Aldermen 'ud also be interested to learn about removal o' t' masonry and furniture from inside t'tower. Sold, I believe, to line your own pocket!"

Redhead swore loudly.

"Now you can all listen to me," continued Sutton firmly. "We'll go together for fresh torches and come back to find that miniature. It must be lying on t'floor in t' tower room. If it's not theer you'll all be searched."

Two or three voices started to object but ceased at the sound of a sword being drawn.

"Lead the way to t'jail for your torches, Maister Redhead,"

commanded Sutton. "I'll go last so that I can keep an eye on yer."

They heard the party of rogues march away.

"There's no honour among thieves," muttered Mark.

"They didn't mention Tom," said Catherine. "I wonder where he is?"

"I'm here," whispered a voice just above them and a small figure slid from the bridge and joined them. They greeted him with delight.

Tom's eyes shone brightly in the dark and he reached for something around his neck.

"I've got this for you," he said quietly, and he gave Mark a miniature on a gold chain.

There was a long silence. Tom watched Catherine and her brother who were looking at the heirloom. To Tom the ornament was a thing of great beauty and craftsmanship. The chain consisted of the letters "H" and "E" linked by small circles of gold.

Catherine and Mark also thought the ornament very beautiful but to them it meant something more. It was an expression in art of their father's love for their mother. The chain of letters "H" for Henry and "E" for Elizabeth linked their names together.

Lodged in the pendant was a miniature painting of their mother. The ornament, first worn by their father and then his heir, would be worn in time by succeeding eldest sons. It was a symbol of family pride and devotion. To a mere collector it was worth a large sum of money. To members of the Kempe family it was above all price.

Mark looked up.

"Thank you, Tom." And he wished the words to express the gratitude of an entire family. At that moment Mark resolved never again to regard Tom as a vagabond. Experience was teaching him that integrity was not confined to his own class. He hung the chain round his neck and slipped the pendant inside his shirt.

It was Tom who brought them down to earth. He peered out over the bridge and said, "They've all gone."

"Yes, but they're coming back with fresh torches," said Catherine. "We must leave here. But where can we go?"

"Let's make our way back towards the cottages and decide what's best to do," suggested Mark.

They crossed the bridge, followed the opposite bank of the

moat around Clifford's tower for nearly a hundred yards and then moved directly towards the river. Finding a concealed spot near a wall they sat down.

Mark reviewed the situation. "We're expected back at the cottages to sleep but Webster's men might come searching. Hugh Scothern might let us board his keel tonight but that's not really safe; Webster's men might go there too."

"If we don't see the people at the cottage they might send out to look for us," said Catherine. "It's already late. And their searchers might meet Webster's men."

Footsteps sounded close by and they stiffened in fear. A figure loomed out of the darkness. Individually the two boys prepared to make a fight of it. The figure stopped close by. There was a faint smell of fish that carried easily on the night air and to their relief they recognised John Sproatley. They rose out of the darkness and startled him.

"I were looking for thee."

"Would you sit with us, please?" asked Mark. Mark explained their immediate problem.

"You can spend t' night o' my boat," said Sproatley. "It's not very comfortable but if these men arrive yer can keep well 'idden until I get rid of 'em."

He led the way to his fishing boat and while Catherine and Tom stowed themselves away Mark accompanied Sproatley to the cottage to thank the people for their hospitality and explain something of their change in plan.

They spent that night in the boat's forward cabin but Catherine and Mark slept fitfully. They woke many times and could not settle. Tom, who was used to sleeping rough, had a good night.

Just before dawn John Sproatley rowed them across the river. The tide was on the ebb and the Ouse was flowing swiftly south towards the Humber and the sea.

Hugh Scothern was already making preparations for the journey to Lincoln. Tom was to share the aft cabin with him while Mark and Catherine were to sleep in the forecastle, which was normally used as a general store and locker room.

They thanked John Sproatley who called out, "Safe journey!" as he rowed back across the river.

Under Hugh Scothern's direction his new crew helped to untie and cast off 'Pyewipe' from the small wharf. Then with the owner at the tiller the keel moved slowly out into midstream and drifted easily on the ebb tide.

They scanned the banks for any sign of Webster or his henchmen but in the pale morning York seemed deserted. Clifford's Tower rose menacingly out of the mist but gave no hint of the previous night's activities.

Half a mile further downstream they looked back at the city but even the huge Minster was hidden in the morning mist.

"We've a long journey ahead," said Hugh Scothern. "So the sooner you lads become familiar with sailing 'Pyewipe' the better. You can begin by steering. Mark, you take the first turn. I'll be alongside to show you what to do. The current's quite fast and there are some tricky river bends to navigate."

For the first few miles the other two walked constantly fore and aft, partly to get to know the feel of the keel that was to be their home for a few days and partly to peer into the water and view the flat countryside from every possible vantage point.

"It's quite a walk around the whole ship," said Catherine. "Like the long gallery of a large house."

Scothern's face showed surprise at the young boy's knowledge of a long gallery. "Sixty feet there and sixty feet back," he said.

The gangways along the sides were narrow and without rails. When passing each other they had to be careful not to fall sideways either on to the covered hold in the central part of the ship, or into the river. Catherine in particular was always relieved to reach the short bow or stern decks. There a low rail provided a further measure of safety.

"What's a long gallery?" asked Tom.

Kay glanced at Mark and then said, evenly, "It's a long room at the top of a large house. It goes from one end of the house to the other. I think people use it for exercise when the weather is very bad and they can't get outside. Look at those sheep," she added, changing the subject lest Hugh Scothern should grow curious about her knowledge of great houses and ask questions.

"This is a strongly built vessel," observed Mark as he shared the tiller. "There's enough wood in the hull to provide the timber frame of a house."

"Aye," said Scothern. "'Tis strong and it's made by craftsmen. When we next tie up have a look and see how the oak planks fore and aft have been bent to make the bows and stern vertical."

"I'd noticed that. And why are the long sides of the hull also vertical and not shaped like other ships?"

"Mainly because these keels or barges are designed for cargo. I carry bricks and sand mostly – even pit-coal at times. Hence the ship needs both strength and space. The design also helps navigation in narrow rivers and waterways. 'Pyewipe' is flat-bottomed as well as vertical sided and she sits nice and squat in the water. There are no projecting bits anywhere to catch on the river banks. Except the lee-board and that can be hauled in. And anyway it's quite flat."

"Is that the board hanging over the larboard side by ropes?"

"That's it. We may use it when we reach the Humber. It's lowered so that it projects beneath the ship's bottom. It acts as a keel and prevents 'Pyewipe' from being driven to leeward when we're close hauled. You'll see," he added with a laugh observing that Mark appeared thoroughly perplexed at the sailing terms.

They passed Stillingfleet where they had landed the day before and just before noon reached Drax village where the river widened. Half an hour later the current began to slacken and they hoisted the square sail on the single mast standing amidships.

Mark, Catherine and Tom sat on the forward deck whilst Scothern skilfully navigated 'Pyewipe' through a lengthy 'S' bend with tricky shallows.

The river Ouse widened still further and suddenly 'Pyewipe' was in the middle of a large expanse of water. Away to starboard they could see the mouth of another large river.

"That's the Trent," called Scothern from the stern. "This point where it meets the Ouse is the beginning of the Humber. The river currents here are tricky – dangerous even." He glanced upwards. "Where's the wind?"

They attempted to assess the wind's direction in various ways. Catherine shut her eyes and turned slowly round; Mark looked at the sail; Tom watched a bird gliding overhead.

'From that direction," said Catherine, pointing.

Tom was pointing a different way.

"What do you think, Mark?"

Mark hesitated and then said, "I'm agreeing with Tom."

"Right! And which direction's that?"

"South-east," said the boys together.

"Splendid! How can you tell?"

"We're travelling east and south is to the right – er, to starboard," said Mark.

Scothern looked at Tom.

"By the sun," said Tom.

The freshening breeze was chopping up the surface of the water and 'Pyewipe' rocked and strained a little.

Catherine took the tiller while Hugh Scothern assisted by the boys adjusted the square sail.

"To make the best headway we want to keep her as near the wind as possible. But being flat-bottomed she tends to drift away from the wind. You can feel her turning away now. So we'll lower the lee board and prevent her from drifting."

As soon as the board was lowered they felt 'Pyewipe' shudder as though taking an extra deep breath. Soon she was bustling and wallowing through the choppy waters.

As they approached the mouth of the Trent the three travellers looked away to larboard and down the stretch of the Humber. Ships of various kinds were sailing up, down and across the river. Their thoughts went downstream to the people of Kingston upon Hull and Grimsby who had so kindly cared for them; and beyond them to the North Sea which had claimed the lives of Simon Lee and some of his crew.

Mark sat with Tom on the forward deck while Scothern stood on the stern castle. Catherine was still managing the tiller under the owner's close direction.

Gradually the anxieties of the last few hours receded in the content of an afternoon's sailing.

"Look at the church high up over there!" called Catherine. The boys followed her gaze high up on Trent's left bank.

"That's Alkborough," Scothern told them. "Built by the Normans. It's standing on a ridge of high ground that reaches all the way south to Lincoln. It's your turn to steer, Tom. Come on, my lad!"

Tom scrambled quickly to the tiller and Catherine walked gingerly towards the bows. "There must be a wonderful view from up there," she said, having seated herself safely on the fore deck beside her brother.

"From the top of the tower you can see the Minster at York and Lincoln Cathedral – on a clear day that is! A little to starboard, Tom." Tom moved the tiller gently and had a feeling of power as 'Pyewipe' changed course at his bidding.

They anchored for the night near a village five miles from Trent mouth. Despite the rather cramped conditions in the forward locker room Catherine and Mark slept soundly and were up and about shortly after daybreak. Together with Tom they walked to the village for fresh eggs, cheese and milk.

After a good breakfast the anchor was hand-winched from the river bed and 'Pyewipe' continued her journey south along the Trent. The day was fine but progress was slower than on the previous day since much of the time they were sailing against both tide and river flow.

There was some discussion on the fish to be found in the Trent and when they anchored late that afternoon a few miles north of Gainsborough Tom suggested they caught some trout.

"How?" asked Mark. "We haven't an angling rod or a hook."

"We don't need a rod," said Tom. "I tickle the trout."

"What is 'tickling trout'?" asked Catherine.

"Come and see," replied Tom. "I don't promise to catch any."

Hugh Scothern excused himself. "I've plenty of things to do. But you all go along. I reckon young Tom'll be worth watching and if his skill is what I think – then you'll taste trout before the night's over."

They left the keel and walked two hundred yards to where a stream flowed into the Trent.

"We'll go up here," said Tom.

They walked along the stream's bank until they reached a shallow pool. Tom led them three yards away from the river bank and motioning Mark and Catherine to remain still he crept forward.

For a while he lay motionless on his stomach. Then he signalled the others to sit down near his feet. He dabbled his arms up to the elbows in the stream and gazed down into the water. There was a small rock in the river bank and with his hands he felt gently underneath it. All the time his hands moved smoothly as his fingers trailed in the water. He remained thus for several minutes.

He could see what the others could not. A large trout was edging towards his right hand. He spread his fingers smoothly as his hand drew very slowly close to the fish. A few moments later his fingers reached the underside of the trout and caressed its slippery body.

The trout backed slowly. The fingers approached again. The fish was entranced. Tom's fingers continued to stroke until the gills of the fish were above the palm of his hand, then, with a confident grab, he took the trout from the water.

His friends were delighted with his skill and he chuckled. "One more and then I'll cook them."

He led the way to another part of the pool just below a section of the river where the water ran shallow over large stones. This time Mark and Catherine lay one on each side of Tom in order to watch him more closely.

A similar period of concentration resulted in another grab and a second trout larger than the first.

They gathered small sticks of wood and then to Tom's surprise Mark made a flame and lit the fire. It was Mark's turn to chuckle. "We live in the country too, you know!"

After the trout were cooked and eaten they rested round the wood fire in the warm early evening air.

"Where did you learn to tickle trout?" asked Catherine.

"My father taught me," said Tom. "I used to watch him when I was a small boy. We travelled from village to village telling stories, singing, performing acrobats, juggling. There were three of us – my father, his brother and me. We went all over the place together."

"What about your mother?" Catherine asked.

"I don't remember her. I believe she died of the plague when I was small."

Mark and Catherine both wondered if Tom had other relations. Then Tom suddenly continued.

"About a year ago there was an accident. A horse ran wild in a Market Place where we were performing. My uncle was trampled and killed and my father was badly injured. Later he found that he would never be able to tumble, do acrobats or even juggle again properly. He was ill for some time. The village people looked after us and I helped with farming and other odd jobs. Sometimes in the evenings I told stories that I'd heard my father tell."

He threw some more sticks on the fire.

"After a long time, when he was better, we left the village and travelled the road with our small cart. Dad would mend pots and pans and I would do odd jobs. In the market place we would tell stories together and I would do tumbling and acrobatics. We were just able to make enough to live. My father had always wanted to travel in the north of England. A little while ago we came up to Corbridge and had a happy time working in villages along the south side of the old Roman Wall. One day Dad decided he would like to go north of the old wall to some remote villages over towards Scotland."

His eyes began to sparkle.

"My father loved a good story. He told them so well. I've seen tough men with fighting scars on their faces and their arms cry like small children when listening to him. He lived his stories as he told them. It was his love of adventure that made him go into the wild country. Only a short time ago we spent the night in a lonely village. In the dark a band of mosstroopers attacked the village, plundering and killing. They set fire to farmhouses and killed all the men they could find. They killed the farmer in whose barn we were sleeping. They were taking his daughter away on one of their horses and my father tried to stop them. I was watching from the barn door. I saw it all."

Tom paused.

"After I had buried Dad I wandered back towards the south. I'd been walking for about three days when those men caught me for the Pits. I didn't care much what happened to me after that – until you came."

A thin wisp of smoke spiralled up from the remains of the fire into the late summer dusk.

Tom felt relieved now that his story was told. He had been afraid to speak before in case he should lose the friendship of Mark and Catherine. He knew little about them but it was fairly obvious that they came from a 'well-to-do' family: Catherine's gentleness and courtesy; Mark's authority and confidence. His own background was nomadic. People like himself who travelled from place to place doing odd jobs were called tinkers. They had a reputation for cheating and stealing and if a crime of any sort was committed they would be the first to fall under suspicion. He could not bear the idea of Mark and Catherine thinking badly of his father or himself. His finding and returning the family miniature had made him feel more secure in their eyes.

Catherine wondered what it must be like never to have had a permanent home; always to be on the road, travelling from one village to the next; never knowing where the next meal would come from. Like they were doing now in some ways.

Mark was thinking what an accomplished young man Tom would have been had he received all the advantages of a good tutor. His own lessons included grammar, arithmetic, geometry, astronomy and music. He received training in fencing, dancing and riding. He learned three foreign languages. 'There must be many boys like Tom who never have a chance to prove themselves' he thought. He was determined that if their journey ended successfully Tom should be taken into the family circle and brought up as one of them.

'If their journey ended successfully!' Mark's thoughts brought him up with a jolt.

"Kay, how long is it since we left Alwinton?"

"That's difficult," replied his sister. "We were five days on the 'Susanna' – weren't we, Tom?" Tom nodded. "Then six or seven days at Kingston upon Hull and three or four days near the pits. Oh it must be about three weeks."

Mark was gloomy. "It may well be another three or more before we reach London."

"Would it be better to make for Warwickshire?" ventured Catherine.

"No, Kay. It would take just as long to reach there and then they would have to get a message to London. That would be another two or three days. In any case Webster might go to Warwickshire." He hit the ground with a clenched right fist. "They must know that Richard is innocent," he cried vehemently.

"Richard is your brother?" asked Tom.

"I'm sorry, Tom," said Mark gently. "I should have told you

before. Prompt me, Kay, if I forget anything."

Tom listened while Mark explained exactly who they were and the reason for their journey to London. He spoke softly but with intensity and authority. So clear were all the details in his mind that Catherine remained silent throughout.

"And your brother is Sir Richard?" said Tom, when Mark had finished.

"Yes. It's because our family own a large amount of land. Under a very old law the head of the family inherits the title. Richard inherited from our father, Sir Henry Kempe, who served with the Earl of Leicester against the Spaniards. The Earl presented him to the Queen when they returned from fighting in the low countries. Richard's been presented to the Queen as well."

"Presented to the Queen!" There was awe in Tom's voice. "What is she like?"

"We've never seen her." laughed Catherine. "She can be very stern I believe. Richard used to say lots of people are frightened of her. She's laughing one moment and furious the next. Temperamental – that's the word for it, I think."

"Will you see her when you reach London?"

"I shouldn't think so," said Mark. "So long as we see an important minister of state, tell him about the plot against the Queen's life, and save Richard – that's all that matters. Of course it would be exciting to see the Queen. She's quite old."

Each of them wondered what they would do if they came face to face with Elizabeth the First of England.

Catherine shivered suddenly for it had grown dark and chilly. They had been so engrossed they had not noticed how late it had become.

"Mark! Tom! Kay! Where are you?" It was Hugh Scothern's voice two fields away.

"We're here!" called Catherine, jumping up.

"Time for turning in," called the distant voice.

Tom threw some loose earth on the wood fire and together they crossed the fields back to 'Pyewipe'.

Chapter Nine

The Road South

There was little wind the following day and progress up the Trent was slow. It was mid-afternoon before they reached Torksey where the Roman-built Foss Dyke canal from Lincoln joined the river.

Steered by Hugh Scothern the Keel turned sharply to larboard and entered the canal. The anchor was dropped and 'Pyewipe' came to rest a short distance from a stone bridge that spanned the waterway.

"There are two things to be done, my lads. First to furl the sail and second to take down the mast so that we can pass under bridge."

The sail was lowered and neatly rolled up. Then, with the aid of wooden winches, the lines attached to the top of the mast were slackened.

"Mark, you can give me a hand to lift the bottom of the mast out of the tabernacle." He pointed to a square socket sticking up from the deck. "When it's out Kay and Tom can slacken the lines still further until the mast is lowered slowly to the deck. We've twice the usual number of crew so we should do it in record time!"

They heaved up the mast and rested the end on the open dock. Then the winches were turned and as the lines slackened the mast tilted slowly from vertical to horizontal.

"How do you get 'Pyewipe' under the bridge?" asked Mark.

"If you look over the side you'll see the canal water is still. There's no flow such as you find in a river. We attach a rope to the bows, take the other end under the bridge and pull hard!"

"You must be very strong," said Catherine.

"Not really," laughed Scothern. "Once 'Pyewipe' begins to move it's quite simple. And there are usually one or two Torksey folk ready and eager to help. This time Tom can take the tiller and you two can help me pull the rope."

A long stout rope was taken from the locker room where Mark and Catherine had slept. It was tied to the bows and passed under the bridge to Mark who was waiting on the other side with his sister. Then Hugh Scothern pulled up the anchor, jumped off the boat and ran to join them. Tom sat by the tiller.

"Heave!" cried Scothern and they pulled until they almost fell backwards. 'Pyewipe' moved slowly towards the bridge. "Take up the slack and then another heave."

The rope was drawn tight again.

"Heave!"

'Pyewipe' moved forward a little quicker.

Tom shifted the tiller slightly, the keel swung out towards midstream and the bows went gracefully under the bridge.

"Well done everyone! Keep her steady Tom lad! Well done! Take in the slack again and prepare to slow her down by pulling gently as she draws level. Then we'll drop anchor for the night. Gently now."

'Pyewipe', now clear of the bridge, drew level and they tightened up on the rope. "A little to larboard, Tom. Keep hold of the line you two. Straighten her up, Tom."

'Pyewipe' drifted towards the bank. "A little more, Tom."

'Pyewipe' slowed as Scothern and his helpers checked her with the rope. Then when she had almost stopped Scothern jumped from the bank on to the Keel and dropped the anchor. There was a splash and 'Pyewipe' came to a halt.

"What a crew!" said Hugh Scothern. "I shall miss you all. We'll just tie her up to the bank and that's that."

After supper, sitting on the canal bank, Scothern asked them if they knew the story of the Lincoln Imp. They shook their heads.

"There are several versions of the story. The one I like best is about the time when work was being done to the east end of Lincoln Cathedral. It's called the Angel Choir because of the carved figures of Angels which fill the framework of the arches."

"The Imp and the Wind had been going round the building when the wind dared the Imp to play tricks on the builders and delay their work. The Imp, a grotesque little chap, accepted the dare. When the builders were busy elsewhere he'd nip up to a new wall and with a magic strength pitch several blocks of masonry on to the ground."

"The builders were mystified and when the Mayor arrived he refused to give them their wages. He said he only paid for work done.   There were some noisy arguments. Then one bright lad kept watch and the Imp was caught. But here's the strangest part. While they were all wondering what should be done with the Imp one of the carved Angels flew down from his arch high up in the triforium, snatched up the Imp and placed him above one of the pillars in the Angel Choir. As the Imp was set down he turned to stone and you may see him there now peering out from the carved foliage and looking as wicked as ever."

"There's another story for your collection, Tom," said Mark. "We think he's a rare teller of tales," he added to Hugh Scothern. "Don't we, Kay?"

Tom looked embarrassed. "You've never heard me, Mark."

"I'm sure you are," said Catherine. "You notice everything, every detail, and you remember everything."

Tom, who felt quite overcome by this sudden praise, stood on his hands and walked upside down around the group. Then he turned two somersaults, did three handsprings and sat down again. The others applauded vigorously.

"If there's a breeze we should reach Lincoln tomorrow in fair time," said Hugh Scothern. "Where do you travel from there?"

"To London,'" said Mark. "We must get there as soon as possible. It's most important. If necessary we'll walk all the way. Have you any idea how we might get there more quickly?"

"That's difficult. You've still a long way to go and the roads are bad – and dangerous. But I expect you know that. I wish I could help – wait a bit though! It's almost Fair time. You should find people travelling to the Stourbridge Fair near Cambridge. It opens in ten days or so. It's one of the biggest fairs in England and attracts buyers and sellers from all over the country; from all over Europe too! You might be allowed to travel with some merchants if you're willing to look after their horses and make yourselves useful."

"How far is Cambridge from London?"

"I couldn't say. But it's about half way between Lincoln and London. I know that because a mate of mine rode here from London and he stopped at Cambridge for the night."

"We'll look out for the merchants then. But we shan't have another journey like this. You have been most kind, Master Scothern. I wish there was some way we could repay you."

"You've helped me no end. I should have found things very difficult with my lad being laid up. I should have had very little sleep and it might well have taken a day or two longer to get here. You've made a fine crew – all of you. I shall miss your company. Now – it's time we turned in. I've a busy day tomorrow and you've a long, hard journey ahead."

Next morning the mast was raised and fitted back into the tabernacle. Both the square mainsail and the smaller topsail were hoisted to make best use of the wind. The anchor was raised and 'Pyewipe' began the final part of her journey to Lincoln along the ancient Foss Dyke canal.

A gentle but steady breeze filled the sails and the Humber Keel moved purposefully forward. There was neither tide nor current to impede them and by late morning they had their first sight of the Cathedral's twin towers high above the city.

In the late afternoon sunshine 'Pyewipe' dropped anchor in Brayford Pool where the canal joined the river Witham. The children offered to help unload the keel but Hugh Scothern said that the people who had bought his cargo would do that. "You'd best be on your way. You've a deal of travelling to do. More than walking in the long gallery!" he said, unexpectedly. "That's your way, to the south of the city."

They each shook hands with him, thanked him again for his kindness and set off.

"We've three or four hours before it gets dark," said Mark. "Shall we stay in Lincoln until the morning or start walking now? What do you think, Tom?"

"In three or four hours we can walk seven or eight miles."

"I agree," said Catherine. "Let's get on our way." They left Lincoln, climbed up out of the Witham valley and walked along the track that had once been the Roman road called Ermine Street. When darkness came they were eleven miles south of the city.

"Let's find somewhere to eat and sleep," said Mark.

They sat in a cornfield, ate the supper, which Hugh Scothern had thoughtfully provided, and spent the warm night sleeping under a hedgerow.

They awoke at dawn and continued walking south.

They had passed through a village with several cottages, a forge and a farm when they heard a commotion from beyond a hedge.

The loud neigh of a terrified horse was followed by trampling and rumbling. Then a horse pulling a cart bolted through a hedge gap and careered towards them. They scattered as one wheel struck a large stone and that side of the cart jerked into the air. The cart ran briefly, balanced on one wheel and then crashed to its side. The drag of the cart arrested the horse, which reared with its legs flaying the air and its eyes rolling.

Catherine approached until the sweating animal threatened to crush her on its next plunge. Her eyes were riveted on the curb-rein and as the horse plunged again she stepped nimbly to one side and took hold of the bridle.

The horse strained upwards and Catherine was almost lifted off her feet. She held on saying softly, "It's all right, boy. It's all right." Mark took the curb-rein on the other side and together they brought the horse under control.

"You're all right now. There's nothing to hurt you. Everything's all right." Catherine stroked its neck down from the ears. "That's better."

Tom, who had been watching with admiration and remembering another incident with a wild horse, said, "The farmer's coming."

"You're a plucky boy," said the man to Catherine. "A snake frightened him. What a mess! Vegetables all over the place. And look at my cart! I'll free him from the shafts."

Catherine, still chatting in a soothing voice, led the horse a few yards along the track whilst the others examined the cart.

"The side's smashed and this wheel is almost off. I'll have to get the Smith."

"We'll look after things while you've gone," promised Mark.

"Will you? That's very kind. I shan't be long."

Nearly two hours later the cart was repaired and reloaded and the horse was back in the shafts.

The farmer's wife gave them some milk and made them stuff their pockets with apples and pears. "And here's some cheese, it'll go down a treat with the apples."

They tramped on along the rough track and just before midday were overtaken by a horse-drawn touring carriage that forced them into a ditch and covered them with dust. Two servants clung precariously to the driving seat white the occupant, a noble looking man topped by a slashed leather hat with a yellow feather, was jolted about inside.

They watched the carriage gradually become a cloud of distant dust.

"How quickly we'd reach London in one of those! Just two or three days," said Mark, wistfully. He removed his jerkin and they crossed the track to walk in the shade of some trees.

They sat under an enormous oak to eat and had just started off again when they saw a horseman approaching very slowly.

"Look at the bundles and the pots and things hanging from the saddle," whispered Catherine.

"It's a tinker," said Tom softly.

"Good-day!" called the-man cheerfully as he passed them. Two pewter mugs were clanking together like a tolling bell.

"Good-day!" they called.

"What a woe-be-gone looking horse," remarked Catherine.

"So would you be if you had to carry all those things!" chuckled her brother.

"Look out! Here's another rider coming at tremendous speed," cried Tom. He leaped into the ditch followed by his friends,

The hoof-beats grew louder and the horse and its rider, bent low over the animal's neck, thundered past stirring up more dust. They watched them bearing down on the tinker who urged his unhappy nag into a ditch the moment before the galloping horse reached and overtook him.

"A messenger I should think," observed Mark as they climbed out of the ditch.

During the afternoon clouds gathered and the air became less sultry. Then a drizzle began.

"It's a relief to feel the cool rain after the heat and dust," said Catherine, holding her face skywards.

But the relief was short-lived. The drizzle increased to a steady fall and rain began trickling down their necks and backs and through to their scalps.

Puddles and tunnels of water appeared in the spoiled surface of ancient Ermine Street and their brisk walk became a slow squelch.

Finally the fall became a downpour. Their clothes became

soaked and heavy and clung to them. Eventually they sought shelter in a church porch.

They each stripped to the waist, wrung out their clothes and sat on a stone bench to watch for an easing of the rain.

Mark became very depressed. They were miles from anywhere. He felt tired and wet. It might rain all night. Where would they sleep? Perhaps they would find a barn. But then the farmer might turn them out or arrest them as vagrants. And why had he hazarded his sister's health in allowing her to accompany him?

The lashing rain continued.

He mustn't allow himself to think this way. Richard's plight was worse than theirs. He fingered the gold chain around his neck and touched the pendant. Keep Faith!

He glanced at his sister and their eyes met.

Catherine smiled. She had been studying his expression for some moments and guessed something of his thoughts. "Don't worry. We'll get there. We've travelled over half the distance and we've come through an explosion and a shipwreck. We know Richard is innocent. They wouldn't do anything to him until they were absolutely sure."

"In ordinary times you might be right," said Mark. "But these aren't ordinary times. People have been plotting against the Queen ever since she came to the throne. Even before she became Queen her life was in danger. It's the duty of her ministers to make quite sure no harm comes to her. If anything were to happen there would be civil war in England again. It would be like the Wars of the Roses but much worse. I remember Richard saying that they had tried to persuade her to name her successor so that when she dies there will be someone to take the throne, but for some reason she won't give a name. She's too old to have children even if she did marry."

Tom listened with interest for he had never heard talk like this. The conversations between his father, uncle and himself concerned the next stopping place: their reception; who was likely to have them put in the stocks or pillory where rotten fruit and vegetables would be flung at them. Food had been another regular topic of conversation. Sometimes they had eaten and sometimes they had not. Tom had learned to pull the string tighter around his small waist and turn his mind to other matters in an effort to forget hunger.

An hour later the rain eased and they set off again in a drizzle. After a mile the drizzle ceased and the sun returned to cheer them. Mark's depression lifted as quickly as it had descended. "Let's walk briskly to warm ourselves and make up some lost time."

After another six miles it began to grow dark. "I'll make a big wood fire," said Tom. "Then we can dry our clothes and get really warm again."

They searched along the edge of a field where the thick foliage of trees had protected a hedgerow from the rain and found plenty of dry sticks.

"I've found some early blackberries," called Catherine.

"There are some over here as well. You manage the fire, Tom, and we'll collect the berries. Put them on my jerkin, Kay," He removed the jerkin and placed it on the ground.

Tom soon had a fire blazing in a corner of the field. Then he found some strong sticks and set them upright in the ground. "We can dry our wet clothes on these. Oh – you've found some windfalls as well as blackberries."

"Yes. It's not the best meal I ever had but it will keep us going.

They stripped off all their clothes except the breeches and hung them to dry. Then they sat around the fire, threw on more sticks and watched the flames leap high in the darkening atmosphere. Wood crackled and spat and sparks floated upwards and jumped out at them suddenly. They toasted themselves, ate their fruit and began to feel more content.

"Would you tell us a tale, Tom?" asked Mark.

"What sort of a tale would you like? Comical? Tragical? Heroic?" These were the words he had heard his father use.

"You choose," said Catherine.

"Something heroic then. The story of a brave young warrior who fought two hideous monsters and a dragon. It happened across the sea –"

"'What was that?" Catherine locked round into the darkness, listening.

"What?" asked Mark.

I thought I heard something behind the hedge."

They listened. The fire crackled loudly.

"Perhaps it was a badger," said Tom.

"Sorry," said Catherine. "I had a nasty feeling at that moment. Silly of me. Please go on, Tom."

"A long time ago Hrothgar, the King of Denmark, built a magnificent Hall called Heorot. All his soldiers gathered in the hall for feasting. But the sound of their merriment was heard by a hideous monster, Grendel, who lived in the murky, swampy fens. He was stronger than ten men and on his hands each claw was a hideous spike. From his eyes there flashed an ugly gleam like a flame. He hated happiness and he set out for the Hall. As he approached he smelled human flesh and blood – his favourite food. He reached the hall and with one blow of his claw-like fist smashed down the huge wooden doors. He seized the nearest warrior and snapped him in two like a twig –"

Three men sprang out of the darkness. Catherine felt herself taken in a cruel grip and could only struggle uselessly with her legs.

Tom soon wriggled from his attacker's grasp and attempted his own style of wrestling. He bemused the man with his feints, somersaults and side steps. But eventually brute force overcame him. He felt a vicious blow on his chin and everything went black. Mark's assailant was the youngest of the three men but also the most brutal in appearance. He was unshaven and had matted straggly hair and several broken teeth. He met his match in Mark who had been trained in the art of self-defence together with his fencing lessons.

Mark knocked his opponent down twice. The second time the ruffian rose swearing and stormed at Mark with his arms flaying the air. Mark dodged the whirling arms but felt the man's knee in his stomach. He doubled in pain and the man seized him but, straightening suddenly, he caught the ruffian on the chin with the top of his head. The man staggered backwards, overbalanced and sat on the edge of the fire.

Instinctively Mark jumped forward to help him but was seized from behind by Tom's attacker.

Mark's assailant scrambled from the fire and beat out his smouldering breeches. "Let's take the gold necklace and get out of here!" Mark was held firmly from behind while the man removed the chain and pendant. "This'll be worth gallons of sack – and an 'ole lot more! 'Ave this in its place!" He welted Mark on the cheek with the back of his hand. Mark neither flinched nor cried out. This seemed to enrage the man who brought back his hand and struck at the other cheek. The blow caught Mark on the chin. Blood flowed from his nose, his ears roared and the man and the fire whirled about in front of him. He felt himself released and slid to the ground in a heap.

Kay felt frightened and angry. Her captor pushed her towards Mark. "Stay there. Don't move or you'll suffer too!" She heard the men crash their way through the hedge and on to the road. She stumbled across to Mark who had recovered sufficiently to murmur, "Look at Tom. I'm all right." She crossed quickly to Tom, who was lying still, took his bare shoulder and moved him gently on to his back.

Mark sat up slowly and wiped the blood from his face with the back of his hand. He felt his chin but nothing seemed to be broken.

Then uproar broke out a short distance away. A deep voice boomed, "Cut-throats! Footpads! Vagabonds! Lay hands upon them!" There followed shouts and oaths and sounds of scuffling and thumps. Then more shouting and the sound of footsteps running away.

"Well done lads!" boomed the same voice. "We have routed the pampered Jades of Asia! What you have there, Ned? Bring a lantern." There was a short silence and then the same voice continued "By the Lord of Ludgate! Here's a thing!"

Mark got shakily to his feet.

"Come lads!" continued the voice. "I think we may find the answer through here."

Mark heard movement beyond the hedge and then the imposing figure of a man came through the gap and into the firelight.

"Good evening, young sir! I am Nicholas Ridley.'" The man bowed. "Might this ornament by yours?"

CHAPTER TEN

Enter Nicholas Ridley

Mark could hardly believe the sudden change of fortune. Moments before he had been lying on the ground, bleeding, the precious family heirloom stolen, and now the footpads were put to flight and the miniature safe.

"Might this ornament be yours?"

"It is."

"Describe it if you will, please."

"The initials of my parents H and E form the chain. The painting by Hilliard in the locket is of my mother."

Nicholas Ridley held out the chain. "Perfectly described," he said. "I am pleased to return it to you."

"Thank you. Could you please help with Tom. He was knocked down by those ruffians."

Ridley looked over at the still form lying near the fire. He walked quickly across and Catherine rose to make room for him. He knelt down and bent over Tom. "At least he is breathing," he pronounced and added in sudden gentle tones, "The wretches – attacking young people in this fashion. What did they do to him?"

"I didn't notice," said Mark. "I was struggling myself."

"He was hit on the chin," said Catherine.

"No bones broken then – unless his chin has suffered. It should be safe to lift him. I'll take him to the props wagon."

So saying he lifted the thin body effortlessly and cradling it in his arms walked towards the gap in the hedge. "Come with me if you will."

Mark and Catherine followed him on to the track beyond the hedge. A few yards away they saw three figures. Two were holding lanterns. In the darkness beyond they could make out the side of a large wagon.

"Stephen! Bartholomew! Quickly lads! Water in a bowl and the 'Elixir of life' for this hurt boy."

The three figures climbed into the front of the wagon. Moments later one of them jumped from the back and set a flight of steps on the ground. Ridley marched up and laid Tom gently on a sack.

"Hold up the lantern, Ned."

Mark and Catherine stood on the steps.

"Where's that Elixir? Bartholomew! Stephen! Late on cue again! And bring me that other lantern. One isn't sufficient!"

From the depths of the wagon emerged a gawkish, red-haired boy clutching a bottle.

"Take out the stopper, Bartholomew," urged Ridley. "I'm supporting this boy; your hands are free."

Bartholomew drew out the stopper and handed the bottle to Ridley who put its neck between Tom's pale lips. Mark and Catherine watched intently and were relieved to see Tom's eyes flicker open.

Stephen, whom Mark thought looked slightly older than Bartholomew, appeared with the other lantern and a rough wooden bowl filled with water. Ridley asked Tom to waggle his chin gently. This Tom did without effort. "Clench your teeth." Tom obeyed. "I don't think there's anything broken," said Ridley. We'll bathe your face in cold water to help bring out any bruising. And you, my young friend," he added, looking at Mark, "also require water. Your face is bloody! Ned, give your lantern to this lad and take Stephen and Bartholomew to collect more firewood."

'It was our fire that attracted the robbers," said Mark.

"And it also helped us to see what was happening," said Ridley.

Catherine held up the lantern and looked round the wagon's interior. There were several large pieces of platform stacked along one side; four large buck baskets; poles, spears and swords; a stout wood table and several stools. There were more sacks, which looked to be straw filled. Hanging from the roof Catherine saw an assortment of articles including two lutes and a tabor.

"Now I think we should introduce ourselves properly. I am Nicholas Ridley, travelling player."

"I'm Mark, this is my s – brother Kay, and this is our friend, Tom."

"Well Tom, Kay and Mark, we shall dine tonight around your fire."

Half an hour later the four players and the three children were preparing to tackle lentil soup with chunks of bacon in it and then bread and cheese, all of which was washed down with ale.

When the meal was finished Ridley dispatched the three players to wash the wooden platters and prepare the wagon for the night. When they had gone he said, "You must forgive my curiosity but it troubles me that three young lads – shabbily dressed perhaps, but with fine speech and manners – should wander the countryside as prey to footpads and worse."

"We are on our way to London," said Mark.

"Indeed! Do you know London?"

"No, Master Ridley, but we know people who live there. I have an urgent message for them. Lives are at stake."

"Urgent messages; lives at stake?" said Ridley. "It has the makings of a Revenge Tragedy. But I shall not enquire further. What supporting roles can you play?"

Catherine and Mark were perplexed. "Supporting roles? What are they?"

Ridley's eyes danced roguishly at their bewilderment. "I am – I should say, we are – going to Stourbridge Fair to play for two or three days. Then we go to Gorhambury House at St. Albans to play for Master Francis Bacon's nephews and nieces. And then, my young friends, to London for a season and also to see a young acquaintance of mine who is doing well as a player and a writer I believe. I like adventurers if they are honest and I am – um – intrigued by this adventure of yours. You could travel with us to London but – " and his eyes danced again, " – you must play your parts. You must support yourselves with supporting roles. Do you sing madrigals? Or dance? Can you erect a Pageant Stage? Of course you may not wish to travel with such as us; I know that we are merely players......" His final words were delivered in a tone of mock apology.

The offer was generous and a solution to their problems. Mark secretly wondered if he might disclose to Francis Bacon his knowledge of Cain Webster's treachery. He had heard his name mentioned in connection with the Court.

"You are most kind," replied Mark. "We would be honoured to travel with players. Tom is a teller of tales and an acrobat. Kay and I are not so skilled but we would help in any way we could."

"We both play the lute and the tabor and we can dance a Pavane, a Galliard and La Volta," said Catherine with spirit. "And I can sew and mend all manner of clothes." She stopped, and thought, 'I shouldn't have mentioned sewing; I'm supposed to be a boy!'

"Can you now," boomed the actor's resonant voice with no hint of surprise. "Then you may join my company of players and journey with us to London. And you may judge for yourselves how undeserving we are of the names of rogues and vagabonds."

Nicholas Ridley looked across the wood fire, no longer ablaze but glowing fiery red, and addressed Tom. "Where did you learn to tell tales?"

"Travelling with my father, sir," replied Tom. "He was the best I ever heard."

"Was he indeed. Well, if it's in your blood, lad, you won't escape from it easily. We shall see. This chance meeting could be a stroke of fortune for you. We shall see! Enough of this. We have a long journey tomorrow and with this evening's excitement you must be feeling tired. I see by your drying clothes that you have endured the foul weather. Tonight you shall sleep in the dry and in safety."

The wagon was large and although it contained so much paraphernalia there was room for the seven sleepers. Nicholas Ridley and Ned lay on their straw mattresses near the front of the wagon while Stephen and Bartholomew were at the back. "You three can rest safely in the middle," said Ridley. "Blow out the lanterns, Bartholomew."

Tom had fallen asleep the moment he lay down and Catherine's eyes closed shortly afterwards. Mark lay for some time looking through the opening at the back of the wagon to the stars far beyond. The events of the last few weeks seemed unreal to him, like an extraordinary dream, and Mark thought that he might yet wake to find himself in the pele tower near Alwinton. But the wagon and its contents were real enough and the snores of Nicholas Ridley were certainly no figment of his imagination. Mark thought of his brother who might be looking at the same night sky from the confines of his cell in the Tower. If only he knew that help was on the way! Mark prayed silently that the nights and days would pass quickly to make their journey to London seem much shorter.

Lying awake with his thoughts made Mark feel lonely and after a time the straw sack seemed lumpy and most uncomfortable. He shifted his position for the umpteenth time and sighed.

Someone moved nearby and a voice close to his ear said gently,

"Have a drop of Master Ridley's elixir." It was Ned, the company's second player. Mark took the bottle gratefully, drank a large draught and then returned the bottle with a smile. Ned nodded and crawled back to his sack.

Mark felt a comfortable warmth spread through him, his eyes closed and all his worries vanished with sleep.

He woke to a sunny morning with activity all around him. Everyone else was up and busy.

Have you groomed Tamburlaine?" Ridley's voice boomed outside the wagon.

"This moment!" replied a thin voice.

"The fire's going well, Kay!" called Tom.

"Thank you!" answered Catherine. "Who is Tamburlaine?" she enquired as she prepared to heat the pottage for their breakfast.

"The horse," replied Ned, cheerfully. "He's named after the warrior in a play by Christopher Marlowe. Master Ridley longs to play the whole part."

Stripped to his waist Mark washed in a bowl of cold water and then prepared to make himself useful.

Nicholas Ridley was talking earnestly to Stephen, older of the two young players. The young man was on his knees holding a sword with the point towards his chest.

"Pyramus kills himself because he thinks his sweetheart is dead. It's a tragic story and you must not play for laughs when you die. It's not like the Turkish Knight in the Mummer's Play. We can only have one death like that on the stage. Now let's do it again."

Stephen thrust the sword rather unconvincingly between his chest and his left arm and toppled forward.

Nicholas Ridley groaned. "Let the audience see what you are feeling," he implored. "You're too quick. Imagine it! Feel it! Suppose you had a sweetheart who you thought had been killed."

"But I haven't got a sweetheart," protested Stephen.

"Imagine you have!" roared Ridley. "Imagine it. When I play the scenes from "Tamburlaine" I imagine I'm a great soldier with a huge army conquering the world. Do it again. We must make it convincing or we shall lose our audience."

Mark left them rehearsing and crossed to where the red-headed Bartholomew was grooming the horse.

"Good morning!"

"Hello," said the boy player.

Tamburlaine, who was cropping the grass turned slowly and looked at Mark.

"He looks strong," said Mark.

"He has to be to pull all that stuff in the wagon."

Ned appeared from inside the wagon and stood on the driver's seat. "Bartholomew, have you repaired Thisbe's dress?"

"Not yet. I haven't had time. I was going to do it last night but the trouble with the robbers stopped me."

Ned shook his head and disappeared back inside the wagon.

"Who is Thisbe?" asked Mark.

"A part I play," said Bartholomew. "It's a girl. I have to play the female parts because my voice hasn't broken yet. It won't be long before it does," he added impressively. "Any time now. Then I shall play young men."

Mark nodded. "I played a girl once, when I was younger."

"Are you a boy player too?"

"No. We used to act plays at home. My brother played a young soldier and I was his sister. I forget the name of the play."

A figure cartwheeled round the wagon. It was Tom who announced that breakfast was ready.

When they had finished eating, the wooden platters were washed and the fire smothered. Then with everything replaced in the wagon Tamburlaine was put into the shafts and the players moved off.

Ned drove. A space was cleared inside the jolting wagon and Nicholas Ridley prepared to rehearse a scene between Pyramus and Thisbe. The three new players sat on buck baskets and watched with interest.

"There will be little time for rehearsal when we reach Cambridge so we must use every available moment," Ridley told them. "We haven't performed this little tragedy since my last Thisbe's voice broke."

"What happened to him?" asked Catherine.

"He went into service at the house of Sir Francis Willoughby near Nottingham. I've lost several young players this way. It has become fashionable for rich men and nobles to have servants who are also actors. When they give a banquet they have a cry of players all ready to perform to their guests. My young friend William, who is playing in London, began that way with the Earl of Leicester."

Ridley ran his fingers through the mass of black and grey hair that tumbled about his ears. "Now let us try the scene where Pyramus and Thisbe meet and declare their love for each other."

The audience was not very impressed with the two young players. Catherine thought Bartholomew's movement and gesture very like that of a young lady but his voice was squeaky and he didn't sound as though he cared much for Pyramus. 'Still, it must be very difficult,' she thought, 'for a boy to pretend to be a girl in love with a young man'. Mark, who watched Stephen carefully, thought his movements wooden and although his voice was manly and pleasant it lacked feeling.

Tom was bursting to jump up and say, "Let me try!" He was experiencing all the feelings, all the emotions, inside himself. How could they not understand and express what Pyramus and Thisbe felt for each other? He watched Nicholas Ridley who was trying his utmost with this pale pair of actors. The experienced player was feeling all the emotions himself. Tom thought he was marvellous. He was too old and too large for either part and yet one could believe him when he spoke the lines.

The wagon rumbled on through the fine September morning and the rehearsal continued with the death of Pyramus and the discovery of his body by Thisbe.

Early in the afternoon Ned handed the reins to Nicholas Ridley and went forward to guide Tamburlaine. Ermine Street was sloping off the ridge of high ground called the Lincoln Edge and descending to the flat lands of the Fens near Stamford. The whole weight of the wagon was now upon the horse and although a brake was applied someone was needed to lead the horse and talk gently to him.

"The Queen's chief minister has a house near here," Ridley observed to Mark who was sitting beside him. "To be invited to play at Burghley House would be a high honour, a very high honour,"

"Perhaps you will one day."

Ridley shook his head. "Time passes and I grow older. Most of all I long to play before the Queen's Majesty. Think of it – Elizabeth of England moved to tears by her humble and faithful player, her most devoted vagabond!"

Mark, watching closely, saw the actor's face flush with pride and his eyes mist with tears. At that moment in his imagination Nicholas Ridley was playing before the Queen. The moment passed and he turned to Mark with a gentle smile. "We all have our dreams," he said.

Late in the afternoon they reached Sawtry. First Tamburlaine was watered and turned to graze. Then the players continued rehearsing with a mummers' play about St. George and the Turkish Knight, Slasher. The children thought this play in much better shape than 'Pyramus and Thisbe.'

It began with the Fool, played by Stephen, asking the audience to clear a space for the actors. He carried an air-filled pig's bladder on the end of a stick and bounced it on their heads. They laughed at his antics although privately Tom thought that he could have made more of his acrobatics and tumbling.

Ned's 'St. George' was every inch a splendid knight, performed with a flourish and spoken with authority.

Then came Nicholas Ridley as the pompous and boastful Turkish Knight. He rolled his eyes, stroked an imaginary moustache and put a foreign accent into his voice which seemed an octave lower than usual.

His fight with St. George was both exciting and funny. At the end St. George appeared to run his sword clean through the Turk. Ridley gasped and groaned and clutched his side. Then with his eyes rolling in agony he sagged gradually to the ground. When the audience thought he was dead he twitched and half rose up again. At last he lay still and Catherine, Mark and Tom broke into spontaneous applause.

Stephen then introduced Bartholomew as the doctor who was to restore the Turkish Knight to life. The boy player was much more convincing as the old short-sighted doctor than as the young lady Thisbe.

The performance ended with a short dance, which Ned accompanied on tabor and pipe. In the middle of this proceeding Ridley called a halt.

"We will test the talents of the unfledged players," he announced importantly. "Master Kay shall play the tabor. Which of you two shall pipe?" He looked from Mark to Tom.

"I've played a recorder," said Mark. "But what about Tom? Can you play the pipe?"

Tom shook his head. "I've never tried it."

"Then you shall learn in good time," said Ridley. "For the present we'll give the pipe to Master Mark and the dance shall be altered to include Ned and Tom."

For the next hour they rehearsed under Ridley's directions until the new arrangement had begun to take shape.

"Splendid!" cried Ridley. "Once more through and then we'll have some food. Keep the rhythm steady, Mark. It isn't easy and you're playing remarkably well. We'll go from the last lines of the play. Mark and Kay, your cue for playing is 'A pocket full of money and a cellar full of beer'. And that's when you cartwheel on to the stage, Tom. Is everyone ready?"

The meal was prepared and eaten with much talking and excitement. They all felt a sense of achievement and were conscious of having worked well together.

After the meal, while the players rehearsed, Mark and Catherine cleared away and Tom attended to Tamburlaine. The voices of Stephen and Bartholomew with occasional interjections from Ridley drifted from the other side of the wagon

Tom finished grooming the horse and looked round for Catherine and Mark but they had disappeared. Mystified he took a wooden bucket and walked through a small thicket to a stream for fresh water.

His two friends were sitting silently together on the bank. Tom stood beside them for several seconds before they were aware of him. Mark looked up dejectedly.

Intuitively Tom knew the reason.

"You're thinking about your brother?"

Mark nodded. "I found the rehearsal tremendous fun but when the excitement was over we both thought about Richard. We seemed to have forgotten the serious reason for our journey and were simply enjoying ourselves."

Tom upturned the bucket and sat facing them.

"I think I know what you mean. You feel you ought to be worrying about him all the time."

Catherine nodded and Mark said, "Yes. I know it sounds silly but he's in the Tower and has no-one to help him. None of his friends know the truth except us and we must do all we can."

"I felt like that once but – well, this is different; my father wasn't in the Tower." He looked away. He mustn't interfere in their private affairs.

"Go on, Tom."

"No, I haven't any right. You wouldn't .." He shook his head gently.

"Please go on, Tom," said Mark. "You may be able to help us."

Tom looked at Mark. "Well, you remember I told you about the accident with the horse when my uncle was killed and dad was injured?" They nodded. "I felt I should stay with him every minute in case he wanted me. He said, 'You won't help anyone by sitting there looking so gloomy, least of all yourself!'"

"Go on," said Catherine.

"Dad said, 'the people here are helping me and you must help them. When I'm better then I shall want you to do all you can for me!'"

A twig snapped and looking up they saw Ned. "Having a private rehearsal?" Then seeing three serious faces he added, "I'm sorry. I didn't mean to interrupt."

Mark smiled and stood up. "You weren't. We were talking over a problem and Tom has helped us."

The others stood and Tom said, "I must fill this bucket."

"And we must finish clearing up," said Catherine.

"Nicholas is still rehearsing the lads, so I'll give you a hand." They waited for Tom to re-join them and returned to the wagon together.

At the end of the day they sat around a fire and Tom held them spellbound with the story of Beowulf, the brave warrior. It was the tale that had been interrupted by the robbers the previous evening.

They heard how the young Beowulf had killed the monster, Grendel, and his hag-mother; how he ruled his people wisely and kindly for many years and finally how he fought a huge dragon that was pillaging the land. The dragon was killed but the aged Beowulf mortally wounded. After his death the people made a huge funeral pyre upon which their warrior-King's body was placed. Then the pyre was set alight and the body burned, as was the custom.

So vividly did Tom tell the story that their wood fire seemed to become the funeral pyre and the listeners watched the flames leap and fall with fascination.

When he finished there was a long silence broken only by the crackling of the fire. No one moved. Then Nicholas Ridley said softly, "Thank you lad. Your father taught you well."

That was the finest compliment anyone could have paid Tom. His dark eyes glowed in Ridley's direction. Such a comment from a professional travelling player! How proud his father would have been.

That night no one had any difficulty in sleeping and at first cock-crow they woke refreshed and ready for the new day's work.

While breakfast was prepared, Tamburlaine was groomed and Ned took Catherine and Bartholomew into the village for provisions and fresh water.

"We should reach the outskirts of Cambridge by dusk," said Ridley when breakfast was over. "Then tomorrow morning we go through the city to Stourbridge Common. There preparations for the Fair will be in full swing. On board the wagon everyone! Ned, take the reins. Stephen, Bartholomew, prepare to rehearse 'Pyramus and Thisbe'. There's much to be done yet!"

Tom held them spellbound with the story of Beowulf.

ChAPTER ELEVEN

Rehearsals

"Alas what chance my Pyramus –"

Bartholomew pitched forward on to the floor as the wagon jolted violently. He resumed a kneeling position.

"Alas what chance my Pyramus
Hath parted thee and me?
Make answer, O my Pyramus,
To her that speaks to thee."

Catherine was watching Tom, who, sitting on a buck basket, was muttering the lines as Ned rehearsed Bartholomew. 'He knows every word,' she thought.

"Thy love hath made thee slay thyself
I swear – I swear – oh, erm…"

"This hand of mine," said Tom, immediately regretting his interruption. He should have given Bartholomew scope to remember the line. "I'm sorry. I couldn't help it."

Ned glanced at him and half smiled. Bartholomew looked reproachful and continued:

"I swear this hand of mine
Is strong enough to do the like er –
Strong enough to do the like' – Oh, bother!"

'My love no less than thine', thought Tom keeping his mouth firmly shut.

"My love no less than thine," prompted Ned.

"My love no less than thine
Shall give me force to work thy wound
I will pursue the dead."

"Let's do that speech again," said Ned.

Bartholomew frowned and repeated the speech with one prompt.

"Why doesn't he put more feeling into 'I swear' and into the last line?' thought Tom.

"Bartholomew, try to put more feeling into 'I swear'. You're not saying it as though you mean it," said Ned. "And the last line – it means you're going to kill yourself. That requires great courage. The way you're saying it doesn't convince me you'd do it. And it won't convince the audience either."

Bartholomew nodded but looked miserable.

"Ned!" called Ridley from the driving seat. "We're just entering Cambridge and the way ahead is very busy. Take Tamburlaine's head would you?"

Ned vaulted lightly over the back of the wagon and ran forward to guide the horse.

"He's a good tutor," said Catherine. "I suppose he once played Thisbe himself?"

"Yes," answered Bartholomew. "He seems to know all the parts we play. Let's join the others at the front."

They scrambled over baskets and props and stood behind Ridley, Mark and Stephen.

They saw carts and people converging on them from both sides. Heavy horse-drawn wagons like their own crunched slowly along the rough-surfaced road. The drivers of smaller carts were trying to weave their vehicles in and out of the slower ones and get ahead of them. Soon the lane was packed and the autumn air was filled with crunching wheels, neighing horses and swearing drivers.

Ridley chuckled. "This is a moment, my young friends, to observe human nature. Not all the red faces and hoarse voices will assist their progress. Patience, my friends, patience."

Stephen turned and winked at Bartholomew.

The vast area of Stourbridge Fields was a mass of activity. Wagons, carts and people were everywhere. Stalls and booths were in various stages of completion. Town officials were hurrying to each new arrival checking licences.

"This row of stalls straight ahead is called Cheapside, the same as the street in the City of London. Here it's the market for cheese and butter. Further on is the large cloth fair called the Duddery. Many of its traders come from Westmoreland. That line of stalls going away to the left from Cheapside and across the fields is called Garlic Row. It runs for a mile down to the river. We turn off left here before we reach Garlic Row."

Ned led Tamburlaine on to the stubble of Stourbridge Fields.

"This part of the Fair is given to the various entertainers," Ridley continued. "Beside ourselves there are Minstrels, Jugglers and Acrobats. Just over there by Garlic Row are the wrestling booths, ninepin bowling and table bowls. You might even find a fortune-telling gypsy though they're in danger from the Constable of the Watch."

"Why is that?" asked Catherine.

"They're not licensed. Come now, we must erect our stage."

Inside the wagon Ned and Stephen shifted the buck baskets in order to reach the three sections of wooden platform that made up the stage and tiring house. They slid out the first of these on its side.

"Take the end, Mark," directed Ridley. "Keep it upright. It's easier to manage that way."

Mark grasped the section of platform and backed away from the wagon until Ridley could take hold of the other end.

"This way." They carried the section a short distance and put it down on its side. The top was level with Mark's nose. "Lay it on the ground. It's the front part of the stage."

A second section was placed beside the first forming a large square platform.

"That's our acting area," said Ridley. "The third section goes at the back and forms the tiring house. It's the place where we dress, change costume and wait for our entrances."

When the third section was in place Ridley said, "Ned, take Mark and Tom to collect the barrels. We'll unload the poles and curtains that enclose the tiring house."

"This way, lads," said Ned. "Down to the river."

"What are the barrels for?" asked Catherine as Ned and the boys walked away.

"To support those platforms so that our stage is about chest high. This enables the people standing at the back of the audience to get a clear view and helps to prevent people climbing on to the stage."

"Why should they do that?".

"Usually because they've drunk too much ale and think they could entertain better than us!"

Four long poles were taken from the wagon together with some lengths of thick material.

"It's old wall tapestry," remarked Catherine.

"Yes. It was left to me by an old man who loved the players' craft. Consequently I have the finest tiring house curtains in England!"

"Do you want the buck baskets out?" called Stephen from inside the wagon.

"Not yet. We'll get the stage erected first. You can find the planks that hold the three sections of platform together."

"Good day, Nicholas!" roared a voice. Catherine looked up and saw a huge man approaching. Stripped to the waist, he wore only woollen tights and soft leather shoes. He was powerfully built with thick forearms and tremendous shoulders,

"By the Lord of Ludgate!" roared Ridley in reply, "Robert Parker." The men hugged each other like two bears.

"You old vagabond," said Parker. "How are the players. Have you had a successful year? Any new blood?"

"A fair year, a fair year. You remember Stephen?" Parker nodded towards the young actor. "Bartholomew there joined us last December. Kay, his elder brother and their friend Tom are travelling with us a short time. He turned to Kay and Bartholomew. "This is Robert Parker, wrestler, part actor and a dear friend of mine."

Catherine feared the following handshake might crush her delicate fingers but the wrestler's grasp was surprisingly gentle.

"Have you news of my rival, Master Mere?" asked Ridley. "His troupe is usually here for the Fair."

"He's staying in the city. There's been some trouble. He had a disagreement with the city fathers and he's been refused a licence. There's also been trouble concerning one of his players but I don't know the facts. It's all hearsay. I haven't seen him or his men. I'm told he's leaving for the west in a few days to play at Bristol and Bath."

"Here come the barrels," announced Bartholomew.

Ned led the horse pulling the barrel-laden cart to a position near the sections of stage.

"We've been to the Hop Fair near the Mayor's house," Tom informed Catherine.

"They had the cart and the barrels all ready for us," reported Ned. "Charles Stockwith sends his greetings. Hello, Robert! How are you?" The two shook hands.

"Setting up the stage?" said Robert Parker to Ridley. "I'll stay and lend a hand."

The twelve large barrels were spaced out carefully: three to support the stage front; three at the back under the tiring house; three supporting each of the joins between the three sections. When these were in position the three sections were lifted and placed on the appropriate barrels. Strips of wood were then nailed to hold the sections firmly together.

"I'll try it out," said Ridley.

"Allow me," cried Robert Parker. "If it will take my sixteen stone it will take even you, Nicholas Ridley!"

Amidst loud laughter the wrestler leaped nimbly on to the stage. Four good strides took him across the front of the stage and six more to the rear of the tiring house. Then he walked to the centre of each section and jumped up and down.

"Firm as a rock!"

"Splendid! Time for food!" announced Ridley and suddenly they all realised how hungry they were..

"Come with me, Bartholomew," said Ned. "We'll buy some hot pies from the vendor in Garlic Row."

"You'll join us, Robert?" asked Ridley.

"Not this time, thanks. I'm meeting some friends at the white leather fair near the old chapel."

"Thanks for your help," called Ridley as his friend jumped from the stage and trotted towards the show booths nearby.

After the meal wooden steps were placed at the rear of the booth stage and the sections of tapestry were hung to enclose the tiring house.

"We'll leave them hanging until nightfall. It'll give them an airing and show everybody that Nicholas Ridley and his players are here. If they remain out during the night thieves may take a fancy to them."

The rest of the daylight was spent in mending costumes, sorting and repairing props and having a word rehearsal during which the actors spoke their lines but did not move or go through the actions. "It's good practice. It fixes the lines in the player's head and sharpens cues."

Shortly after dusk they turned in, exhausted but content with a good day's work behind them and with three days intensive rehearsal ahead before Stourbridge Fair was officially opened.

The next day Ridley announced, "We're going to rehearse three short plays this morning. We've been presenting them in towns and villages during our summer tour. They are merry pieces by a man called Heywood. See what you think of them."

With a background of voices and banging from the stalls in Garlic Row the small audience sat on the ground in front of the stage and prepared to be entertained.

They watched as Nicholas Ridley and Ned playing a Pardoner and a Friar, had a fierce argument and then a fight, pulling each other's hair, scratching and biting. This was uproarious and soon Mark, Catherine and Tom were shouting with laughter. Stephen as the curate and Bartholomew as a villager then attempted to separate the combatants but got soundly beaten for their pains. This too was quite hilarious but somehow the comic business did not come so naturally from the young players.

Then Stephen stepped forward and announced, "'The Four 'Ps'. A very merry Interlude concerning a Pardoner, a Palmer, a Pothecary and a Pedler."

The three members of the audience grinned at each other and leaned forward in anticipation.

The four characters debated and talked individually at great length but there was little movement and no comic business. Mark chuckled occasionally but Catherine and Tom found their attention wandering. Catherine became fascinated by a beetle clambering over the mountains and through the valleys of a furrow beside her. Tom split a straw in two down the middle and tied sea-knots with the pieces.

The third play concerned a man called John, his wife, Tyb, and the local priest. Ridley played the priest and Stephen the husband, John, but it was Ned's performance as the shrewish wife, Tyb, that amazed and delighted the small audience. His voice and movement were so wonderfully changed in his presentation of the chiding, brawling wife, that he became rather than acted the part.

In the afternoon Stephen and Bartholomew joined the audience to watch the experienced players rehearse a series of short farces and some knockabout sketches. The success of all these pieces depended upon the perfect timing of speech and movement. Nicholas Ridley and Ned went through certain parts again and again until they were satisfied.

Mark remembered Ridley's words, spoken to him when they had first met, "You may judge for yourselves how undeserving we are of the names of rogues and vagabonds." The artistry and devotion he witnessed that afternoon gave him a new respect for the players' craft.

Rehearsals continued the following morning with 'Pyramus and Thisbe'. Ridley presented the tragic story in a brief prologue and then appeared as Thisbe's father, a harsh man who would not let his daughter marry Pyramus whom she loved. A scene between the young lovers followed, during which they arrange to meet outside the town near Ninus' tomb. Then Ned told the audience how Thisbe arrived first only to be frightened away by a lion which had just torn a young deer to pieces. And how, in her flight, Thisbe lost her cloak that was then ripped to shreds by the bloody jaws of the lion.

They watched Stephen enter as Pyramus. Seeing the cloak torn and bloody and supposing Thisbe killed he cried out:

> "I wretch hath been the death of thee
> Which to this place of fear
> Did cause thee in the night to come.
> Receive thou my blood too!"

Then Stephen drew his short sword and stabbed himself.

The children watching thought that Stephen spoke the words well but his death was unconvincing. Ridley took him through this several times, "It's lacking truth."

Bartholomew entered as Thisbe.

> "Thy love hath made thee slay thyself:
> I swear this hand of mine
> Is strong enough to do the like.
> My love no less than thine
> Shall give me force to work my wound.
> I will pursue the dead!"

Mark, unmoved by this, turned to grimace at his sister only to discover she was watching Tom. Mark looked across at him sitting cross-legged on the ground, intent upon the stage and quite unaware anyone was watching him. He was speaking Thisbe's lines to himself; expressing her agony in his face and in slight movements of his shoulders and arms. Mark glanced at Ned and noticed that he too was watching Tom.

At the end of the scene Mark saw Tom shake his head discontentedly. 'Tom should be playing Thisbe,' thought Mark. 'He'd be much better than Bartholomew.'

Nicholas Ridley, who had been watching the rehearsal from behind the children, climbed up on to the stage. "You're not feeling it; either of you. The death is unconvincing and you speak Thisbe's lines as though you were reading from a list of items. Let's do it again."

They went several times through the earlier scenes where they declare their love and later where they arrange to meet at the tomb. After a break for food they returned to the death scene. Mid-afternoon Ridley said, "That's a little better. It will pass although I doubt whether it will move the audience to tears. I have to see a town Alderman about next year's licence so the rest of the day is your own." Then in kindly tones he said to the two young players, "But think about your parts: think and feel. Tomorrow morning we'll rehearse the Mummers' Play."

Ridley left for the city Guildhall; Ned went to find Robert Parker and some other friends at the show booths and Catherine, Mark and Tom walked through the nearly completed stalls of Garlic Row and along by the river.

When they turned in that night there was no sign of Stephen. Nor did he appear the next morning in time for the rehearsal.

Ridley looked grim. "He knows we were to rehearse St. George and he also knows it's to be played at Gorhambury within the week. They'll expect a first rate performance."

"Let Tom stand in for the Fool," said Ned quietly.

Ridley looked from Ned to Tom as the suggestion sank in. "By the Lord of Ludgate! That's an idea," he cried. "Give him the lines to read."

Tom blushed and began stammering, "I – I can't…"

"He has difficulty with reading," interposed Catherine kindly.

She had no intention of saying 'He can't read'. Tom had received no tuition since they were at Kingston upon Hull.

"If someone would read the part aloud to me I think I could

learn it quickly," said Tom.

"He has a marvellous memory," added Mark.

"See what you can do while Ned, Bartholomew and myself rehearse the other parts," said Ridley, giving a tattered and badly written script to Mark.

The children sat on the ground some distance away and Mark began to read the Fool's part aloud while Tom listened with concentration.

After a short while Catherine saw Stephen striding across the field. As he passed them Catherine said, "Are you all right?"

Stephen, looking confused, said, "Yes. I visited friends last night and we caroused until cockcrow and then I fell asleep."

'That wasn't very convincing,' thought Catherine.

"Now to face Master Ridley," said Stephen, grimly.

The children continued their rehearsal as Stephen approached the stage. They felt that this domestic trouble was no concern of theirs. Even so the words 'unprofessional', 'discipline' and 'punctuality' carried clearly to them as Ridley castigated Stephen.

When the admonishment was over the four actors continued rehearsing.

"Read the Fool's part again," asked Tom. "But this time let me see the words as you say them."

By midday Tom was almost word perfect and during the afternoon the children watched full rehearsals of 'Pyramus' and the Mummers' Play of St. George.

The rest of the daylight was spent in putting the finishing touches to costumes and props so that all would be quite ready for the first public performance the next afternoon.

Across the whole fair hundreds of stallholders, Mountebanks, wrestlers and others were preparing for the great opening the next morning and there was an air of excitement late into the night.

"Come along, young people, it's time for sleep!" Ridley yawned majestically. "Where on earth have Stephen and Bartholomew got to? Do you know where they went, Ned?"

"They set off towards Cambridge about two hours ago."

"They'll have to discipline themselves better than this. I'm all for carousing at the proper time but the night before an opening performance is the wrong time. When will these youngsters learn! I suppose nothing's happened to them?"

"Here they are, now," said Ned.

The two players appeared in the firelight. "Sorry we're a bit late," said Stephen..

"Come along, lads, come along! We've an important day tomorrow. There'll be plenty of opportunity for enjoyment when we reach London!"

Bartholomew glanced at Stephen who said imperturbably, "I'm sorry, Master Ridley."

Ridley grunted. "Smother the fire, Ned. Into the wagon all of you!"

"Smother the fire, Ned. Into the wagon all of you."

CHAPTER TWELVE

Stourbridge Fair

Mark put the trumpet to his lips and blew a loud squeal. "It's too soon after dinner," he protested.

Everyone laughed.

"Try again," urged Nicholas Ridley.

Mark blew another squeal.

"It sounds like a hunted pig," observed the actor. "Once more, if you please."

Mark blew again.

After wavering uncertainly the note steadied and trumpeted across the fair field.

The company applauded and Catherine said, "Your face has gone red."

"So would yours," gasped Mark.

"Can you remember what to shout?" Ridley asked the three children. They nodded.

"Project your voices and speak clearly so that everyone will understand when and where the plays are to be performed. Walk along Garlic Row to the river. Then go to the Hop Fair and the Mayor's Booth where we saw the opening ceremony this morning. Return up Garlic Row and finish at Cheapside and the Duddery. Call 'one hour' on the way to the river and 'half-an-hour' on the way back. Have you got both drumsticks, Master Kay? Splendid! Here's an hour-glass, Tom. Return when it's run."

Walking one behind the other Mark, Catherine and Tom struggled through the clamorous throng milling round the stalls and stood together in Garlic Row where they were jostled from all sides.

"We shall never be heard above this noise," said Catherine who, like Mark, was feeling acutely self-conscious.

"They'll hear the trumpet," said Tom.

"If I blow it properly!"

"You will! As soon as Mark's blown, give two bangs on the drum, and then I'll shout."

"Right you are, Tom. Here goes," muttered Mark. He moistened his lips, lifted the trumpet and blew.

The splendid sound brazened its way through the surrounding uproar and there was a momentary lull.

"Boom! Boom!"

"Come to the play! In one hour! At the show booths!" cried Tom in his high-pitched voice.

Many people were looking at them and some were pointing and laughing.

"Come to the play at the show booths in one hour!" repeated Tom.

The sounds of the sellers rose again and people turned back to the stalls and continued haggling over prices.

"Let's move on," said Mark.

They fought their way a hundred yards along Garlic Row and stopped.

"Are you ready?" asked Mark. The others nodded.

The trumpet squealed but few people paid any attention.

"Try again," said Tom.

Mark blew; the crowd hushed.

"Boom! Boom!"

"Come to the play! Merry Interludes and Farces! In an hour at the show booths!"

"Huzza!" cried someone and there was a scatter of applause. Feeling more confidence Mark blew again on the trumpet.

At the next stop the others joined Tom in shouting.

"Nicholas Ridley and his players!"

"Last performance before London!"

"Boom! Boom!"

"Come to the play!"

By the time they reached the river they had stopped ten times to cry the players, had lost and recovered a drum stick, been separated, cheered, pushed, applauded, kicked and sworn at. The close atmosphere reeked of all manner of smells: people; horses; fish; leather.

"There's the Horse Fair" said Catherine, "Where those boys galloped this morning shouting that Stourbridge was open. I hope they got their cakes and ale at the Guildhall!"

"Let's cross over to the Hop Fair and the Mayor's booth,"

suggested Mark. "How's the hour glass, Tom?"

"Half run."

"That's good timing."

They threaded their way into the Hop Fair, cried the Players for half-an-hour's time and pushed through the crowds towards the Mayor's Booth.

"Shall we cry from the platform where the vice-chancellor declared the Fair open?" suggested Catherine, surprised at her own audacity.

"Why not!" said Tom and Mark together.

They all felt part of the fair now. They belonged to Nicholas Ridley's Company of Players! They mounted the dais.

"When Kay has banged the drum, blow the trumpet again, Mark. Let's do that three or four times before we shout. It might get us a larger audience."

They blew and banged alternately and some people drifted towards the dais.

"News of the Players!" repeated Tom several times.

More people gathered.

"Plays begin in half-an-hour! Come to the show booths! Nicholas Ridley and the Players! In half an hour! Come to the plays!"

Mark blew a squeal and there was laughter and mock applause.

"Have another go!" shouted someone.

Mark blew another squeal.

"I hope the plays are better than that!" roared a good-humoured voice and there was more laughter.

The laughter drew more people towards the dais.

"We've got our audience," said Catherine.

Mark blew a perfect call on two notes and a cheer arose.

"In half-an-hour at the show booths! Nicholas Ridley and the players! Interludes and Farces! Last performances before London!"

"Good old Nicholas! We'll be there!" yelled a voice.

The children descended from the dais sounding the drum and the trumpet. This time the crowd parted to make way and the three marched triumphantly and rather breathless back to Garlic Row.

"People are already going towards the show booths," said Tom excitedly. "We've done it!"

After eight more stops in Garlic Row they reached Cheapside and the Duddery where, seeing the hour-glass had almost run, they made their last cry.

"We'd better get back," said Mark. "Let's walk through the show booths."

They passed skittle alleys, two small tents with queues of people waiting for their fortunes to be told, jugglers, a performing bear, acrobats and a man with two performing monkeys.

Then they heard a familiar voice rising above the tumult and saw Robert Parker standing on a raised platform. "Come up! Come up! A flagon of ale for the man lasting three minutes. Who'll take the challenge? A penny a try! You look strong sir. Step up!"

Several men in the crowd attempted to push one of their number on to the platform, but the man struggled and ran off between two tents.

"A flagon of ale for anyone lasting two minutes!" Parker winked at the children as they passed.

Approaching the props wagon they could see a crowd already gathering around the three sides of the stage.

Ridley stepped out of the wagon. He was dressed as a rude rustic with rough, brown breeches, an old jerkin and a straw hat.

"Well done! Well done! There's a good crowd already. We'll have twice the number when we start. Give me the drum and trumpet. Go and find yourselves places to stand in the front row. The crowd will let you through." He climbed into the tiring house.

Mark led the way along the side of the stage. "Pardon me, masters, may we pass?"

"Make way for the youngsters!"

"It's the trumpeter! Let them through to the front!"

They stood near a corner of the stage.

The crowd along each side thickened and spread further back until a huge audience awaited the entertainment. From many comments the children heard it was apparent that Ridley and his players were a popular annual attraction.

The audience grew restive.

"Come along, Nicholas, we're waiting!"

"He's forgotten his words!"

"Too much ale after dinner!"

"Too big to get into his costume!"

Each remark was greeted with laughter.

Then there was movement in the tiring house curtain. The centre slit parted and Ridley stepped through. There was a loud cheer and applause. Ridley beamed, bowed and held up his hands. The noise died away.

"My friends, may I say how delighted we are to be playing once more at this great fair? Known throughout these islands and Europe not only for the quality of its goods but also of its audiences."

Applause was accompanied by a shout, "You said that last year!" "So I did, and – By the Lord of Ludgate! – I meant it then and I mean it now." There were more cheers. "Otherwise why would I return each year? Enough of this – on with the entertainment. Shortly you will witness the lamentable tragedy of 'Pyramus and Thisbe' but first an old favourite – 'The Farce of the Rustics!"

Ridley stepped to one side and Ned, dressed in similar rustic fashion, came on to the stage and was greeted with applause. He bowed swiftly and the farce began.

The audience had obviously come to enjoy itself and the combined artistry of the two experienced players soon had people laughing and shouting encouragement.

Mark and Catherine were startled by the interruptions from the audience during the action. They had only seen plays presented in the hall of their Warwickshire home where everyone listened in silence.

Neither player appeared to mind the comments and several times even replied to them. This delighted the crowd still further.

Tom found the scene familiar. He had watched players when travelling with his father although he had never seen actors to compare with the skill of Nicholas Ridley and Ned.

By the time 'Pyramus and Thisbe' began the crowd was in a most receptive mood and ready to enjoy almost anything the players offered. However, during a scene between the young lovers the children noticed some coughing and fidgeting and when Pyramus stabbed himself someone made a remark that they could not hear and there was laughter.

The tragedy was followed by three short farces and an Interlude. Then during another farce Stephen and Bartholomew passed among the back of the crowd with the rustics' hats to make a collection.

Finally the four players danced a jig while the audience clapped in time and cheered themselves hoarse when it was over.

Ridley stepped forward. "Gentles all, I thank you for your kind attention. Tomorrow afternoon we have a complete change of plays. Come and enjoy more of your favourite farces together with Master Heywood's interludes of 'The Four 'P's' and 'John, Tyb and Sir John'. And now if you will show your appreciation in the usual way?"

Tom knew what was coming but Mark and Catherine were astonished when the crowd began to throw money on to the stage. Ridley bowed and waved his thanks while the three players collected the money from the floor.

Gradually the crowd dispersed and the company gathered in the tiring house.

Ridley looked at the rustic's hats that were overflowing with coins. "Splendid! Splendid! A good crowd this year – appreciative and discriminating. More work is required on 'Pyramus and Thisbe'. I heard laughter in the wrong places. We'll rehearse again tomorrow."

Next morning the children watched Ridley direct his young players.

"Look at Tom," whispered Mark to Catherine. "He's taking it all in; he's not missing a detail!"

Ridley stood between Stephen and Bartholomew, "Try to look at each other's eyes and not into the far distance. You are supposed to be in love. And keep still. When you fidget the audience fidgets and their concentration wanders."

When the rehearsal was over the children walked to Cheapside and through the Duddery where the merchants from Kendal were selling their cloth. Then to the White Leather Fair and the Wool Pair where Catherine was intrigued by the knit stockings offered for sale.

"This must be the boundary of the Fair. Let's look at that small chapel."

"It can't be a chapel, Mark, they're selling ale. Look at those men coming out with tankards. Oh – there's Ned."

The player detached himself from a group nearby and walked

over to them. "Hello! You're looking surprised."

"We thought that was a chapel but it seems to be an ale-house."

"It was a chapel. It used to serve a leprosy hospital nearby. King John allowed the priests to hold a fair in aid of the lepers and that's how Stourbridge began."

"When did it become an ale house?"

"It's only that during the Fair. The present Queen's father closed the hospital so the chapel wasn't needed. The nave is normally used as a store room and the chancel for stabling cattle! Come and have a look at the Norman arches with their patterns."

'The present Queen'. Richard was seldom from Mark's thoughts but those three words reminded him that his brother was only one element in the conspiracy against Queen Elizabeth and her ministers.

They walked round the chapel to the south wall where Catherine pointed to a stone carving below the roof. "It looks like a pig's head. It's both funny and hideous at the same time!"

"It's probably the stone mason's trademark," said Ned. "They used to carve effigies of people they knew. They'd make fun of them by taking a feature – say a large nose – and make it even larger. Some of the masks we use in the farces have been copied from effigies."

Mark heard none of this. He was lost in his own thoughts to a growing feeling of frustration. 'Two more days here. That'll be almost a week in one place, performing plays, when we might have been travelling towards London. We might have been there now! No! That's silly! If it hadn't been for the Players' timely arrival a few evenings ago we might not be this far. It's better to suffer the delay and be certain of a safe arrival!'

They were walking towards Garlic Row.

"How long before we reach London?" asked Mark, trying to sound casual, and fingering the chain around his neck.

"Let's see – we leave here in two days – that's the twenty-first. We play at Gorhambury on the evening of the twenty-third and leave the following morning. We should be in London on the twenty-fifth of September – in about six days."

Mark made a swift calculation. The journey from Alwinton to London would have taken from five to six weeks. "Sir Richard

Kempe has five or six weeks to live." Those were Webster's words on that fateful night in the pele tower.

"Only another six days," said Catherine. She was smiling and sounded confident.

'Does she believe that everything will be all right or is she trying to cheer me up?' wondered Mark. 'Well, I can do nothing to hasten the journey. Tom's right – I'll put all my energy into helping the players.'

That afternoon another huge audience assembled, and the plays began.

The children watched, first with apprehension and then with amusement, as two drunken men, who had filched a short ladder, tried to climb on to the stage during a knockabout farce. They expected Ridley to order the men away but he and Ned improvised dialogue and action to include the interlopers.

The audience was delighted with this unrehearsed incident and the hilarity increased when the owner of the ladder arrived.

"They nimmed my ladder," the man complained, "And I want to use it!"

A tug of war began with the owner on the ground pulling against one drunken man who was sitting on the stage. The other drunk, lying full length along the ladder and groaning, was being jerked about in mid-air.

Eventually they were removed by the Constable of the Watch and the players proceeded with the next play.

At the end of the entertainment the crowd showered the stage with coins. Ridley was delighted. "We'll rehearse the Mummers' Play in the morning and play it tomorrow afternoon after the first farce. It will help us to get the feel of an audience before we play it at Gorhambury."

Before the rehearsal next morning Ridley said, "You three can watch until the Doctor enters. Then come and wait in the tiring house until your cue __"

"A pocket full of money And a cellar full of beer!" they chorused.

"There are players for you!" said Ridley with pride. "During the final farce this afternoon you can help the boys to collect money from the back of the crowd."

They watched the players rehearse in costumes that were covered with long hanging ribbons. Even their hats had ribbons that hung down and concealed their faces.

When the rehearsal was over the actors renovated props and masks, Tom went to buy provisions in Cheese Row and Mark and Catherine fed and groomed Tamburlaine. The horse flicked his tail and stamped gently with pleasure while they brushed his coat.

Tom returned with the provisions, which he dumped in the wagon and then came straight across to his friends. He looked very serious. "You know that man who was in Clifford's Tower? I think I've just seen him!"

"Where?"

"In Cheapside with two other men."

"Did he see you?"

"No. I was behind a stall and he was busy talking."

"Are you certain it was Webster?"

"Almost. It was dark in the Tower but I don't forget a face."

"We must keep out of sight as much as possible. He's not likely to come round this part of the Fair. He doesn't care for plays or wrestling and such entertainment. But we can't be sure."

Catherine gasped. "The dance – we shall be on stage in front of everyone!"

"We can't let Nicholas Ridley down," said Mark firmly. "We'll have to take a chance."

Instead of watching the plays they remained concealed in the wagon until they heard Bartholomew's voice piping the doctor's lines. Then they walked quickly to the tiring house. Catherine handed the pipe to Mark and put the tabor cord around her neck. She felt sick. Mark's mouth was dry with apprehension and he was sure that he would never get a note out of his pipe. Tom was afraid for his friends: he knew how much depended on their reaching London safely. They stood together immediately behind the centre slit in the curtain.

"If Webster sees us and makes a move run as fast as you can into the crowds and around the stalls. He'll lose us there with any luck. Make for the chapel: we'll meet there," whispered Mark.

It all felt so unreal. They heard their cue and went on stage. A mass of faces looked up. Was Webster's among them? For a long moment everything seemed to stand quite still. No one moved; no one spoke.

Then Tom somersaulted forward to join the actors and his movement broke the tension. Catherine and Mark played and the dance began. The audience clapped in time. Webster was almost forgotten as they concentrated on entertaining the audience. They left the stage to a tremendous burst of applause, and stood in the tiring house feeling exhilarated. The applause continued.

"They enjoyed that!" said Ridley. "We'll do it again! Follow me."

As he led the way back on stage the feeling of sickness returned. Suppose Webster had seen them and was drawing near the stage? They went through the curtain and the dance began again.

"Splendid!" beamed Ridley, breathing hard with the extra exertion. "Well done everyone!" He was changing his costume as he spoke and by the time the applause had ceased he was back on stage with Ned ready to begin the next farce.

Stephen and Bartholomew were changing for the first Interlude as the children peered cautiously out of the back of the tiring house. There was nobody about. They hurried down the steps. "We'll stay out of sight in the wagon," said Mark.

They sat among the baskets and props half expecting Webster to appear at the back of the wagon. After a few minutes Mark stood up and looked out. "There's no sign of him."

"Let's stay here until we help Stephen and Bartholomew collect the money," counselled Catherine.

Mark nodded. "That would be best. You've saved us again, Tom. Thank goodness you have such a memory!"

Applause marked the end of the farce and the first of the afternoon's Interludes began. The children waited, listening to the actors' voices, and to the laughter, applause and occasional interpolation from the audience.

As the final farce began they left the wagon, went into the tiring house to collect a hat each and then pushed their way among the people standing at the back of the huge crowd.

When the farce was over coins hailed on to the stage as Ridley and Ned stood bowing and waving.

Finally Ridley stepped forward and held up his hands. "Gentles all, it is difficult for me to express in words how much we appreciate your hospitality. The visit to this Fair is the most enjoyable stay of our tour. The audience is generous and yet discriminating."

"That's quite right," yelled a voice, and there was laughter.

"A good critic," observed Ridley to more laughter. "We leave tomorrow for St Albans and then on to London where a young friend of mine has just built a new and permanent playhouse called 'The Globe'. Next year we shall return with new plays and old favourites. Until then – fortune be with you all and God save the Queen!"

Tumultuous applause followed and many people crowded along the sides of the stage to shake Ridley's hand. All the money had been picked up from the stage before he was able to withdraw and change out of his costume.

"We'll pack all the costumes and properties away in the wagon now, but we'll leave dismantling the stage until the morning."

When the packing was finished Ridley said, "Ned and I are taking the ferry to Chesterton to visit a grand old gentleman who was Mayor of Cambridge many years ago. He has been a good friend to me and to all players and I always pay him my respects. A grand old gentleman! Alas, now confined to his bed. Who will stay with Tamburlaine and the wagon?"

"It's my turn to groom Tamburlaine," said Stephen rather unexpectedly. "Bartholomew can help and we'll guard the wagon."

"Splendid!" Ridley turned to the children. "Perhaps you would like to come with us? Old Matthew would be pleased to see some young folk."

"Do go," said Stephen. "We can take care of everything."

Mark thought quickly. The visit would get them away from the Fair until after dark. If Webster should chance by – "Thank you. We'd like to come."

They walked over the common and passed close by the Mayor's house where the ground began sloping gently towards the river. They crossed Brush Row and reached the ferry, which was moored in a short inlet below Tallow Hill.

Most of the stalls they passed were shut but there were still groups of people discussing the day's events. Across the inlet the Oyster Fair was still busy and they could hear shouting, laughter and raucous singing.

"The Oyster and Hop Fairs continue late into the night," Ridley explained. "Much of the money made by the stall holders during the day changes hands once more and there are many fuddled heads in the morning!"

They crossed the river in the rowing boat and walked the mile to the village of Chesterton.

Old Matthew Hobson was delighted to see them and proved a most entertaining host with several amusing stories about Nicholas Ridley.

"Oh, you exaggerate, Matthew!" the actor repeated on several occasions but he was clearly loving every moment of it.

It was quite dark when they returned to the Fair and they were surprised to see neither lantern nor fire as they approached the props wagon. They could hear Tamburlaine cropping the grass. Sensing their approach he whinnied gently and trotted towards them, stretching his tether rope to its limit.

"Stephen? Bartholomew?" called Ridley. There was no answer. A short distance away torches flickered among the show booths.

"Prepare a fire," said Ned to Tom. "I'll get some light." He took a lantern from the back of the wagon and walked swiftly towards the show booths.

"I'm very surprised that they should leave Tamburlaine and the wagon unattended. And why no fire? What can have happened to them?"

Mark and Tom had just built a fire when Ned returned with Robert Parker. They each carried a lantern and looked serious. "It's bad news, Nicholas. Tell him Robert."

"Your two young players have gone," said the huge wrestler in his gentle voice.

"Gone?" Ridley looked incredulous.

"To Bristol with Master Mere and his players. They left about an hour ago. I was in the city and heard the full story from one of the Aldermen. You'll remember I told you that Mere had been refused a licence to play here; and that one of his players had left? Apparently Stephen saw him two nights ago and fixed everything then."

"It was the following morning when he was late for rehearsal," said Ned.

"Gone?" muttered Ridley. He sat on the tiring house steps looking dazed and hurt.

"Light the fire, Tom, and heat some broth," said Ned, quietly.

"But why?" said Ridley, looking from one to the other. "They seemed contented."

"You'll probably never know," said Robert Parker. "But I know this. They've left a first rate player for a fourth rate one. No doubt Master Mere's smooth tongue and promises had much to do with it, but they'll regret it."

"But we play at Gorhambury in two days," said Ridley, "And I've lost half my company!"

"Much of the money made by the stall holders during the day changes hands once more and there are many fuddled heads in the morning!"

CHAPTER THIRTEEN

The New Players

The fire flickered into life and highlighted the figure of Nicholas Ridley sitting dejectedly on the steps of the tiring house.

None of his friends moved.

Tom, who had set the broth to heat, crouched by the fire and looked beyond the flames to the actor's melancholy face. He desperately wanted to say, 'I could play the Fool and Thisbe, if it would help,' but he felt too modest to speak.

"Tom," said Ned and Mark together. Ned smiled and said, "Go on, Mark."

"Tom knows the Fool's part."

"And Thisbe's as well," added Catherine.

They watched Ridley. His grim set expression gradually relaxed as he lifted his head and looked beyond the fire to Tom. "By the Lord of Ludgate! That's it!"

Everyone felt the atmosphere lighten. Ned was beaming with delight and Robert Parker was smiling too.

"Tom plays the Fool's part but what about the Doctor?"

"I used to play the Doctor," said Ned. "Could Mark play St. George?"

"Oh yes!" cried Catherine.

Mark felt all eyes upon him.

"Could you, lad?" asked Ridley, standing up. "Would you?"

"Yes, but could I play it well enough?"

"How could you doubt it?" cried the player. "With Nicholas Ridley as your tutor?"

"But what about 'Pyramus and Thisbe?" asked Catherine. She wanted Tom to have the chance to prove himself for she was sure he would make a splendid boy player.

"We don't play that at Gorhambury," answered Ridley. "The entertainment is for Francis Bacon's nephews and nieces. They specially requested the mummers' play, which was the reason for my great anxiety a moment ago. We shall include some clowning and two knockabout farces – suitable for young ladies and gentlemen. But don't worry, Master Kay, your friend Tom will get his chance!"

Ned fetched some bread from the wagon and they sat round the fire to eat the broth.

Catherine looked at Tom and thought how full of vitality he was; such a contrast to the pale, silent boy of a few weeks before. He was looking at Nicholas Ridley with something approaching adoration. She thought how Mark too had changed. He was more sympathetic, more thoughtful. She glanced at her brother who was looking into the fire with a faraway expression. 'He's with Richard,' she thought. At that moment he looked up and smiled.

Mark was reflecting how strange life could be. His sister, who might one day marry a nobleman, was travelling the length of England disguised as a boy. And he had just agreed to perform with a company of travelling players! Such a thing would have been unthinkable a few weeks before. Yet he was the same person. He was still the boy from Alwinton and Warwickshire. But no! – he wasn't. He had changed. His attitude to Tom was different for one thing. Perhaps Tom had changed. Perhaps they all had.

Nicholas Ridley looked round at the company. How precarious was the life of a travelling player. Five minutes before his plans had all seemed wrecked and now all was well again. What a life! Yet he wouldn't change it for another. There was Ned – a splendid actor; loyal, compassionate; perhaps lacking self-confidence if he was to become a leading player. Yet he was only in his twenties and he had talent and that was what mattered most.

He looked at Mark and Kay. They were a mystery. Two young brothers travelling to London; a miniature by Hilliard; Mark's authority; Master Kay who sewed so well! But they were honest and hard working. Let time untangle the matter! His gaze rested on Tom for a moment. There was a born player if ever he saw one...

"That was good broth," said Robert Parker, wiping his wooden bowl clean with a piece of bread.

They all looked up.

"And good company to eat it," added Ridley.

Catherine stood. "Give me the bowls. I'll clean them."

"Is there anything else to be done?" enquired Mark.

"No lad, we'll dismantle the stage first thing in the morning and leave as soon as we can afterwards."

"When shall we rehearse our parts?" asked Tom.

"We'll break our journey some time to-morrow afternoon weather permitting!"

"Can we rehearse our words on the way?" Mark was anxious. "There isn't much time."

"By the Lord of Ludgate! Asking for extra rehearsals! What d'you think of that, Ned?"

Ned laughed. "We can have a word rehearsal in the wagon tomorrow morning. I think Master Bacon's nephews and nieces are going to enjoy their birthday entertainment!"

"You'll excuse me," said Robert Parker, "I'm sleepy. I'll come back at dawn and help with the stage."

Dismantling the stage was easier and quicker than erecting it. The wrestler lifted the heaviest things with consummate ease and skill. The barrels were returned to the Hop Fair and everything else was stowed on the wagon in an orderly fashion.

They took their leave of the gentle wrestler. Ridley hugged his friend and thanked him.

"I shall stay here another week," said Parker. "Then I shall visit the Fair at Ely and other fairs in East Anglia during October. I hope to be in London by the new Year."

"You'll find me in Southwark," said Ridley, climbing on to the wagon and taking the reins.. "Ask for me at the Globe – it's a new playhouse. Or at the Mermaid Tavern!" he added with a laugh.

The children waved from the back of the wagon until Parker was out of sight.

"I've heard about Cambridge," said Mark as the wagon trundled through the city streets, "but I had no idea that the college buildings were so magnificent. I should like to come here. What a marvellous place in which to study."

Ned joined them holding two battered scripts of the Mummers' play. "You have one, Kay, and prompt. Mark, you take the other and read St. George. It will help you to become familiar with the words."

"How should I play the part? In my own voice?"

Ned nodded, "Don't try to do anything unusual with your voice. Just remember you're a gallant Christian Knight who defeats the cruel, savage Turk."

"Who is to read the Turkish Knight?" asked Catherine.

"I thought you might like the chance," grinned Ned.

"Oh I would!" Catherine was delighted. She felt most important to be taking the word rehearsal.

To give the play a good start Tom spoke his opening lines with great attack. Mark thought of St. George as representing one of England's great warriors of the past like Henry V and delivered his speeches with authority. Catherine could not resist the opportunity to give an impersonation of Nicholas Ridley's performance as the Turkish Knight, Slasher.

"In come I ze Turkish Knight," she cried, rolling her 'r's. "Come frrom ze Turrkish Land-a to fight!" And she twirled an imaginary moustache.

"By the Lord of Ludgate!" roared a voice from the front of the wagon. "I shall-a lose-a my-a part-a!"

Catherine grew bolder and more dramatic. Tom thought she was quite excellent and lost his own concentration.

"This is the-a challenge that I do-a geev!" cried Catherine, adding in her own voice, "They fight."

There was silence.

"That's your cue, Tom," she said.

"Oh! Oh – yes – er I've forgotten." Tom blushed with embarrassment. Everyone else laughed but he looked very serious.

"Oh cruel Christian " suggested Catherine.

"Oh cruel Christian, what hast thou done?"

Thou hast wounded and slain my only son."

He required no further prompting. Ned's interpretation of the Doctor had them helpless with laughter.

When the run-through was finished Tom said, "How does the Doctor bring a dead man back to life?"

"That's difficult to explain, Tom. There's an element of mystery, even magic, about Slasher's revival. The play is probably based on an old Spring Festival from ancient times."

"What was a Spring Festival?"

"A religious ceremony which included dancing and singing. People thought of the land dying in winter and being reborn in the spring. In some way that primitive thought has become expressed in this Christian play and the re-awakening of the earth from the death of winter is enacted with human characters."

Mark asked for St. George's lines to be read to him. "That's how Tom learned the Fool's lines and it worked:"

Mid-afternoon they reached Westmill, a small village standing along the old Roman Ermine Street. They leaped down excitedly from the wagon as it stopped near some trees just beyond the village. The day was warm and peaceful. The sound of pigeons and rooks was in contrast to the noise and bustle of the trades-people at Stourbridge Fair.

"We'll have a rehearsal with moves and hand properties but without the costumes. They might need altering and we can do that afterwards."

Catherine sat enthralled as she watched them go slowly through the play under Ridley's direction.

"Try an extra tumble on your entrance, Tom. And when you clear a space in the hall at Gorhambury for the actors to perform don't be afraid to wave your stick with the pig's bladder at the guests' heads. Then dodge away with a leap and a twist. Try it again."

Tom nodded and grinned and took a firmer grip on the stick with the pig's bladder containing dried peas that was tied to the end. It was one thing to use the stick against imaginary people but he wondered if he could do it to the guests at Gorhambury. 'Well perhaps the young nephews and nieces won't mind,' he consoled himself.

"Won't it seem strange for me to win the fight?" queried Mark. "I'm not as big as you."

"Not at all, my boy. It will emphasise the great strength of the Christian knight. Take up your sword and we'll try the fight but do consider that it's a wooden sword and will break if you grow too violent. And pray take care of my own person," he added with a wink at Catherine. "I yet hope to play before the Queen's Majesty!"

The dance was changed to suit four performers. Catherine played the pipe while Ned danced and beat the tabor.

After three more complete rehearsals Ridley was satisfied for that day. "We'll light a fire now and attend to the costumes while it's still light. First thing in the morning, if the weather's fine, we'll have a dress rehearsal."

They took the be-ribboned costumes from a buck basket.

"Why they're ordinary clothes underneath all the ribbons,"

observed Catherine. "And the hats are like those you wear for the rustics. Try this on, Tom."

Tom put on the hat and the ribbons fell down in front and hid his face.

"Why is the character's face hidden behind the ribbons?" asked Catherine.

"The villagers who took part in the primitive rites believed that if they were recognised the magic power of their rite would be broken and the earth would not be reborn. In other words their crops would not grow. So it's become traditional for the mummers to keep their faces concealed," Ridley explained. "Here are the Fool's doublet and breeches. Try them on."

Tom put on the rest of his costume and Ridley stepped back a few paces.

"It'll need altering. You're much smaller than Ned. The ribbons from the breeches are trailing all over the ground. St. George will need altering too by the look of it."

"We've got a smaller doublet and breeches that might fit Tom but it would mean transferring all the ribbons," said Ned, who was wearing the doctor's long, loose, beribboned gown.

Catherine began "I could easily" and stopped. Boys did not sew easily. She noticed Mark frowning at her. "As I have no words to learn I could spend my time changing the ribbons. It shouldn't be very difficult."

"The doublet's in here somewhere," said Ned, throwing open a basket lid. They searched among a pile of costumes with a strange musty smell.

"It's going to be difficult leaping and tumbling in all these ribbons," remarked Tom.

"And fighting," added Mark, parting the ribbons in front of his face.

"These should fit Tom," said Ned. " Take off my old costume and try these."

Tom changed costume.

"That's splendid," observed Catherine. "I'll start on the ribbons now."

"I don't think Mark's will need too much alteration, Nicholas. I'll see what I can do," said Ned.

The next morning was crisp and clear. Mark, carrying a small wooden pail, walked through the early autumn dew to buy milk from a farm near the village. He wondered what he would have been doing were he at home in Warwickshire. 'Working at Latin or Greek perhaps, or fencing, or riding. It's a fine morning for a gallop through the great forest near home. The groom will be giving my horse, Malory, plenty of exercise. But I expect he misses me,' thought Mark.

The farmer's wife poured the fresh milk from a large wooden pail and Mark paid her.

"Are you travelling players?"

"Yes. We're on our way to Gorhambury."

"I saw the wagon pass yesterday afternoon. How many are you?"

"Five.

"I think I can manage an egg each!"

"Thank you!"

"Is there room in your pouch? It'll take three all right. Carry the others in your hand."

Mark thanked her again and walked carefully back towards the wagon.

Warm sunshine filtered through the trees encouraging doves and pigeons to 'coo' and 'burr' high above. Rooks cawed hoarsely from a distance.

After breakfast they donned their costumes and began the first dress rehearsal.

Tom and Mark thought it a disaster. They forgot their words and Tom was unable to twist and tumble as swiftly and surely as before. The ribbons showered over him as he somersaulted.

"It's like moving in a pile of hay! And they're not even all sewn on yet!"

Mark was equally put off and made a mess of the fight.

"I think-a I won-a that-a time," mocked Ridley. "Don't worry," he continued kindly seeing the two downcast faces in front of him. "It always happens the first time with costume. The next dress rehearsal will be better. You'll see."

"And you both look splendid," encouraged Catherine. Tom and Mark were unconvinced.

"It was awful," said Mark, who realised that acting was more difficult than it looked.

"I've forgotten everything," muttered Tom. As in all moments of crisis he thought of his father. How ashamed he would have been of his son's bungling performance.

"Enough of this self-pity!" cried Ridley "Prepare for another run-through!"

Sitting with the script Catherine felt as involved as the players. She thought that if she concentrated on the words the actors would not forget them. She fancied she had proved this when she had allowed her own concentration to be broken by some comic action from the Turkish Knight. She had giggled at Nicholas Ridley and Mark had forgotten his next words.

She concentrated all through the second dress rehearsal and there were no lapses of memory.

"What did I tell you," said Ridley when it was over.

"My tumbling is still clumsy."

"But it's better. Next time it will improve still further and it will continue to improve each time we rehearse. We'll have another rehearsal now and then we must be on our way. We rehearse again tonight and if there's time and if it's necessary, to-morrow morning as well. We should reach Gorhambury in the early afternoon and we can hold the final dress rehearsal there in the great hall."

Later that morning on their way through a village Mark pointed to a large Inn sign. "There's a Turkish Knight."

"That's an inn called 'The Saracen's Head'," Ridley told them. "In one room there's a bed ten feet wide and eleven feet long!"

The children exploded with laughter.

"It's quite true – I've seen it. It's known as 'the great bed of Ware'."

Catherine, who had just finished sewing the ribbons on Tom's doublet, wondered at the size of the sheets for so great a bed.

The wagon rumbled on through pleasant wooded country. The sun shone upon the trees and the players looked down on a constantly changing pattern of shadows.

"We'll stay the night in a field just below Hatfield Palace," Ridley informed them. "That's where the Queen lived as a young girl and where she heard that she had become Queen. A good day for England that was!"

Ridley directed two more rehearsals before dusk and they had a further run through the next morning. As the experienced player had promised, both boys' performances improved. Tom, a natural player, was now using his costume to help him when before it had been a hindrance. What Mark lacked in natural ability he made up for in dignity and authority.

"Then guard thy body and mind thy head,
Or else my sword shall strike thee dead."

The words rang out loud and clear across the field and startled a tribe of rooks into loud conversation high up in the tree-tops.

Ridley was pleased and confident.

"You three can rest while Ned and I rehearse our clowning and the Farce."

For the next two hours the men worked; improving the timing of their lines and actions. The children realised how easily laughter could be killed by mistiming; by reacting too quickly or not quickly enough.

They groomed Tamburlaine, had a meal and set off on the last eight miles to Gorhambury House.

At midday they saw the Cathedral of St. Albans on a hill ahead.

"Let's get down and lighten Tamburlaine's load," suggested Mark. Leaving Ridley to hold the reins, they dismounted from the wagon and joined the horse as he began to plod up the steep hill.

They passed the tower near the east end of the Cathedral and walked in the shadow of the massive building. "What a long nave," observed Mark. Eventually they reached the end turned through the old Abbey gateway, descended a hill and crossed a river.

About a mile further on Ridley reined in Tamburlaine and dismounted..

"You see those humps in the ground?" He pointed to a field by the track they were travelling. "This may be the site of an old Roman theatre where people used to watch plays and take part in religious ceremonies."

They followed him along a ditch and climbed on to a long straight mound.

"This was probably the stage and those low mounds making

a semicircle the audience. Imagine the people sitting on rows of benches rising many times the height of those mounds. They would hear perfectly every sound from this stage. An actor could whisper and be heard quite clearly!"

They watched as he stood looking out from the stage towards an imagined audience. Then he said very softly:

> "The man that hath no music in himself,
> Nor is not moved with concord of sweet sounds,
> Is fit for treasons, stratagems and spoils;
> The motions of his spirit are dull as night,
> And his affections dark as Erebus:
> Let no such man be trusted."

Nicholas Ridley looked at them. "My friend, William, wrote that. He spoke it to me himself just after setting it down."

He walked along the edge of the mound.

"Just think. Over a thousand years ago other actors walked across this stage. We are the heirs of a craft as old as man himself."

They returned to the wagon, climbed aboard and set off towards Gorhambury.

"We won't rehearse again until we reach the house."

Sitting at the front of the wagon they waited eagerly to catch the first glimpse of the Elizabethan Manor House.

"There it is," said Catherine and Mark together. The wagon had just emerged from a wood and away to the right was the long white front of the house. In the middle and on the right of the building were two battlemented towers and between them an ornamented archway.

"That's the original building between the towers," said Ridley, "The other part to the left was added between two visits of Her Majesty."

"You mean the Queen stayed here?" asked Tom, open-eyed with wonder.

'Yes. In Sir Nicholas's time. He was the father of Anthony, the present owner, and of Francis, who invited us here. We are to perform to their nephews and nieces. One of them – I think it's Nathaniel, has a birthday."

"Yes, Nathaniel," confirmed Ned. "It was he that specially asked for the mummers' plays."

They drew close to the new part of the house. The two storied building was supported above an open-sided gallery with a series of arches. They passed to the rear of the building and drew up by the servants quarters and the kitchens at the back of the original house.

The children were pleased to see the two actors greeted warmly as old friends by the household staff.

It seemed strange to Mark and Catherine, despite all they had been through, to enter by the servants' door. It was even stranger to be introduced informally to the servants. But they did not mind. They had both learned that people should be taken for what they are, not what they do.

The steward of the household arrived. He was a dignified and courteous man and he lead them from a kitchen, through servery doors and into the Great Hall.

Tom gasped with wonder and everyone smiled. Mark had seen larger halls but this was beautifully proportioned. Its tall, mullioned windows reached almost to the ceiling and made the interior extremely light. The children looked up at the ceiling shaped like a long arch with curved wooden beams and white plaster between them.

Tables and benches stood along the sides of the hall and at the far end was a table with chairs standing upon a low platform.

"The young ladies and gentlemen will be having a party here in the early evening," the steward informed them. "I imagine that you would like to begin your play as they finish eating?"

"Thank you," replied Ridley. "That will do well. It will be your task, Tom, to clear a space between the tables. You will have to move the young people to the sides thereby giving us room to perform. Don't worry," he added, seeing Tom's expression. "We'll rehearse shortly."

The servants were delighted to assist the players. Tamburlaine was taken to the stables to be fed and groomed while the necessary costume and property baskets were unloaded from the wagon and hauled into the kitchen that was to be used as the tiring house.

The players changed into their mumming costumes and Ridley directed the final dress rehearsal.

"When you make your first entrance, Tom, come in as though

you own Gorhambury. Don't be modest or shy. Do everything you've learned at rehearsals and it will be an excellent performance. I'm not worried but I know that you are. That's because you're a professional – because you care. If you decide to continue as a player you'll go through the agony of uncertainty before each performance. But you must learn to live with it. Once on stage you'll feel fine."

Tom nodded. He understood perfectly. How wonderful that someone else should know exactly how he felt. He was determined to do his best for this man. He remembered Ridley's words spoken at the Roman Theatre, 'We are the heirs of a craft as old as man himself'.

The rehearsal went well. But the new players found it very strange indoors. Their voices seemed much louder and their actions bigger.

"Don't worry. The children will enjoy it."

After Nicholas Ridley and Ned had rehearsed some of their trickier pieces of clowning they all changed out of their costumes and went into the garden to relax.

It was apparent to Mark and Catherine that neither the late Sir Nicholas Bacon nor his son Anthony were much interested in gardens. Bushes, shrubs and trees needed pruning and the grass was long and tangled. However there was a small Knot Garden with its clusters of shrubs and herbs neatly tended just outside the north windows of the hall. Beyond this they found a maze built of box and densely growing shrubs.

"We'd better not go in there," said Ridley. "We might not find our way out in time for the performance!"

They returned to the kitchen, put on their costumes and waited. They could hear laughter from beyond the serving doors leading to the hall. Tom watched the variety of sweetmeats taken through on trays with considerable wonder. There were jellies and meringoes; tiny rabbits, geese and ducks made of almond paste and marchpane mixed with isinglass and sugar; ginger, pine-comfits and sugar loaf. Each fresh tray was greeted with acclamation. Even Catherine and Mark could not remember such a variety at one time. They were offered a choice of sweetmeats but with the tension mounting before the performance felt they could eat nothing.

Neither could they remain still. Ridley and Ned were sitting on stools looking unconcerned, but Catherine, Mark and Tom sat down, stood up, walked round the large kitchen table, crossed to the window, sat down, stood up and went through the whole process again and again.

'I cannot imagine why I'm worried; I'm not performing,' thought Catherine. 'Well, I am playing the pipe at the end. Oh dear!' She really felt nervous for the boys.

The steward entered. "They're almost finished. Are you ready?"

The moment had come. They all stood up looking at Ridley.

"Ready Tom?" he said.

Mark and Tom sat down, stood up and went through the whole process again and again.

CHAPTER FOURTEEN

The Entertainment

Tom nodded and took a tight grip of his bladder stick.

"Good lad! Don't forget – you own this house! On you go – and good luck!"

Tom felt dizzy with excitement and slightly sick. He took a deep breath. Catherine opened the servery door. Tom leaped through and somersaulted into the group of children who were playing in the middle of the hall, which was now lit by two large candelabra hanging from the ceiling.

Catherine, dressed in her usual boy's clothes, followed with script, tabor and pipe and sat on a bench at the side of the hall.

"It's the Fool!" cried a fair-haired girl.

Eight children cheered lustily.

"It's the Fool: Oh!" squeaked a small boy as Tom tapped him on the head with the bladder.

> "Room, room, brave Gallants all,
> Pray give us room to rhyme;
> We come to show activity
> This merry birthday time."

"Hurrah."

"Ouch!"

"Oo!"

"Make room for the players!" commanded the tallest boy.

Tom leaped, somersaulted, turned, twisted and bounced the bladder on the head of a fat boy and a girl with dark hair and beautiful eyes.

"Move back! Give them room!" repeated the tall boy.

"Nathaniel says 'Move back'," insisted the fair-haired girl.

> "Activity of youth,
> Activity of age,
> The like of this was never seen
> Upon a common stage."

Seven of the children were now sitting on the floor in a semi-circle. Tom skipped up to the eighth, a freckle-faced boy who was still standing, and tapped him on the head with the bladder.

"Ha!" cried the boy.

"Sit down, Diccon!" commanded a plump, rosy-faced girl, tugging at the boy's doublet and breeches. Diccon thumped to the floor.

As Tom twirled he glimpsed several older people standing the semi-darkness at the back of the hall. 'Everyone in the house is here,' he thought.

On the other of the servery door Mark awaited his cue. He was standing astride a Hobby Horse. His left hand, which held the stick horse below the head, was clammy with nervous sweat. For the third time he felt for his wooden sword with his right hand. It was still there! He swallowed nervously and coughed for the sixth time.

> "Step in St. George, thou champion
> And show they face like fire."

A push on the back from Ned sent him through the door and into the hall.

"Hurrah for St. George!" The three girls and Diccon wriggled with delight.

Mark rode his hobby horse around the children, the joy on their upturned faces giving him confidence.

> "In come I, St. George,
> That man of courage bold.;
> With my faithful horse and sword
> I wore a crown of gold."

Mark swung his leg over the hobby horse and 'stabled' it against the wood bench near Catherine.

> "I fought the fiery dragon,
> And drove him to the slaughter,
> And by those means I won
> The King of Egypt's daughter.
> Show me the man that bids me stand;
> I'll cut him down with my courageous hand."

Tom, crouching by the fat boy, jumped up. "Step in, bold Slasher."

A large figure strode into the hall. The top half of his face was concealed by ribbons and the lower half by a huge moustache, which he twirled.

"Scabby Slasher!" shouted Nathaniel. The other four boys yelled with laughter and the plump girl grinned.

"Nathaniel!" protested the fair-haired girl.

"Pooh! Scabby Slasher!"

> "In come I, ze Turkish Knight
> Come a-from ze Turkish land to fight.'"

said the vast figure in stentorian tones, silencing Nathaniel.

> "I a-come to fight St. George,
> Ze man of courage bold;
> And if his a-blood be hot, Ha! Ha!
> I soon will make it cold."

St. George turned boldly upon Slasher.

> "Stand off, stand off, bold Slasher,
> And let no more be said,
> For if I draw my sword,
> I'm sure to break thy head.
> Thou speakest very bold
> To such a man as I;
> I'll cut thee into eyelet holes,
> And make thy buttons fly!"

The fat boy chuckled and patted his doublet, tight over his stomach.

Slasher twirled his moustache and appeared to swell.

> "No a-satisfaction shalt thou have
> But I will bring ze to zy grave."

St. George drew his sword and a boy missing some front teeth clutched the plump girl.

> "Battle to battle with thee I call
> To see who on this ground shall fall."

Slasher drew his sword and waved it in the air.

> "Battle to battle vith ze I pray
> To see who on zis round shall lay."

St. George circled Slasher and the girls hugged themselves in anticipation of a fight.

> "Then guard thy body and wind thy head.
> Or else my sword shall strike thee dead."

Slasher twirled his moustache once more:

> "One a-shall die and ze other shall a-live;
> Zis is ze challenge zat I do give.'"

St. George and Slasher circled, watching each other closely. Their swords clashed and they circled again. Then with a shout St. George thrust his sword between Slasher's chest and his left arm. Slasher cried out. St. George heaved out his sword and stood back.

Slasher clutched his side; staggered back two steps; tottered forward two steps; swayed; sank slowly to his knees; swayed to the left and then to the right; collapsed on to his left side and rolled on to his back.

Nathaniel led a burst of cheering and applause.

The Fool left the semicircle and walked towards St. George.

> "O cruel Christian, what hast thou done?
> Thou hast wounded and slain my only son."

St. George sheathed his sword,.

> "He challenged me to fight
> And why should I deny't."

The Fool appealed to the upturned faces.

> "O is there a doctor to be found
> To cure this deep and deadly wound?"

Tom knelt by Diccon, the freckled boy, who grinned and tried to inspect the pig's bladder.

"Here's the doctor," announced the fat boy, as a spectacled figure in a long ribboned gown shambled in and immediately tripped on to his face.

"Ha!" shouted Diccon while the rest giggled.

The doctor scrambled to his feet and peered about for the Fool.

> "Yes, there is a doctor to be found
> To cure this deep and deadly wound."

He tripped over Slasher's legs.

> "I am a doctor pure and good
> And with my hands can staunch his blood."

The Fool helped him to his feet.

> "What canst thou do and what canst cure?"

From the pocket of his gown the doctor pulled a length of bandage.

"It's got sticky stuff on it," whispered Nathaniel to the dark girl with beautiful eyes,

> "All sorts of diseases,

Just what my physic pleases;"

The bandage stuck to his fingers.

"The itch, the stitch, the palsy and the gout

It stuck to his chin.

"Pains within and pains without."

The bandage became inexplicably wound around his neck.

"If the Devil is in I can fetch him out."

With the bandage wound round his neck and stuck to his chin and hands the doctor fell flat once again.

Tom, praying inwardly that the next piece of business would work, rushed to the doctor's assistance. Mark and Catherine watched. The Turkish Knight lying on the floor opened an eye and watched too.

"He'd better mind that sticky bandage," said the fair-haired girl.

"It's stuck to his elbow already," observed Nathaniel.

"And his right hand!" shouted Diccon.

"They're getting all mixed up!"

"They'll never get free!"

"Where's the Fool's head?"

"They'll be stuck together for ever!"

"Ugh! How awful!"

Then everyone gasped as the Fool and Doctor suddenly separated.

The fat boy gaped and Diccon led the loud applause.

Catherine applauded too and even Mark forgot he was St. George and clapped twice.

The doctor produced a small medicine bottle from his pocket and held it to Slasher's mouth.

"I have a little bottle by my side;

The fame of it spreads far and wide,

The stuff therein is elecampane;

It will bring the dead to life again."

Diccon stared in wonder as Slasher twitched into life and slowly sat up. St. George and the Fool lifted him on to his feet and the four players joined hands and faced Nathaniel.

"We wish you a Happy Birthday and a joyful year;

A pocket full of money and a cellar full of beer!"

The players bowed and Nathaniel, beaming at the compliment, stood and led the applause.

Catherine handed Ned the tabor and put the pipe to her lips. The players bowed again. Then Ned glanced at Catherine, nodded, and together they struck up the dance.

"Come on!" cried Nathaniel, pulling the dark-haired girl to her feet. "Let's join in!"

"Yes, come on!" squeaked the small boy.

Three girls and four boys jigged madly while the fat boy sat and clapped his hands in time.

As the jig finished, the exuberant Tom led the players through the serving door and into the candlelit kitchen.

"One more bow!" cried Ridley and led them back into the hall where the children were applauding and jumping up and down with excitement.

Back in the kitchen the two older players removed their mumming costumes and returned quickly to the hall to continue the entertainment.

The boys removed their ribboned hats and felt their faces hot in the cooler air.

Mark and Catherine flopped on a bench and leaned on the huge kitchen table in the middle of the room. They felt exhausted after their concentrated effort.

Tom was standing quite still. He felt exhilarated. This was the most important moment of his life. He wanted nothing but to become a professional player.

The door from the inner courtyard was opened and the flames of the four candles in their pewter sticks flickered wildly and recovered.

A servant entered, closed the door and the flames steadied.

"You remembered your parts well! The steward thought you might like some food now."

He opened the doors of a ventilated store cupboard and set a large platter of sweetmeats on the table.

"There you are. I'm going back to watch Master Ridley."

As the kitchen door was opened and shut the candle flames danced again.

They gazed at the sweetmeats.

"Don't they look delicious," said Catherine. "I don't know which to choose first!"

"What are those little animals made of?" asked Tom.

"Marchpane," replied Catherine. "It's almond and sugar. Try one, Tom. I'm going to."

Tom ate a 'rabbit'. "Umm. Isn't it sweet!"

"Too sweet for me," said Mark. "I think the Pine-comfits are nicer. Whew! I'm hot in all these ribbons. Help me off with my costume, Kay."

The boys removed their costumes, put on their everyday clothes and sat down again.

The actors' voices and the children's laughter sounded from beyond the serving door.

Tom wished that he could get into the hall and watch the actors. He was anxious to learn all he could about his chosen craft.

Catherine looked round the huge kitchen. It was bigger than theirs at home in Warwickshire. Her thoughts wandered as she considered the size of Gorhambury. 'What was it like to belong to a really famous family and live in such a huge house? How many servants were there? And what happened when the Queen paid a visit on one of her progresses?'

Mark, head in hands and elbows resting on the table, looked at the scrubbed table-top with its channels of grain running along its length. Near his right elbow was the letter 'R' carved by someone in an idle moment. Mark thought of his brother. They would reach London the next day or the day after. What should he do? Go to the Tower? No, that wouldn't be any use. He must see a Minister of State. The Palace of Whitehall was not far from London Bridge. Perhaps Ridley would have some idea.

The candles flickered wildly as the door from the inner courtyard crashed open.

"You may have been covered in ribbons, Master Mark, but there was no mistaking your voice!"

It was Cain Webster.

Mark recovered first. "Outside – into the garden!"

Webster moved into the room and three men crowded the doorway behind him.

Tom leaped for the garden door and wrenched it open.

Catherine and Mark dashed through into the darkness outside and Tom followed. They heard a stool crash over as the men stormed across the kitchen.

"Get a lantern!" yelled Webster.

Mark and Catherine stumbled through the Knot garden with small shrubs and dwarf box impeding their haste. Tom ran to the left, clear of the knot garden.

Mark and Catherine blundered out of the ordered garden and ran towards some bushes just visible in the light from the hall windows.

"Villains! Where's that lantern?" shouted Webster.

Catherine tripped and fell. Mark helped her up and they plunged into the darkness.

"Spread out and find them!" yelled Webster.

Mark grabbed his sister's hand and they pushed between two large bushes and stumbled on for several yards only to find their way blocked by a thick hedge.

"We're in the maze! Back this way!" whispered Mark.

They retreated, moved to their right and hurried on. To their left someone was crackling twigs and swishing bushes as he moved.

The maze led them to the right and then another hedge barred their way.

"Back. We've missed an opening. Feel for a gap on the left."

They retreated a few paces.

"Here it is. Come on!"

Keeping contact with the hedge they walked in a curve to the left and then they were forced to turn sharply to the right.

"I've lost all sense of direction," confessed Mark in a whisper. "Which way is the house? Let's wait and listen."

They heard a shout and an oath. "I've got one of 'em!"

"They've caught Tom!" faltered Catherine.

They heard struggling and the same voice yelled, "Come and help! I can't manage this little swine!"

"Don't let him go but keep your voice down!" Webster sounded frighteningly close.

"Let's try and get back to the hall and find Nicholas," whispered Mark. He was afraid they would harm Tom.

"I've got his legs," rasped a new voice somewhere on their

right.

Mark gripped Catherine's hand tighter as they stumbled forward.

Then a man holding a lantern reared up suddenly in front of them. "I've got 'em! Here!"

"Don't let them go!" snarled Webster nearby.

"Run for it, Kay!"

Mark released his sister and hurled himself at the lantern in an attempt to knock out the candle. At the last moment the man lifted the lantern high into the air. Mark cannoned into him and was gripped round the waist.

"Run, Kay!"

He struggled, freed himself and started forward only to run into another man and held tight.

"Bring the light here!" commanded a cold and familiar voice.

The lantern was held close to Mark's face.

"Well – it's Master Mark. All the way from Alwinton."

Someone close by shrieked.

"Let me go! How dare you! Let me go!"

"Keep still you little brat! Ouch! Hold still!"

"That's all three taken care of by the sound of it," said Webster.

They were marched roughly into the stables where Tom was sitting on the floor, his arms bound to his body and his ankles tied.

Webster faced Catherine. "Well, Mistress Catherine, your cropped hair and boy's clothes didn't fool me for very long. When you came into the hall I thought there was something familiar about you and when I heard your brother's voice I was in no doubt." He turned to the men. "We must leave immediately in order to be in London the day after to-morrow. It's fortunate I called here otherwise our plans might have been spoiled by this clever whipster!" He hit Mark across the cheek with the back of his hand.

"Beast!" shouted Catherine.

"Keep quiet, my lady," mocked Webster.

"Don't you touch her," shouted Tom, struggling with his bonds.

"I don't know you, boy. It's a pity you've got mixed up with these two. I shall deal with you all in the same way."

"How shall we get rid of 'em?" snarled Tom's captor.

"With Sir Nicholas Bacon in the house we daren't dispose of them here. We can't take them to London on horseback; it's too risky; they're as slippery as eels. Tie them up. We'll take all three in the players' wagon. You can drive, Fletcher. Leave your mare in the stable. The rest of us will ride on horseback. Gag the brats."

"What about the players?"

"We'll be away before they know what's happened. Quick! Harness that horse to the wagon and we'll leave now!"

Mark and Catherine were bound like Tom and all three were heaved into the props wagon.

They heard Tamburlaine harnessed and then Fletcher climbing on to the wagon.

"Giddup!"

The wagon crunched forward.

"Where d'you think you're going?" It was Ridley.

"Out of the way!"

"Get off my wagon!"

They heard a whiplash and a cry. Then Ned's voice shouting, "You devil.'"

"Deal with them!" commanded Webster.

"Get off my wagon!"

Sounds of scuffling were followed by a loud groan. Then the wagon jolted as someone clambered up in front. They heard more oaths, a muffled cry and the wagon shook again.

"Find some more rope. Tie them up and sling them in with the brats."

There was considerable movement outside and finally two of the men clambered into the back of the wagon and the bound bodies of the two players were heaved aboard.

"Now – are we finally ready?" Webster rasped. "No stopping until we reach London."

CHAPTER FIFTEEN

London Bridge

The wagon and its escort left Gorhambury without further delay.

The ropes binding Mark's arms to his body formed a painful ridge between his back and the wagon floor and the tight gag dragged the corners of his mouth. He strained his neck to look out of the back of the wagon but everywhere was blackness. He wondered how Catherine was feeling. He knew she was lying between his head and the front of the wagon. If only he could talk to her; and talk to Tom. He thought of the players. Had they been badly hurt in the struggle?

The continuous rumble of the wagon was accompanied by Tamburlaine's rhythmic clip-clop.

Someone on Mark's right shifted and knocked his foot. Feeling relief in the physical contact he pushed sideways with his feet and felt a push in response. There was further movement and a body rolled against him. Hair tickled his right ear. He guessed it was Tom.

The wagon jerked violently and settled again, scrunching and rumbling.

Mark wondered where they would be taken when they reached London. No doubt Webster would kill them at the first opportunity. But there was always hope.

Catherine lay on her side across the wagon on a large bundle of material. She fretted and fumed. If only she could bite through her beastly gag and talk to someone. If Tamburlaine would stop! If he would refuse to pull the wagon any further! Catherine willed him to stand still but the clip-clop continued. Perhaps Webster's horse would bolt suddenly and throw its rider whose neck would be broken!

Tom wished he had succeeded in drawing the men away from his friends in the maze. But the deliberate noise he had made among the shrubs had not fooled Webster. He shifted his position and felt his head against Mark's shoulder.

The wagon rumbled on through the darkness.

Mark awoke and felt the rope under his back. He was cramped and cold. What a hotchpot it had turned out! He drew up his knees and arched his back. He could not stay long in that position but it would ease his back for a while. It was still quite dark. He wondered how long he had dozed and how far they had travelled. He felt Tom lying beside him. Was Richard lying awake, wondering and hoping? Perhaps it was already too late to save him. In desperation Mark shifted violently and strained at his bonds causing them to cut into his flesh. No! He must not think that Richard was dead; he must not give up hope. Hope was his spur for action; his spur for saving Richard and his Queen.

Mark's sudden movement awoke Tom who stared into the darkness and listened to the familiar rumble and clip-clop. He thought of the players. Had they been injured in the struggle? Would Nicholas Ridley have a plan for their escape? He had many friends in London; would he be able to get in touch with them?

Tom wondered what London was like and if he would ever see the Globe Playhouse and meet the actor, Will, whom Nicholas Ridley so often mentioned. He felt Mark moving and guessed that his friend was awake. He tried to recall the song his father had often sung to keep their spirits up. "Greensleeves" – that was its name. 'Well I can't sing it,' he thought, 'but I can hum it.'

Tom began softly. It sounded very thin against the rumble of the wagon. He had just decided it was pointless continuing when to his great joy first Catherine and then Mark joined in. The shared experience cheered them. They repeated the tune with more confidence and hummed a third time quite loudly. Then Catherine hummed a tune that Tom did not know. Mark, who seemed unsure of the piece, joined in occasionally. But there was no sound from either Ridley or Ned.

The wheel rumble suddenly echoed loudly and harshly and Mark guessed they were passing through a village.

The next time he woke Mark could just make out the outline of the back of the wagon.

He dozed again and awoke in a chill grey light. Through the back of the wagon he could see trees the colour of pewter. He moved his knees up and down several times in an attempt to get warm.

The wagon rolled on and Mark watched the light change slowly from grey to white and saw the trees lose their leaden appearance as the russet dawn touched the golden-brown leaves. The wagon slowed down as a long steady ascent began. 'Poor old Tamburlaine,' thought Mark.

After a long climb the ground levelled out and then Mark had the curious sensation of his feet being higher than his head as they began a very steep descent.

The wagon slewed sideways and stopped.

"If someone doesn't put the traps on the front wheels and take the horse's head the whole lot will run away."

It was a relief to hear a voice even if it was one of Webster's men.

Distant shouts followed together with the stamping of hooves.

From the wagon floor Mark could see two chestnut trees burning gold in the morning sun. A fair breeze was disnesting a few leaves and they twisted and swirled towards the ground.

Then he heard someone tampering with the front wheels. After a short while Tamburlaine neighed and the wagon straightened up and rolled downhill crunching and occasionally sliding.

Eventually it levelled out again and stopped. "You can leave the horse now," called the wagon driver. "And I'll remove the wheel traps."

Arching his neck Mark looked back towards Catherine and near her saw a large bundle of material. If he pushed it with his feet he could prop his back, take the his weight off the ropes and see the road out of the rear of the wagon. He moved backward in a series of jerks and propped himself against the bundle just as the wagon moved off again.

He looked at his sister who nodded vigorously. 'Kay seems all right,' he thought with relief. Looking out of the wagon he saw they were passing through a village. A church appeared on the right, then fields and then a hill topped with a windmill. Single cottages and houses appeared to left and right.

The wagon lumbered on and Mark saw the bright midday light lose its radiance as vaporous autumn clouds chased each other across the sky.

The number of houses gradually increased. The road became busy with people most of whom were walking in the same direction as the wagon. Mark guessed they were approaching the city boundary.

A few minutes later the wagon passed under an arch and Mark's saw a battlemented wall stretching away on each side. They had reached London at last!

The wagon swung to the left and one of the horsemen appeared at the back. Roofs and windows were crowded together on each side of the streets and there was an unhealthy smell. They clattered on through several streets. Then Mark felt the wagon take a sharp right turn and they entered what he thought to be an arch but which turned instead into a tunnel. The noise of the wagon's rumble and the horse's hooves echoes loudly from the walls and roof and it grew dark and dank. They emerged from the tunnel and Mark saw that they had passed through some tall buildings. Seconds later that they entered another tunnel and the noise increased again, echoing and re-echoing.

They came into the light again and a loud rumble signified that the hard surface of the road had changed to wood. Then the wheels crunched again and almost immediately a voice cried "Whoa!"

The wagon stopped in the shadow of another arch and Mark heard the men dismounting. They appeared at the back of the wagon and one climbed on board.

"Get them upstairs quickly, there's no-one near," commanded Webster. "Carry the brats but free the men's legs; they can walk up!"

Tom was lifted roughly and carried to the back of the wagon. He looked down at Nicholas Ridley. The player's eyes were closed and on his forehead there was a gash with dried blood.

Ned, who was looking up at him, nodded and winked.

Then Tom was seized by a man outside the wagon, carried through the small doorway of a building nearby and up a steep narrow staircase. He counted four flights before a small but stout door was pushed open and he was dumped on to a rough wooden floor. He lay and listened to the man's footsteps dying away down the stairs.

Tom looked around. The room was smaller than their stage at Cambridge and smelled dusty. There was one window.

Footsteps grew loud and another man appeared with Mark over

his shoulder. He pitched his load on to the floor and left the room. Seconds later, Fletcher arrived with Catherine.

"Webster'll be up in a minute so don't go away." He laughed and went down the stairs.

After a long pause there were sounds of several footsteps and Ned stumbled into the room with his arms still bound. A man following threw him to the floor and stood beside the doorway.

They heard thumping on the stairs. Someone swore loudly and the thumping grew closer. A man backed into the room supporting Ridley's body under the armpits. Another man was holding the player's ankles. Both men were gasping with the exertion. They half carried, half dragged the heavy body into the room and dropped the player on the floor. Ridley seemed quite lifeless.

Webster appeared and stood in the middle of the room. "You'll remain here until tomorrow. I have important business that cannot wait. I'll deal with you all when it's successfully completed." He turned to the men. "Get downstairs. I'll lock this door." He turned outside the doorway. "Fletcher will be guarding the front entrance so you'll be quite safe!"

They heard a key in the lock and listened as Webster's footsteps died away; a dull boom as the entrance door was closed. Then silence.

Mark looked at the grubby plaster ceiling and wondered what they could possibly do to escape. He heard movement and saw Tom rolling towards him.

Tom reached Mark, rolled away and then rolled back again. At first Mark was thoroughly perplexed but then he realised that Tom was trying to reach his gag.

After several attempts Tom achieved his aim and Mark twisted his head so that the knot was close to Tom's tied wrists. He felt Tom working at the knot with his fingers for about a minute or so but with no success.

Tom was still for a while resting his fingers and then he began working again. Mark felt his hair being pulled but the knot remained tight. There was another pause.

Then Tom began again, working with forefingers and thumbs. Suddenly Mark felt the gag loosen and then give. Tom jerked away pulling the gag with him.

"Oh – well done," muttered Mark, working his jaw to remove the stiffness.

Tom rolled towards Catherine who, seeing what had happened, was already trying to move herself round.

Mark struggled with his bonds but they remained tight. He looked across at Ned who was also striving to free himself.

After a little while Tom rolled over and Mark heard Catherine say "Thank you, Tom. Oh, that's better."

"Are you all right, Kay?"

"Yes, except that I'm stiff. Are you?"

"More or less. If only I could get free."

Tom rolled towards the still form of Nicholas Ridley. He was afraid the player was seriously hurt.

The quite suddenly Ridley sat up, jerked his arms up and down very slightly and eased them out of his bonds. Then he untied his gag.

"Thank you, Master Tom, I can manage by myself! Allow me to help you!"

Soon they were all free and massaging their limbs.

"We thought you were hurt," said Tom.

"I was in repose; a useful practice."

"But how did you free yourself?" asked Mark.

"To tell would give away a secret."

"Were you stupefied?" enquired Catherine, looking at the gash on Ridley's forehead.

"Not quite, although one of those braggarts struck me with some force. I should have been overpowered eventually so it seemed useless to struggle. Discretion is the better part of valour as you will learn, my young friends. So far as freeing myself is concerned, shall we say I learned a trick or two from Robert Parker who can perform the most extraordinary feats with his body. I shall say no more. I wish though that I had not allowed those fellows to drag me up the stairs. I feel extremely bruised." He surveyed them all with a smile. "It was a good performance of the play at Gorhambury, wasn't it, Ned?"

"Most certainly, Nicholas. Most professional!"

"And now, Master Mark, I think Ned and myself are entitled to further explanation. You told me once that you were on your way to London with an important message. From the first I have been aware that you and your – um – sister are neither waifs nor vagabonds but come of a good family."

"How did you discover that I was a girl?" asked Catherine with some indignation.

"If you had directed as many boy players as I have you would understand! Do you agree, Ned?"

Ned grinned broadly. "Yes, Nicholas."

Mark knew that the time had come to explain everything.

"Kay and I were staying at Alwinton near the Cheviot Hills......."

At the end of the story Ridley looked very serious.

"Then her Majesty's life is in danger, as well as your brother's? We must find a way out of here. It's useless to attack that heavy door; we should be heard by the guard below. And it's useless waiting for someone to come. Your man, Webster, is not returning until to-morrow. Did he not say, 'I have important work which will not wait'?"

"Yes."

"Then if we can't go down, we must go up. I have an idea where we are and you can confirm it. Look out of that small window, Mark.

Mark rose from the floor and crossed to the window. Rubbing the dirt from the pane with his sleeve he peered through. "We're over a river – the river Thames. I can see it flowing beneath us!"

"It's as I thought. We're imprisoned at the top of a house on London Bridge. What else can you see?"

"Away to the left beside the river is a large tower and I can see walls with battlements." Mark's voice altered suddenly. "O – is that where Richard is?"

"Yes, lad," said Ridley, gently. "We'll try to climb out of here and on to the roof and then we'll look for another window to enter. When we find one we'll break into the house and get down to the street. If there is trouble you can rely on Nicholas Ridley to talk us out of any awkward situation."

"Who is going out first?" said Catherine, quietly. She was looking out of the window and down at the enormous drop to the river beneath.

"I will!" Tom and Mark spoke together.

"Look, Tom, Richard is my brother. It's my charge."

"But Mark, I'm the only one...."

"Just one moment," interposed Ridley, "Let us discuss the venture sensibly. Let us consider 'how' rather than 'who' for a moment. We'll join together the pieces of rope used to bind us. That will make a safety line. We'll tie one end round the waist of the first person out of the window. The other end will be held securely by those in the room. The one on the roof will tie his end around a chimney – there must be one nearby – and the others can use the rope to climb out and join him. As far as 'who' is concerned it should be myself or Ned. We are taller and the added height may prove an advantage."

Ned nodded agreement. "I'll go: I can give you a few years, Nicholas!

"By the Lord of Ludgate!"

"It's my charge," said Mark firmly. "I must 'Keep Faith!' He fingered the chain and pendant around his neck.

Catherine felt proud of her brother and fearful for him.

Tom, whose inclination had been to volunteer because he had no family, tried to imagine himself in Mark's place. How would he have acted? He hoped that he would do as much for a brother. It was Mark's charge.

Nicholas Ridley and Ned looked at one another and nodded. They too understood.

'We'll have to break the glass," said Ridley. "No one below will hear it and the pieces will fall into the river."

He smashed the window pane with his elbow and carefully removed the jagged pieces round the sides. A swirl of wind filled the room and disturbed the dust of months.

Ned helped to secure the rope round Mark's waist while Ridley craned his neck out of the window which was just big enough to allow his shoulders through and looked in all directions. He drew his head in again. "Have a look outside, Mark. It's going to be difficult but not impossible."

Concealing his nervousness Mark crossed to the window. The wind took his breath away. He saw first a long, sheer drop to the river, with the water rushing away from him on an ebb tide. Above he saw the roof ridge from which the two sides sloped steeply away forming an inverted 'V'. Immediately to the left was the end of the building. Looking right Mark saw another window some distance away with a similar inverted 'V' roof above. Between the two windows was a gully where the rain water from the sloping roofs collected and drained away. If he stood on the window sill outside he might just be able to reach the gully.

The wind made his eyes water. Blinking away the tears he looked once more at the Tower fortress. Was his brother still imprisoned there? Was he still alive? To whom should he tell his story when he did escape? He drew in his head and turned to the others in the room.

"What do you think, lad?" asked Ridley.

Mark explained his plan and Ridley nodded. "It's the only way I could see. Are you ready to try?"

Mark nodded and felt a pounding inside his chest.

"We'll need to know when you've secured the rope. Make the signal four long pulls." Mark nodded again. "Take hold of the rope everyone. Ned and myself nearest the window; Kay and Tom at the end. Out you go, lad!"

Mark swallowed, took a deep breath and clambered on to the sill. The rope felt secure about his waist. He climbed outside and hung on for a moment swaying in the wind. Slowly he stood up facing the outside wall with his fingers still inside the room holding the lintel of the window. The wind swirled again and threatened to blow him sideways towards the corner of the building. He shifted both feet along to the left and then did the same with his hands. He wanted to get as close as possible to the gully between the sloping roofs.

Gripping tightly with his right hand he released the other from the lintel, and moved his arm sideways and upwards trying to feel the tiled edge of the roof. His hand struck something and he looked slowly upwards. The eaves overhung the wall about six inches and he had to reach his arm slightly backward to clear them. Slowly he leaned his body outwards away from the building. The wind swirled again and he braced his body to counter its sudden force. His fingers touched the edge of the roof above the eaves and he slid them downward to the left.

'Will I reach the part where the other roof slopes to meet this one?' he thought.

His body jolted as his right foot slipped slightly. He closed his eyes and remained motionless. The wind swirled again and his right hand felt cold.

'I must keep moving. At least I've got a rope tied round my waist.'

His left hand found the gully between the roofs.

'Now the difficult part. I must transfer my right hand to the roof edge.'

He released his hand, felt for the eaves above his head and slid his right hand towards his left. He was now leaning to the left with his body projecting even further outwards, and away from the building.

'So far so good. But I can't stay like this. I've got to hoist myself upward by the arms and to do that I've got to take my feet off the windowsill. Left foot first.' The wind shook him again. 'Now the right.'

His whole body swayed to the left as he swung from his hands and for a moment he thought that he would fall. But he clung to the edge of the roof and steadied himself.

He put all his strength into his arms and pulled his body upwards until his chin was level with the gully. There was safety! He pulled until his shoulders were above the level of the gully, then he pushed on his hands and arms to raise himself further. He brought up his left knee until he felt it against the roof edge. A push on his wrists and on his knee and he lay in the gully with his legs sticking out over the edge of the roof.

He hauled himself along on his stomach and lay still for a moment. 'I've done it!'

He rolled over on to his back. Above his head on the right he saw a short chimney stack. He stood up, untied the rope and clambered up the steep roof. Embracing the chimney he passed the rope from one hand to the other. He tied it securely, tested it, slid down to the gully and pulled deliberately four times. Then he sat down and waited.

Back in the room no one had spoken since Mark had crouched on the sill. Then came the signal.

"He's done it!" said four voices together.

"Tom next, I think," said Ridley. "Then you, Kay. Ned or myself will go last."

Mark crouched between the roofs and watched the white clouds racing away beyond the Tower fortress. Suddenly gusts of cold wind whipped around him.

Then he saw the rope tighten. First one hand came over the edge and gripped the rope, then another and then Tom's face appeared. Mark leaned forward and helped him on to the roof.

"Kay's next."

They lay waiting near the edge of the roof. Both were thinking the same: would Kay be strong enough to pull herself from the window to the roof? The wind swirled and the rope moved slightly and tightened again.

A hand appeared and the boys leaned forward as far as they dared and took Catherine under her shoulders. After two good heaves she was lying beside them in the gully.

"The players insisted on tying the other end of the rope round my waist – just in case. We've got to dangle it back for them."

She untied the rope and it was dropped over the edge and swung to the left. At the third attempt they felt it tighten and soon afterwards Nicholas Ridley appeared followed almost immediately by Ned.

"Haul up the rope," said Ridley when Ned was safely with them. "It may come in useful and will prevent anyone following."

They coiled the rope, which Ned then slung over his shoulder and under his arm. Meanwhile Mark had climbed slowly beyond the chimney and on to the roof ridge. "There are many more roofs like these," he called back. "Shall we cross them all?"

"We might as well get as far as we can before descending," bellowed Ridley against the wind.

They followed one another slowly up and down each of the roofs. First Mark, then Ridley followed by Catherine, Tom and Ned. The fierce wind gusted into them and several times they crouched low to save themselves being blown over. Writhing snakes of smoke blew from the chimney stacks.

At the top of each steep roof Ridley waited until Catherine was safely beside him, then together they slid down and waited for Tom and Ned to follow.

Half an hour later, with chilled fingers but with bodies warm from their exertion, they moved away from the river side and looked down on to the street that ran across the middle of London Bridge and divided the houses. Ahead of them was a new building that stretched across the width of the bridge and had a central archway for carts to pass through.

The ridge of the final roof ran with the bridge instead of across it. In a strong wind and with the afternoon sun showing only fitfully through the clouds, they moved slowly along on all fours with a foot on each side of the ridge itself.

Mark reached the end first and looked down several feet to the top of a semi-circular tower with battlemented parapets. He heard Catherine give an expression of disgust. "Oh! How horrible!"

Ahead of them and beyond the new building stood a great stone archway at the southern end of London Bridge. Sprouting from its battlements were many long spikes sticking into the air. Impaled on the end of each spike was a rotting human head. Large rusty-brown birds were tearing at three of the heads.

"The fate of traitors, spies and heretics," said Ridley.

Tom had seen similar sights though never so many heads in one place.

Mark thought of his brother and then averted his gaze to the semicircular roof of the building immediately below. "It's too far to jump. We'll have to use the rope."

Ned secured one end around the nearest chimney-stack and then Mark dropped the other end towards the flat roof below.

"It doesn't reach all the way down," he announced. "It's difficult to tell just how far it does go. We'll have to take a chance."

"I think it would be common-sense if I went first this time," said Ned. "I'm the tallest and have least distance to fall. I can also help the rest of you down."

Ned grasped the rope, eased himself over the edge and slid out of sight.

Holding on to each other Mark and Tom peered over. They could see the top of Ned's head descending by the rope. For a moment it was still and then it dropped suddenly and Ned landed on the semi-circular flat roof and fell over backwards.

He picked himself up and waved to them.

"He's all right," said Mark. "I'll go next."

He slid down and the rough rope fibre chafed his hands.

Ned half caught him as he dropped from the end of the rope.
Catherine followed, then Tom and finally Nicholas Ridley.

Let into the flat roof was a trapdoor.

They followed one another slowly up and down each of the roofs.

ChAPTER SiXTEEN

Mark versus Webster

"I've just realised where we are," said Ridley. "We're standing above the practice rooms owned by Vincenzo Saviolo. I visited him several times with my friend William. Saviolo is his fencing master."

They watched Ridley bend down, grasp the iron ring in the trap door and heave. They peered into the rectangular opening and saw a ladder leading down to a room with some large baskets and wooden chests. They followed Ridley down and looked up at Ned who was closing the trap carefully in order to avoid a loud bang.

Ridley, who was already descending a flight of wooden stairs to the next floor, called up, "Here's a sight for a sore body!"

The scrambled down the creaking stairs and saw four truckle beds standing close together.

"After last night's cramps and cricks I'm tempted to rest here for an hour or two!" Ridley opened a door and sounds of clashing steel came from the floor below. "Saviolo has three or four large fencing rooms. Let's see if we can find him." A feeling of tension rose with each step taken down the dark staircase.

They crowded into a doorway, with Catherine and Tom on tiptoe trying to see past Nicholas Ridley, and then jostled through to stand in one corner of a large room.

In the centre two men faced each other. Each was armed with a rapier in one hand and a dagger in the other. The outer wall of the room was all windows and the bright light, reflected from the flashing blades, danced about the room.

Rapiers and daggers clashed together and slid smartly away as the fencers parted and circled one another. Then they closed together and the weapons locked above their heads.

"Nothing neither way!" laughed one and they parted and lowered their weapons.

"Well, again."

The men crouched for another bout.

Ridley stepped forward and froze as one fencer saw him and straightened up.

"Nicholas!"

"Harry! By the Lord of Ludgate! Henry Condell! Harry, you rogue! How are you?"

The children watched with amusement as Nicholas embraced the fencer who was still holding his weapons.

"Nicholas, how good to see you! And Ned! How are you Ned?" Henry Condell released himself from Ridley's embrace, tucked the rapier under his left arm and took Ned's outstretched hand. "Where have you all come from?"

"From the heavens like Greek Gods." said Ridley. "What fortune finding you here. Do you remember the fights we had in Will's plays about King Harry the Sixth? How the groundlings cheered!" He looked at the three children. "You should have seen us! Come – you shall testify. You fence of course, Mark?"

"I do – though I'm sadly out of practice."

Ridley crossed to a long wooden chest and took out two light weapons with small bell guards and tapering blades. "Here's your foil!" The weapon flashed towards Mark who caught it by the hilt. "Prepare to defend yourself!" cried Ridley, walking swiftly to the other end of the room and swishing the foil through the air.

Henry Condell winked at Catherine and Tom. "Nicholas goes wild when he has a sword in his hand but he does no harm."

"On guard!" cried Ridley from the far end of the room. With his foil held upright and the hilt touching his chin he saluted Mark who responded in like manner. Then Ridley lowered his foil to the attack, held his left arm in a curve behind him and advanced on Mark in a most curious fashion. 'Rather like a crab skipping,' thought Mark and he wondered how to counter Ridley's extraordinary attack. However when his opponent reached him and their foils engaged Mark realised that behind the nonsense and show was an expert fencer. The player lunged to the left and to the right of Mark who retreated slightly beating away his opponent's blade. Ridley stormed in again shouting "Huzza!" Mark held his ground as the foils clashed to his right, to his left and again to his right. Then Ridley feigned another attack to Mark's right. Mark was caught off balance and before he could recover he felt the player's foil touch him near his left shoulder.

"A palpable hit!" cried Ridley, adding in the same breath, "Well done! I think we're both out of practice but you have a skill, Mark. I can tell even from that short engagement. But I waste precious time with my foolery – we have serious work in hand."

Ridley turned to Henry Condell. "I also forget my manners. Mark, Catherine, Tom – this is Master Henry Condell, a colleague of my friend Will's in the Lord Chamberlain's Players at the Globe Playhouse. Harry, it is vital that my young friends have the ear of a Queen's Minister. They have a serious matter to divulge. Something that affects the very life of her Majesty, the safety of the realm and this young man's brother."

Condell looked surprised and his fencing partner rose from one of the three-legged stools and walked over to join them.

"Then you are in luck," said Condell. "Sir Robert Carey should be with Master Burbage at the Globe Playhouse this very moment. And this young man," he continued, indicating his fencing partner, "is on the staff of Sir Robert Cecil the Queen's Private Secretary. May I present John Fairfax."

"Then take us to your new playhouse, Harry. I'm longing to stand on its stage and speak a speech."

"You'll like the Globe, Nicholas," said Condell, as they prepared to leave. "It's built from the timbers of the old theatre at Shoreditch. And Will is writing plays all the time. Splendid plays with marvellous acting parts for all the company."

Condell led them out of the room and down two flights of stairs.

"I think this young man is hoping to become a player," said Ridley, putting an arm round Tom's shoulders. "We must see if Master Burbage requires any new boy-players."

They stepped into the open air on London Bridge and the children looked up at the huge stone gateway that stood between them and the south bank of the river. Catherine shuddered once again at the sight of the mouldering heads on the steel spikes and at the birds pecking and ripping the rotting flesh.

On their left they saw a woman in the pillory with her head and arms through three holes in a wooden frame. Next to her a man was wedged in a wooden cage with his arms extended through the bars hoping for food.

They were passing under the stone archway when Mark

suddenly put a hand to his neck. "The locket! It's gone!" He turned to Ridley. "The chain must have broken during our fencing match. I thought I felt something when you claimed the hit. It's probably lying on the floor of the practice room. I must get it. Wait for me at the end of the bridge."

Mark dashed back and hurried up the two flights of stairs. Entering the deserted room he began searching anxiously for the precious family heirloom.

Unable to find it he became both worried and perplexed. Had it fallen into the chest when he replaced his foil? He looked inside but could not see it. He began to search among the thin steel blades thinking it might have fallen and slipped down between them.

"Are you looking for this?"

Mark swung round in the direction of a familiar voice.

In the doorway stood Cain Webster, a sword in one hand and the locket in the other. He advanced two steps into the room and pushed the door behind him with his right foot. It slammed with a crash that echoed through the room.

Mark watched Webster put the heirloom in his jerkin pocket and walk towards him.

"Now, Master Kempe, I'll put an end to your meddling."

Mark felt no fear, only determination. He snatched a foil from the chest, moved swiftly to the centre of the room and took guard.

Webster attacked and Mark realised at once that the man's extra weight and experience would tell heavily upon him. He decided to parry the attack as long as he could and then try other means.

The swords clashed together and Webster attacked Mark's head, stomach, chest and then his head again. Slowly, Mark felt himself being forced back to a corner of the room. If he lacked experience and weight he had sufficient agility to surprise his opponent. He continued backing away until he was almost trapped in a corner and then suddenly he flung down his foil and dived under Webster's sword arm.

Mark's timing was perfect. The man was completely surprised and caught off balance. Webster had lunged for what he thought would be Mark's death and ran his sword into the wooden wall panelling. He swore in fury, wrenched the sword out of the wall and turned to face Mark.

In those precious moments Mark had scrambled across the room and seized one of the three-legged stools.

Webster advanced with his sword raised and his eyes on the stool. He was waiting for the moment it was thrown so that he could dodge out of the way and move in to kill.

He drew closer. Mark watched and waited. Webster was three sword lengths away – now was the moment.

Mark moved as if to throw the stool and Webster, deceived by the feint, swerved to his right. Before he could regain his balance Mark hurled the stool with all his strength.

It caught Webster on the side of his head and he fell heavily to the floor with sword and stool clattering beside him. Mark leaped forward, seized the sword and stood back.

"I think he won't move for a few minutes."

Mark turned quickly, his sword ready to parry any attack. Was this one of Webster's men? The stranger, who was unarmed, approached Mark.

"That was a well aimed throw. I was next door at the mercer's choosing some material and came here expecting to find two friends practising – not a man attacking a youth armed with a stool."

Mark relaxed a little. "Two men were here. They left a few minutes ago."

"Do you know if one of them was Henry Condell?"

"Yes!" Mark looked at Webster, who lay as he had fallen, and lowered his sword. "This man took something that belongs to my family. I must have it." He knelt down, felt inside Webster's jerkin, drew out the locket, opened it and held it in his left hand.

"She is very beautiful," said the stranger who was looking over Mark's shoulder.

"That's my mother," said Mark, proudly.

"It is also a beautiful miniature. Is it by Nicholas Hilliard?"

"It is. How do you know?"

The stranger smiled. "It's not very difficult. I've seen other paintings by him and there are few, if any, as clever as he."

Mark looked up from the miniature to the face of the man above him. He thought him in his late thirties. He wore a beard and a moustache and had a high domed forehead. His dark hair tumbled over his white shirt collar. In his left ear he wore a small gold earring. But it was his eyes that fascinated Mark. It was not their colour but their quality. Mark felt as though they were looking right inside him. As though this man could see his innermost thoughts. Yet they weren't inquisitive eyes, but kind and generous. Mark felt he would trust this man completely.

He slipped the heirloom in his pocket and stood up. "I must find my friends: they'll wonder where I am."

He felt no sense of achievement. He had reached London and his enemy lay unconscious at his feet. But was he in time to save his brother?

There was a commotion on the stairs. Mark gripped his sword firmly. "That man has friends," he said, looking at the body of Cain Webster.

The stranger moved swiftly across the room and took a rapier from the chest. "We'll manage them," he said. Then he returned to Mark's side, smiled, swished his rapier through the air and stood in a relaxed manner. Mark waited for the worst to happen with a new surge of confidence. With this man one could achieve anything!

The sounds outside increased and suddenly there was a rush of people into the room.

"By the Lord of Ludgate!"

"Nicholas!"

"Will, it's good to see you!"

The two men clasped hands while Ned and Henry Condell stood by Webster's body.

Catherine and Tom ran to Mark. "Are you all right? What happened?"

"I'm all right," Mark replied. "I'll explain later." He turned to Ridley. "We must do something about my brother."

"Something is being done. Young John Fairfax has gone to the Globe to tell Sir Richard Carey we are on our way to see him. Having delivered that message Fairfax is going to ride as fast as he can to Whitehall Palace to find Sir Robert Cecil." Ridley turned to his friend. "It's life and death, Will. His brother's life is in danger and so is the Queen's."

Mark felt some sense of relief. Important people were being alerted. But only he knew all the facts. He must see Sir Robert Cecil himself and explain everything.

Ridley sensed his anxiety. "Will, take the young people to the Globe. The rest of us will remain as gaolers. We cannot leave this villain unguarded and his accomplices may come in search of him. I suggest we arm ourselves with foils."

"Certainly, Nicholas. But you have not introduced me to your young friends."

Ridley stepped forward majestically.

"This is Mark Kempe; his sister, Catherine; and a fledgling player called Tom. My young friends, allow me to introduce you to Will Shakespeare."

It caught Webster on the side of his head and he fell heavily to the floor with sword and stool clattering beside him.

chapter seventeen

Journey's End

"Did Nicholas say your name was Kempe?" asked Shakespeare as they descended the stairs. Mark nodded.

"Where's your home?"

"In Warwickshire."

"'Was your father Sir Henry Kempe?"

"Yes!" said Mark and Catherine

"Did he serve with the Earl of Leicester in the Low Countries?"

"Yes, he did!"

"What an extraordinary coincidence! I met him once."

"Where?"

"In the Low Countries. When I was a young man I served the Earl as soldier and travelling player. Your father attended a council of war and I was overjoyed to learn that he lived only ten miles or so from my home at Stratford. It was like meeting a neighbour."

"Did you know him well?" asked Catherine as they stepped from the building and on to the bridge.

Shakespeare laughed. "No, he was a Captain and I was an ordinary soldier. I only spoke to him for three of four minutes."

"And yet you've remembered him."

"Your father was a courteous gentleman. And I seldom forget a name or a face." Shakespeare looked hard at Catherine with her untidy mop of short hair and her boy's clothes. "Nicholas did call you Catherine, didn't he?"

Mark and Tom chuckled and Catherine nodded.

"I'm used to boys playing the parts of young ladies," Shakespeare continued, "But this is the first time in real life that I've met a young lady dressed as a boy!"

"We've travelled from the north of England and thought it safer for Kay," explained Mark.

"I felt like a girl inside though," confessed Catherine.

"No one would have guessed," said Tom. "I thought you were marvellous."

"And in my heart lie there what hidden woman's fear there will, we'll have a swashing and a martial outside!" said Shakespeare.

"That's exactly how it was. That's how I felt. How well you said it!"

"It's from a play I'm writing," said their new friend, almost apologetically.

They reached the end of the bridge but instead of following the main road, which lay straight ahead, Shakespeare led them to the right. "Keep close to me. If one of you gets separated in the crowd call out immediately. Mark and I have our foils but keep close." They entered a narrow way where the houses on each side seemed to lean towards each other, making it a tunnel rather than a street. People looked out of first floor windows and chatted to their neighbours opposite. In the street a host of people jostled, shouted and swore. There was a stench of rotten garbage.

At the corner of an alley a crowd of people dispersed suddenly to disclose a man with blood oozing from his chest slumped against a wall. A man holding a knife scuttled away up the alley.

Catherine stopped and stared with horror at the figure on the ground.

Will Shakespeare put an arm round her shoulders and drew her away. "That happens once or twice every day. It's the usual way of settling a score in Southwarke! But don't imagine all the people here are bad. There are many good-hearted honest folk. If it weren't for them we should have poor audiences for our plays."

They reached the end of the street and emerged from the noisome crowds to open ground. The air became sweeter.

"There's the Globe Playhouse," said Shakespeare, pointing to a building with a thatched roof about half a mile away.

Tom leaped into the air with excitement.

"You want to join the players, Tom?

"Yes, Master Shakespeare, more than anything!"

"He's a rare teller of tales," volunteered Mark.

"And he was a splendid Fool for Nicholas Ridley," added Catherine.

Shakespeare smiled. "We'll see what we can do about it."

They crossed a stretch of rough grass and entered the playhouse through a small door.

"Where are you, Dick?"

"In here, Will."

They followed Shakespeare into a room lit by a standing candelabra. Seated at a table strewn with papers and set with a flagon of wine and several tankards was a bearded man. He rose to greet them.

"Have you seen Fairfax?" asked Shakespeare.

"I have. Carey had already left here so John saddled his horse and rode off to Stanegate stairs. He'll row himself over to Whitehall Palace if there's no ferryman and find Sir Robert Cecil. I've never seen him in such a hurry. He rushed in, muttered something about 'treason' and galloped away before you could fill a flagon! It all sounds like one of your plays, Will!"

"Can I get to Whitehall Palace tonight?" asked Mark. Shakespeare and Dick Burbage looked at each other and then at Mark. "It's extremely urgent. It could mean my brother's life!"

"You can ride?"

"Of course!"

"Then I'll go with you," said Shakespeare. "Dick, will you look after Catherine and young Tom here?"

"Catherine?" said Burbage, looking at the 'boy' standing before him.

"Yes," said Shakespeare. "He is Mark's sister!"

"Couldn't I go with you, Mark?"

"No, Kay. You wait here and get some rest. I promise to come back as soon as I've seen Sir Robert."

"I'll fetch two cloaks," said Shakespeare. "The evening air will be damp and chilly."

"Come and sit down you two," said Burbage. "Are you hungry?" Catherine and Tom nodded. "I'll get some food in a moment."

"Come along, Mark!" called Shakespeare from the corridor.

They hurried outside the playhouse, saddled two horses and set off in the fading light westwards across St. George's Fields by the Lambeth marshes to Stanegate Stairs.

Mark's thoughts raced as they galloped along. Would there be a boat to take them across the river? Would Sir Robert Cecil be at the Palace? Would he see them immediately? Would he believe such a story from a bedraggled young man? Was his brother – ?

"It's not far to the river."

An evening mist swirled low over the ground and they eased their horses to a trot.

"Where did you first meet Nicholas Ridley?"

"On the way to Stourbridge Fair. He's been a good friend to us."

"He has a great heart; we all love him," said Shakespeare, warmly.

Mark saw the river swirling in front of them. They dismounted, tethered their horses to a post and walked down the bank to the short wooden pier. A rowing boat was tied up alongside.

"Thank goodness the tide is full; it'll make it easier to row."

Mark wrapped his cloak tightly about him as Shakespeare rowed into midstream. The last streaks of day had almost gone when they passed beneath a wooden bridge and entered a narrow inlet of water. Shakespeare rowed to a landing stage and Mark grabbed a rope that was dangling down into the river, stepped up on to the wooden platform and tied up the boat. Shakespeare shipped the oars, climbed out of the boat and led the way along a gravel path.

"Who's there?" demanded a gruff voice.

"Friends! Will Shakespeare and Mark Kempe to see Sir Robert Cecil on urgent business."

"Follow me. I'm to take you to Master Fairfax."

They followed the armed sentry along the path, through an archway and across a broad quadrangle to a heavy wooden door, which the sentry struck twice with his pike. A few moments later the door swung open to reveal John Fairfax.

"Ah, Will! I left word with the sentry that you might follow tonight. Good even, Mark. I've seen Sir Robert and the news is good. He'll see you straight away."

Fairfax led them along numerous corridors and up a grand staircase until they came to a wooden door exquisitely carved with oak leaves and acorns. Fairfax paused before the door, glanced back at Mark, winked, and then knocked twice very deliberately.

"Enter!"

Fairfax went into the room and closed the door behind him.

Shakespeare smiled at Mark. "Sir Robert is a strange looking man but honest. He'll listen to you."

The door re-opened and Fairfax motioned them to enter.

By the light of a candelabra standing on a desk Mark saw they were in a large study with heavy wooden furniture. Near an open fireplace with several logs smouldering in the grate stood a bearded man with a slightly hunched back.

"Good evening, Master Shakespeare."

The actor bowed slightly. "Good evening, Sir Robert."

Sir Robert Cecil looked steadily at Mark for some seconds.

"You are Mark Kempe?"

"I am, Sir." Mark bowed.

"And you are the brother of Richard Kempe?"

"Sir Richard Kempe."

"Sir Richard Kempe," repeated Cecil, dryly. "I am told you have information regarding a plot against Her Majesty?"

"Yes, Sir, and against my brother. Has he – is he alive?"

"I must confess myself more concerned with the Queen than with your brother," answered Sir Robert, though not unkindly. "I am sure you will understand that the safety of this realm is of more importance than the life of one man, even though that man is your brother."

"Yes sir. But I have been travelling for weeks – from Alwinton in Northumberland – with my sister – because we heard he was in the Tower and was to be executed for treason."

"From Northumberland? I thought your home was in Warwickshire?"

"It is sir, but we have a house near the border as well."

Sir Robert Cecil crossed to Mark and looked steadily at him. "I think you had better begin at the beginning." Mark thought his voice sounded warmer. "Give him a chair, Fairfax; sit down, Master Shakespeare."

Mark sat down and watched Sir Robert throw a log on the fire. A shower of sparks shot upwards and a smoky smell drifted into the room. Then the Queen's secretary sat in a large chair and looked earnestly at him. "Now, young Kempe, let me hear the whole story."

Mark's narrative was interrupted three times. Sir Robert invited Mark to repeat the conversation between Webster and Ford at Alwinton, and he asked for full descriptions of Ford and then of the men with Webster at Gorhambury. Fairfax was commanded to take full notes.

Mark concluded his story and the silence that followed was broken only by the spurting logs in the fire.

When Sir Robert finally stood up the others rose also.

"Sit down, my boy, sit down." Mark felt Sir Robert's hand on his shoulder as he pushed him gently back on to the chair. "Your brother is alive though he is still confined to the Tower." He looked up. "Fairfax, there is much to be done. I think that you and I will get no sleep tonight." He looked again at Mark. "You shall have all the food you require and then you shall sleep the night here at the Palace."

"Sir, I promised my sister that I would let her know what happened."

"I am sorry, but your life is in danger until this plot is unravelled and its leaders caught."

"Excuse me, Sir Robert." Mark heard Shakespeare's voice behind him. "With your permission I can return to the Globe and deliver the good news."

"You may, Master Shakespeare. Fairfax, take this young man to Davy. He is the steward, Master Mark, and will give you food and a bed for the night. I will see you tomorrow."

An hour later, refreshed and fed, Mark climbed into a large four-poster bed with crackling clean linen sheets and was asleep upon the instant.

Late the next morning he was summoned to Sir Robert Cecil's study.

"Thanks to your resolve we have uncovered the whole plot. Naturally I cannot give you all the details but your tutor, Cain Webster, is in the Tower and five others were arrested only an hour ago at a house in Walworth. I have signed the order for your brother's release. He will be here shortly. Do you wish to wait for him or go to your sister at the Globe playhouse?"

"I'll wait here, Sir."

"I thought you might," replied a smiling Robert Cecil.

That afternoon Mark fidgeted in a parlour off the great hall. He felt apprehensive. Richard had been under sentence of death for over two months. What would be the effect of such an ordeal? Had he been tortured? Would his appearance be much altered?

Mark heard footsteps and turned to face the door. It swung open and Richard walked firmly into the room, his sword swinging at his side. His cheeks were pale and drawn but his eyes were keen and his head erect.

"Mark! It's good to see you!"

"Richard!"

The brothers hugged each other affectionately. Mark felt the burden of responsibility that had weighed on him for the past weeks lift suddenly and he clung to Richard and wept with relief and joy.

There was a knock on the door and John Fairfax entered. "Sir Richard, you are commanded by the Queen to attend her Majesty at Nonesuch Palace. You must leave within the hour. A messenger has gone to fetch your sister that you may see her before you go."

Forty minutes later Catherine, who arrived with Shakespeare, was just in time to greet Richard before he climbed into a coach with Fairfax. Both young men looked splendid in their court dress and waved their feathered hats gaily as they were driven away.

Then Mark, Catherine and Shakespeare returned to the parlour and sat by the crackling wood fire.

"How's Tom?" asked Mark.

"Splendid," replied Catherine. "When he heard the good news he somersaulted all round the Globe stage! He sends greetings."

"He spent the morning watching a rehearsal and saw a play this afternoon," said Shakespeare.

"So did I. It was about a rich lady whose suitors had to choose one of three caskets. If they chose the right casket they could marry the lady. Nicholas Ridley and Ned send their greetings also."

"They're going to stay with us and play at the Globe for a while," said Shakespeare. "And we've given Tom a small part in a new play. He'll rehearse in the mornings and help in the tiring house during the afternoon performances."

"Good old Tom," said Mark. "Where's he going to live?"

"With Henry Condell. Harry's got several children of his own and Mrs. Condell is delighted with the idea of adding to the family!"

"Did Nicholas find Tamburlaine and the wagon?"

"Yes. They'd been left at the George Inn near the bridge. The Inn Keeper recognised them and came to the Globe last night.

Nicholas wept for joy when he heard the news and rushed off with the Inn keeper!"

Mark and Catherine spent the next four days at the Globe Playhouse and returned each night, to sleep at the Palace.

On the fifth day, as they were sitting in the second gallery watching a rehearsal, John Fairfax came up to them.

"You are commanded by the Queen to Nonesuch Palace. She wishes to hear your story."

The children were both excited and fearful. The Queen was rumoured to have a fiery temper.

"What about Tom" asked Mark. "He is part of the story."

"Tom is included in the command," said John Fairfax.

Dressed in borrowed clothes, Mark, Catherine and Tom travelled from Whitehall by coach to the Palace of Nonesuch near Ewell in Surrey.

They were given hurried instructions to bow on entering the room and to bow again when they reached the Queen. They were to speak only when commanded.

Feeling extremely nervous they ware admitted to the Queen's presence. Sir Robert Cecil ushered them in and they saw everyone in the room turn to look at them.

They bowed and walked forward. A dozen pairs of eyes watched them. They approached the raised throne at the far end of the room. On reaching the first of the four steps leading up to the Queen's chair they bowed again. Sir Robert Cecil introduced them.

"Your Majesty, may I present Mark Kempe, Catherine Kempe and Thomas Langley."

How odd to hear Tom called by his full name. It made a strange event even stranger.

They gazed in awe at the woman seated before them. She was wearing a magnificent dress of silver cloth embroidered with pansies and butterflies. The red curls on her head were set with pearls and her cheeks were rouged.

"Mark, Catherine and Thomas," she said, looking at each one as she spoke their name. "Sir Robert tells me that you have done great service both to your Sovereign and this realm. I should like to hear your adventures. I am ever anxious to learn about my people and you can teach me. Come and sit by me on the steps.

Sir Robert, I fancy you have urgent matters to attend to. You have our permission to withdraw; so have you all. I wish to remain alone with my young friends. Sir Richard Kempe, you may stay. You are no doubt as anxious as I to hear the full story."

Cecil and the other courtiers and ladies in waiting withdrew.

The Queen smiled. "Now Mark, Catherine and Thomas, I want to hear everything."

As they told their story the children grew more relaxed. They took it in turn to narrate but often interrupted each other when some detail was forgotten.

At length they came to the end.

The old Queen leaned back in her chair and looked from one young face to the others in turn.

"So you, Master Tom, want to become a player?"

"Yes, your Majesty."

"It is a fine profession. The players have given me many hours of entertainment and much food for thought. You will need to know a great deal about life if you are to portray characters on a stage. Master Shakespeare knows more than most of us, I suspect; he will be a good tutor for you. I shall look to see you when the players visit me here or at Whitehall or at Greenwich."

She turned to Catherine. "And you, young lady! Travelling through my realm dressed as a boy! What stories you will have to tell your children and your grandchildren. That is something I have never known; something that I have missed; although I would not admit it to everyone. I should have liked to share experiences with children of my own. But it was not to be."

She sighed gently and looked at Mark.

"How proud your father would have been. What, I wonder, will you most treasure from your journeyings?"

"Meeting so many different kinds of people, your Majesty. Finding help and kindness where I would not have expected it."

Elizabeth of England nodded and smiled.

"I had many adventures as a young girl. Indeed, like your brother, I was imprisoned in the Tower and did not know if the next day would be my last. I found my early adventures helped me later on – and one is learning all the time. Experience is the best tutor, you know."

On the last day of the year the players from the Globe performed at Whitehall Palace. Mark, Catherine and Richard were present to see Nicholas Ridley granted his wish to play before 'The Queen's Majesty'. Ned too was in the company and also Tom who was now a professional boy player.

Early in the new year Mark and Catherine said goodbye to their many friends and returned, with Richard, to their home in Warwickshire.

Although time would erase much from the children's memories, the whole adventure would prove a source of enrichment for the rest of their lives.

Mark often recalled the Queen's words, "Experience is the best tutor, you know."

"there's the Globe Playhouse," said Shakespeare.